Break Point

by Amelia Grace Seiler

The characters in this novel are figments of my imagination as are the liberties I've taken with the geography of Rochester, New York and the details of Highland Hospital.

ISBN-13: 978-1480244863
ISBN-10: 1480244864

Dedicated with all my love to my husband, Bryan Seiler, for the innumerable times during my writing career he has resisted joining the French Foreign Legion.

Heartfelt gratitude to Dorothy Dessloch, Doris and Jules Cohen, Miriam Grace Monfredo, and the many others whose encouragement and enthusiasm convinced me to keep writing.

Prologue

And thus the heart will break, yet brokenly live on.
~ Lord Byron

Snow matted the young woman's wild black hair as she inched along the treacherously slick sidewalk that curved up to the main entrance of Rochester's Highland Hospital. Ambulances rushed past, their strobe lights and sirens assaulting her overwrought senses like physical blows. Suppose the hospital wouldn't admit the tiny baby she had hidden inside her coat? Suppose the man who was tracking her had staked out the hospital? Suppose the police locked her up for what she had done?

These were all risks she had to take.

In the ER waiting room she balanced the unnaturally still child on her lap and tried to fill out the paperwork thrust at her by a harried Admissions clerk. She printed her own name on the first line and "homeless" on the second. When a third line demanded her child's name, tears trickled down the woman's face and dripped onto the filthy blanket that swaddled the baby. She paused and then wrote a name. It was Christmas, but a name was the only gift she had for this newborn child.

She waited an eternity before they let her see a doctor, but when he began asking questions she dared not answer, she clutched her stomach and told him she was feeling sick. Then she ran down the hall towards the women's restroom, bypassed it, and vanished into a night so cold that salt spread by city trucks could not melt the ice on the streets.

1

Chapter One

From a tiny table in a warm corner I idly watched a man wrestle open the Bishop and Wolf's ironbound door, fighting the wind that threatened to rip it from his grasp. A blast of cold, salt-edged air muscled its way ahead of him into the room.

For a brief moment the regulars glanced up. It was rare for a stranger to show up on St. Mary's Isle this time of year. In the summer, the village would be overrun by day-trippers and tourists visiting the Isles of Scilly. But during winter months, only native islanders were willing to endure the storms that beleaguered the chain of small islands that sat along the bleak Cornish coast.

The man unzipped his leather jacket and glanced around the room as if searching for someone. When his gaze lit on me, his eyes locked on mine like a poacher spotlighting a deer.

"Kate Scholfield?" he said as he approached my table where it sat in isolation under one of the pub's mullioned windows. I could tell from his accent that he was a New Yorker.

I nodded. What choice did I have? No one would track me all the way to the Isles of Scilly to tell me I had just won the New York State Lottery.

The man draped his jacket on the back of the chair and sat. He was about my height, maybe five-four, olive skin, and graying hair slicked carefully back. Behind thick glasses were expressive Latin eyes that corresponded with a dominant nose and an aggressive chin.

I stuck my fork into the steak and kidney pie congealing

on my plate. "Do I know you?"

His face was grim when he reached across the table to offer me his ice-cold hand. "My name's Aguilar. Joe Aguilar." He leaned back in his chair and reached into the pocket of his Levis. Out came a neatly folded fax which he handed to me. "I need to explain a few things before you read that."

I ignored him and unfolded the fax. It was a newspaper article dated January 5 from the *Rochester Democrat & Chronicle*, something about a dead girl pulled from the Genesee River. My hands began to shake. I tossed the paper on the table. "What exactly does this have to do with me?"

"I have a niece on the Rochester police force who goes to the same church as your sister-in-law, and, well...."

"It's Darla, isn't it?"

"Hey, are you gonna be okay? You look kinda pale. You want a glass of water or something?"

"Why would you be here if this is not about Darla?" I picked up the fax, read it a second time, and tossed it across the table at him. "There's nothing in this article that indicates it's Darla."

"Your sister-in-law is Caroline Scholfield, right?"

I nodded and felt my stomach clench in fear.

"Well, her daughter's been missing since sometime before Christmas...."

"I know that. She's run off before. It's not a big deal." I said it to convince myself rather than to convince him.

"Your sister-in-law is afraid the girl they pulled from the river might be her."

"No! That's ridiculous! It couldn't be!"

"Look, lady. I'm not making this up. The cops think the girl in the morgue might be your niece. How can I make it any plainer than that?"

"Dear God! Caroline must be frantic. Darla is her life!"

"Yeah. That's why I'm here. Your sister-in-law's blind,

right?"

I nodded.

"So she can't identify the body, and she won't trust anyone else to do it. She wants you to come home."

"But...I...."

"Look, I don't know how to say this nicely. The body had been in the river a long time. Ice, debris, fish. Eventually they can use DNA to identify her, but, thanks to the jokers in Albany, the lab's budget has been cut and they're backlogged til the Fourth of July. It isn't like a TV series where you get results before the next commercial break. Someone's got to identify this girl before your sister-in-law falls apart at the seams."

"Do they...know if she...was it suicide or...."

"The police either don't know what happened to her or they aren't saying. My niece didn't tell me anything except it was urgent someone find you and tell you to get back to Rochester as soon as possible. Your sister-in-law collapsed at her job last week, and they put her in the hospital, but she checked herself out six hours later. Said there was no one to take care of her guide dog. I don't know what she thinks will happen to the dog if she ends up in the morgue next to her daughter."

I stared at the bearer of this frightful news. "Thank you for tracking me down." My voice was not as emotionless as I might have wished. "I'm sorry I was rude to you, Mr. Aguilar. I need to find a phone and call Caroline." I grabbed my trench coat and slipped my purse onto my shoulder, fumbling in it for my wallet as I hurried out the door. As I left the pub, I glanced back and saw Aguilar reach down to pick up my hat which had fallen onto the wet floor.

The street was deserted except for gusts of wind ripping along the narrow cobbled way. I ran to a phone booth just up the block where I could call Caroline in privacy. A solitary

4

street lamp, unaided by moon or light from neighboring windows, struggled to illuminate the area. Buildings hovered desolate and untenanted in the light's feeble glow, their planked construction devoid of both paint and ornamentation.

Inside the phone booth, the temperature felt well below freezing. I no longer had the benefit of motion to help circulate my blood, and I stamped my feet to no avail as I punched in access code, country code, area code, Caroline's phone number, and then my well-used AT&T calling card number. Finally I heard Caroline's voice on the line.

"Kate! At last! Where are you?"

"I'm still on St. Mary's Isle. Darla...?

"Oh, Kate! I didn't know how to reach you. They've found the body of a girl, and I...I know it's her! When I described Darla, the police said it could be a match. But she...the body...Oh! If you only knew! The body had been in the river and...." Caroline, who never cried, started to cry. "Father Donnelly tried to help, but he couldn't be sure if it was Darla or not. And he's been our priest for years. If he can't identify her, nobody can. Except maybe you. You know she's all I have. I'm going insane not knowing!"

"What about dental records? Can't they identify bodies by using dental records? You've had the same dentist since Darla was a baby."

"Doctor Wagner? Don't you remember the fire in those offices behind the Renaissance Hotel in Pittsford last fall? I know I sent the newspaper article to Whit. Maybe he didn't show it to you. Three people were killed in the blaze. Doctor Wagner was one of them. He would have celebrated his seventy-fourth birthday this year. All his records were lost. He never switched over to digital records, said he was too old for computers. Maybe it's just as well he died in the fire. He adored Darla. It would have killed him to have to identify

5

her."

"Oh, Caro!" I stood in the cold phone booth in stunned silence and listened to Caroline's broken-hearted sobs.

After a few moments I heard her blow her nose. Then she said, "Kate? Are you still there?"

"I'm still here." My fingers were growing numb from gripping the phone. I changed hands and stuck the frozen one inside my coat under my arm. It felt like an ice cube in my armpit.

"I know you're going through a..." Caroline's voice faded in and out as the storm disrupted the lines and gusts of wind and rain assaulted the phone booth."

"What, Caroline? I can't hear you."

Caroline's voice came across the line, louder, bitter and shaken. "I said I need your help with this. I know you're going through a rough patch, but this is one thing I can't manage on my own."

I knew what a concession it was for Caroline to ever admit she needed help. "Of course, I'll come," I said, dread washing over me.

"You were planning to come back soon anyway, weren't you?"

"Yes," I lied. "I have to empty out Aunt Myla's house and put it on the market. And the lawyers have been on my case to deal with...Whit's estate. But give me a minute to think. The mail boat won't depart from here until three tomorrow afternoon. If the boat can sail in this weather, I'll get into Penzance tomorrow evening and catch an overnight train to London tomorrow night. I'll call you the minute I get to the airport to give you my flight information."

"Oh, Kate. Thank you!"

"Now stop worrying. I'm sure it's not Darla."

"Hurry. There's more...and it's even worse!" Caroline said, and then she hung up.

I stared at the receiver in my hand, bleakly wondering what could possibly be worse than not knowing if the body of your only child was lying in a morgue. I considered calling her back, but then decided against it. I would be at her house soon enough. And I'd had all the bad news I could take at the moment.

Outside, icy rain stung my face and streamed down the cobblestone street. By the time I re-entered the pub, I was shivering from cold and reaction to Caroline's story.

Aguilar had been keeping patient watch over my sodden hat.

When I threw myself into my chair, he said, "You look like you could use a drink, lady."

"Brandy sounds good." I clenched my chattering teeth.

"How about if I order you some dinner, too?" He picked up my plate and put it on the next table. "Yours is cold now."

"I don't want dinner. I'm not hungry anymore. Brandy will be fine." I used my napkin to wipe cold rain off my face.

"Well, you should eat something," he said. "You're pale as a ghost." He pushed away from the table and persisted, "You want the same thing as before or something different?"

"Just brandy. Thanks." I slumped down in the chair, unbuttoned my coat, and brooded over the phone conversation.

Caroline had been a nurse working with Doctors Without Borders in Cambodia and had been blinded by fragments from a land mine that detonated near her jeep. Earlier that day, before the land mine shattered her life, she had delivered the baby of a village woman who had been brought to the field hospital as a last resort. The woman had been in labor for almost twenty hours. Both mother and baby survived, but the mother was terrified to return to the village with the newborn because it was obvious the father of the baby was not her Cambodian husband but an African

7

American she had accommodated for a little pocket money.

Caroline had decided on the spot to adopt the baby. A tiny affirmation of life in a land of death, she called her. When the helicopter came to evacuate her and the other casualties of the land mine, Caroline fought the morphine that threatened to put her under and refused to leave without the baby. She later adopted the baby on the grounds of humanitarian parole, and Darla, a bright, manipulative child, had been the center of her existence ever since.

Aguilar came back to the table juggling a lager for himself, my brandy, and a slice of chocolate cake which he set down in front of me. I struggled out of my slouched position. "I didn't order that."

"I know you didn't order it. It comes with my dinner. I don't eat dessert, but there's no sense letting it go to waste." He went back to get flatware. When he returned, he handed me a new napkin and a fork. Then he said, "Listen, let's move to that table by the fire."

I pushed myself upright, stuck my wet pea cap in my pocket, and picked up my brandy. At the moment I personally didn't care if it was cold at this table, but I was too distraught to argue, and the man had come all the way out here to find me.

Aguilar followed me with the cake and his jacket.

When we had settled at the new table, he said, "So, my niece said your sister-in-law is a pretty special person. What a terrible thing to happen to her!"

I told him about Caroline and her adopted daughter. I paused in my narration while the pub owner set down Aguilar's dinner. The man ate fastidiously while I finished the story, sipped brandy, and picked at the frosting on the cake. When he pushed his empty plate aside, I said, "I really do want to thank you for tracking me down."

He shrugged. "Someone had to do it." Then he leaned

back in his chair and said, "So what exactly are you doing out here on this frozen rock in the middle of winter?"

"I'm researching an article for a travel magazine," I answered, giving him only part of the truth.

"Yeah? Well, why in hell didn't you wait for summer to do it?"

I felt the unaccustomed tug of a smile at the corners of my mouth. I shrugged and said nothing.

"So what are your plans now?"

I ran my fingers through my hair. The rain and salt air had given it new definition. "Pack and head for New York." I changed the subject. "How did you find me?"

"My niece called me at my hotel in Madrid. I spend two weeks in Spain every winter. And, I have to say, it certainly beats this place for a winter vacation. At any rate, my niece said she was faxing the newspaper article and your photo to me. According to your sister-in-law, you were somewhere in the Isles of Scilly - pronounced with the "c" silent - but you didn't have a mailing address or phone number. My niece had no idea where in hell the Isles of Scilly were, but she looked on a map, and they didn't seem to be very far from Spain.

"When I got as far as Penzance, I talked to the captain of the mail boat. He said there weren't many places you would be staying in the Isles this time of year, and if I checked at the hotels, someone might recognize your picture. This was the biggest island, so I tried the hotels along the waterfront. When I got to the Bishop and Wolf Inn, I got lucky. The man behind the counter said you usually show up in the pub for dinner, and bingo."

"I'd like to reimburse you for your expenses."

"Don't worry about it. The flight from Madrid to London cost less than fifty Euros, and from London I just caught a train."

"Where are you staying tonight? At least let me pay for

your hotel room."

"You don't need to do that. I got a room here. I just hope the heating system works. The joint looks like it was built in the Middle Ages, and this isn't exactly the tropics."

No, I thought, *this isn't the tropics. But I didn't choose this island for its climate. I chose it because I was desperate for sea birds and solace.*

Chapter Two

It was after nine when I left Aguilar in the pub nursing his lager by the fire and climbed the narrow stairs to the second floor where I had a room. In all probability, Aguilar and I were the only guests that night. I washed in the dreary bathroom down the hall and crawled into bed.

Sleep was impossible. I'd never had a child. I could only imagine what Caroline was going through. At length I switched on the bedside lamp and lay staring at the time-darkened beams of the low ceiling. The room's plastered walls were painted ivory, but beneath the paint the ancient surface was warped and uneven. Heavy green drapes provided privacy from the street below and made a feeble attempt to subdue the icy drafts that crept through antiquated, ill-fitting windows. On the floor, wide floorboards not covered by the rug leaked not only cracks of light from the public room below but also its sounds and odors. I didn't mind. The proximity of the pub and its regulars countered my self-imposed isolation.

Long before dawn I pushed back the covers and struggled out of the overly soft bed. The room was icy, but I smoothed out the down-filled duvet and resolutely opened my suitcase on top of it. After setting aside jeans, pullover, and a heavy gray sweater, I spent the next hour trying to condense my clothes and photographic equipment into the available space of one suitcase and a carry-on.

In the end, I determined I would have to wear my bulky hiking boots if I wanted to shut the bags. It didn't really matter. The boots would be necessary for the long walk along the rough coastal path to the bench overlooking the sea where I intended to spend my last few hours on the island.

At first light I dressed, ignored the unruly state of my frizzy hair, and made my way down the ill-lit, narrow stairway to find the pub owner and pay my bill. The stairs were uneven, the narrow treads worn concave by innumerable footsteps over the centuries.

The proprietor, with whom after a month I was on nodding terms, took my credit card and said, "Going back to America, then, are you?"

"Just for a while to sort out a few things," I replied, ever the optimist.

It was cold outside, but a weak sun was struggling to reverse five days of stormy weather. The wind, though still a factor, had moderated and was content to whip pockets of litter and winter leaves into minor whirlwinds in alleys and doorways. A stray lid from a dustbin clattering against the door of the tiny post office, the raucous cries of gulls, and the monotonous squeak of an ancient sign swinging back and forth over an ironmonger's shop were the only sounds that greeted me.

It took me about forty cold minutes along a narrow bracken-edged path to arrive at the solitary oak bench which overlooked the prehistoric cairns and ragged rocks in the sea below. I sat on the bench, drawing my knees up to my chest for warmth, and looked down on the dramatic panorama.

Man at the dawn of time, even then possessing insight of life beyond death, had heaped plinth upon plinth to construct a group of burial chambers that had outlasted many of modern man's more elaborate memorials. The cairns faced the wind-torn sea and the elemental beauty of the offshore rocks. There could be no more beautiful place to leave the dead to wait out eternity.

I huddled there in the cold for perhaps twenty minutes

before a solitary figure climbed into my line of vision. Joe Aguilar. I should have expected it. The cairns were one of the major attractions listed in the island guidebooks. I couldn't very well run from him after he had given up the last days of his vacation to search for me, so I waited reluctantly as he made his way up the rock-choked hillside.

"I hope I'm not interrupting your solitude," he said. He had his hands thrust casually in the pockets of his leather jacket and a Nikon slung around his neck. His eyes raked across my face. "What's the matter?" he asked in alarm. "Have you had more bad news about your niece?"

I hadn't realized there were tears on my face. I swiped at my eyes with the back of my hand and gestured mutely at the brass memorial plaque on the back of the bench.

Whitney Scholfield, Requiescat in pace.

"Who was he? Your husband?"

I tried to answer in a matter-of-fact voice. "Yes. My husband. He died in November."

Aguilar sat down on the edge of the bench. "I'm sorry. What happened to him?"

I shrugged. "He was in Iraq – he worked for an oil company. One of those roadside bombings that seem to happen every day."

"Well, you picked a beautiful spot to put a memorial. In fact, before I realized it was you, I got some pretty good shots of you sitting here. Maybe you'd like to have a copy of them."

I just shrugged again because his sympathy was threatening to unleash a renewed onslaught of emotion.

He checked his watch, obviously ill at ease and wondering what to do. "Look," he said, "we're going to have to get back pretty soon. If we miss the ferry, we're stuck on this island until tomorrow. I wanted to get some pictures of the prehistoric burial ground. Want to walk down there?

13

Maybe you can fill me in on it. I haven't had a chance to read the guide book, but it must be what, two or three thousand years old?"

He looked relieved when I stood up and walked down to the cairns with him. He hadn't come prepared for a woman in the throes of a crying jag.

Thirty minutes later as we climbed back up toward the inland road, he offered me one of two candy bars he pulled from his pocket. "I hope this doesn't ruin your lunch."

I ripped off the wrapper and bit into a Cadbury Crunchie, savoring its honeycombed center. "Thanks," I added with my mouth full. "I skipped breakfast."

We continued up the steep hill, avoiding outcroppings of granite thrusting randomly through the grass. When we reached the pebble path, I checked my watch and said, "We can catch the island bus at the end of this lane if we hurry. It only passes by every two hours, so if we miss it, we'll have to walk back to town." Then in belated reply to his query about lunch, I added, "But I'm not in any hurry to get back for lunch. I'm skipping it."

"Well, you've got to eat something. You didn't eat your dinner last night, and you skipped breakfast. Right?"

"True."

"Brandy and frosting last night and now a candy bar. You're going to die of malnutrition and need a goddamned commemorative bench of your own."

The same smile that tugged at the edges of my mouth last night threatened to reappear. The wind whipped hair into my eyes, and I brushed it back. "I get seasick on boats, so just mind your own business. Okay?"

"Mind my own business? Whose business do you think it will be to haul your ass back to town if you pass out?"

I turned my back on him. "Set your mind at ease," I called over my shoulder. "You won't have to do any hauling.

14

Here comes the bus."

The ferry ride to the mainland was not an auspicious beginning for the trip home. I arrived at the dock at the last minute still wearing this morning's hiking boots, my face devoid of make-up and my hair wild from the wind. Aguilar looked me up and down. "Not exactly Fifth Avenue, but what the hell."

I laughed in spite of myself.

By the time the Scillonian III was ready to depart, the weather had cleared, but the seas were still rough. I downed two Dramamine and waited until the last second to board. The steward had informed me on the trip over to St. Mary's that in the roughest weather the mail boat might sit offshore for eight hours or more until the seas calmed sufficiently to allow her to safely dock. I had vowed then I would never board the inter-island vessel without first checking the forecast. Today I didn't have that option.

I left Aguilar on the main deck and slipped down to the bowels of the ship where the British, in uncharacteristic compassion, had installed bunks along the walls and supplied not only blankets but also motion sickness bags. I climbed onto one of the bunks in the all but empty room and lay there numbly as the boat slipped its mooring and headed out to sea.

Whit had died in an agony of flames in a hellhole in Iraq. There had been nothing left to bury. Dramamine kept my nausea at bay but it did nothing for the devastation I felt leaving his memorial behind. Nor did it mitigate my dread at being forced to stand next to Caroline in a morgue and identify the body of her only child, a child whom I also loved.

An hour and a half later, I came up on deck as the boat slowed to enter the harbor at Penzance. Aguilar was hanging over the rail snapping pictures in spite of the cold. The setting sun had transformed the sea into a shimmering, shifting cloth of gold. The few boats still out had become mere charcoal sketches backlit on the horizon, but a myriad fishing vessels sitting in port were washed in a glory of color. It was a canvas worth braving the frigid wind to catch on film. Normally I would be berating myself for having packed my camera. Today, however, the only pictures on my mind were horrific images of a dead girl, and I was desperate to keep them suppressed.

As we prepared to dock, the Scillonian gave forth one long blast of her whistle. Choppy water sloshed roughly against the pilings and salted the air with brine. As soon as the gangway clanked down, a crewmember released the gate and let us file off. I was first on shore. Last on and first off. My motto for all sea-going ventures.

The overnight Intercity train was already warming its engines at the Penzance Railway Station by the time Aguilar and I wheeled our luggage down the center platform to board. As the train headed south along the spectacular coast of Cornwall, a Pakistani steward came by with the tea trolley. Aguilar bought egg mayonnaise sandwiches and barely chilled Chardonnay in plastic glasses, a repast which effectively dispelled any illusion of the Orient Express. When he opened his wallet to pay the steward, I caught sight of his badge.

"You're a cop?" I said in surprise as the steward continued down the aisle of the train.

Aguilar smiled condescendingly and held up the badge. "Read the fine print, lady. United States Department of Agriculture. That doesn't even come close to making me a cop, although there are times when I wish it did."

I unwrapped my sandwich and stared at it. The thought of eating made me ill, but it would be rude to throw the thing away. I took a small bite and tried not to grimace. "So what exactly do you do for the Department of Agriculture?"

"Inspect meat plants and slaughter houses, make sure everything's up to standard. I used to own a meat market with my brothers, but this is a better fit. Every time I have a save, I feel like I've done something worthwhile."

"What's a save?"

"It's what I call it when I stop tainted meat from hitting the market or make some bastard clean up the rat feces in his plant. Anything that prevents someone from getting hurt? I call it a save."

I did not know then how desperately I would be needing saves of my own.

Chapter Three

Due to a security alert at Heathrow, my flight arrived late into Chicago's O'Hare Airport. Wearing hiking boots and lugging a carry-on full of duty free liquor, I raced through O'Hare like a linebacker, arriving at the American Eagle gate with only minutes to spare.

Two flight attendants were standing outside the cockpit door. One smiled serenely and said, "Going to Rochester?"

I nodded.

"No need to rush, dear. Our departure time just got pushed back because of lake effect snow between here and New York."

Suddenly I knew exactly how Medusa felt when her hair turned to snakes.

Wordlessly I turned and walked down the aisle of the plane, plucking airsickness bags from seat pockets on the way to my seat. No sense telling the stewardesses how desperately I needed to be in Rochester, and no sense telling them how grateful I was for the reprieve.

Ninety minutes later, when the plane finally lurched into Chicago's stormy stratosphere, I pulled the airsickness bags from my purse and stacked them on my lap. The businessman in the seat next to me glanced over at them and swiveled around to check out the full aircraft. His face sagged in resignation when he realized there were no other available seats.

Sorry," I muttered. "I took Dramamine, but when it's really rough, nothing helps."

"Try thinking of something else to take your mind off of

it," he said brusquely. Then he clamped a pair of Sony earphones on his head and shut his eyes. An irritating reggae beat leaked from his earphones.

Turbulence buffeted the plane. The pilot's voice came on overhead instructing everyone to keep their seatbelts fastened. I heard glasses rattling on a beverage cart and a crash as something heavy fell to the floor. I shut my eyes in resignation. Right now even puking up my guts seemed preferable to thinking.

When the American Eagle jet finally shuddered to a standstill in Rochester, I dragged myself down the concourse to baggage claim, my spirits lifting somewhat as my feet registered contact with solid ground. Outside the terminal a bitter west wind was blowing. A snowplow grazed past, taking with it three inches of freshly fallen flakes.

I rented a mid-sized vehicle with four-wheel drive and was soon glad I did. Icy roads made driving treacherous, and I was grateful Caroline's house was only fifteen minutes from the airport. She lived in the Ellwanger Barry section of the South Wedge, a neighborhood of century-old houses on small city lots. Even in the storm her green two-story house was easy to find. It was the only one that still had Christmas lights twinkling merrily on the porch. I skidded into her unshoveled drive and honked twice.

"You finally got here!" Caroline cried as I struggled in the side door with my luggage.

In the kitchen I hugged her under the watchful supervision of Nomad, the elderly Golden Retriever who had been her faithful guide dog for several years. Since I had last seen her, Caroline's well-endowed frame had become almost skeletal.

"You're so thin!" I exclaimed.

"Yeah," she responded in a voice that shook. "I guess worrying about your child will do that to you. I'll be fine. I just need to know whether or not Darla's...dead."

Caroline wrapped her arms across her stomach as if to contain her pain and started to cry. She shook her head and pulled off her dark glasses to wipe her eyes. "Sorry," she said. "I need to pull myself together. I called the...morgue...to let them know we were coming tonight. We just have to give them a time."

Forty minutes later we pulled into the parking lot of the Office of the Medical Examiner. In spite of blowing and drifting snow, it was not difficult to find the place. The building was located on a well-lit government campus on East Henrietta Road just a few blocks from Monroe Community Hospital, an extravagant structure built during the Great Depression and impossible to miss even in a blizzard. By contrast, the Medical Examiner's Office was a low, modern brick structure with a V-shaped entrance. It's only distinguishing feature was a lit flagpole with a large American flag whipping in the wind.

A cop met us at the door. I could not imagine what Caroline was going through, but I knew I was there only because I had no choice. As we followed the man's broad back into the bleak recesses of the building, I desperately tried to see nothing, smell nothing, and feel nothing.

The body, even viewed remotely, was every bit as horrific to look at as I had anticipated, a mangled and chewed gray-green corpse with stringy patches of long, curly black hair and the ruined eyes of the truly lost. I bit my lips to prevent myself from gasping. Bile filled my mouth, but I dared not retch because Caroline was sitting next to me gripping my arm fiercely and dreading the news I could deliver. "Tell me," she hissed. "Tell me what you see. Don't make me sit here not knowing!"

I shook my head even though I knew she couldn't see me. "Caro, I've been your eyes for a lot of things, but not this."

"Is it Darla?" she cried. "Just tell me! Is it Darla?"

I stared helplessly at the image on the monitor. *Oh, Darla! Is that you?* The girl had skin that might once have been the dusky color of Darla's, and beneath her bloated body was a frame every bit as delicate. What was left of her face hinted at Asian features, her coarse black hair was as curly as Darla's. Her body with small breasts, fragile limbs, and nibbled fingers could easily be Darla's. But there was not enough of the girl's features left intact to definitively identify her. Tears slipped down my face as I shook my head mutely at the cop. "I just can't be sure."

I stood and looked down at Caroline's bowed head and could think of nothing more to say. In my mind I heard Darla's teasing voice, mocking me as she often did when I told her that her behavior left me at a loss for words. "Come on, Aunt Kate," she would say, "you're the most literate person I know. You're never at a loss for words unless you're keeping one of my secrets."

An image flashed through my mind of Darla in a bikini a few summers ago, poised at the edge of Lake Ontario as Caroline and Nomad waded nearby in gently lapping waves. Darla was shivering and laughing, and she had her finger to her lips. "Shh," she had mimed to me and had pointed at her newly pierced navel. I rolled my eyes and shook my head, and that made her laugh even more.

I turned to the cop. "Do you know...could anyone tell if the...girl...had a ring in her navel?"

Caroline's head snapped up. "Darla didn't have a ring in her navel. I forbade her to have anything pierced besides her ears."

"She had her navel pierced, Caro," I said. "She just never told you."

"Obviously there were a lot of things she never told

me," Caroline responded bitterly.

The cop glanced through the papers he had in his hand. "Give me a minute," he said. He disappeared through a door that exhaled cold, morbid air, and I prayed once again it was not Darla lying on that gurney, naked and ravaged and dead.

About ten minutes later the cop reappeared. He put a gentle hand on Caroline's shoulder. "The girl did not have her navel pierced. I even called to double check with the medical examiner. I guess that means, Ms. Scholfield, she's not your daughter."

Chapter Four

Darla was still missing, but for the moment Caroline was manic with relief. When we returned to the house, she left me to haul my luggage upstairs to the guest room. I could hear her slamming cupboard doors and rattling glasses in the kitchen.

"You want Lady Grey tea or cheap Merlot?" she called.

"I have Glenmorangie in my carry-on for you and Gentleman Jack for myself. Just bring glasses, and kindly put ice in mine." We'd been arguing over the merits of ice in our liquor since we became roommates our freshman year in college.

Caroline appeared in the living room with two glasses but no ice. "Aside from the fact that there is more than enough ice outside to freeze hell over, we both know it's sacrilege to put ice in good liquor!" she said.

"For some inexplicable reason, I assumed you would be gracious to me because I have jet lag and have come all this way to straighten out your life," I told her.

"Oh, Kate, don't I know it!" She felt her way into one of two overstuffed chairs and reached down to pat Nomad who curled up at her feet. "Thank you more than I can say for flying home. And thank you, thank you for bearing good tidings. I wonder if they'll ever figure out who that poor dead girl is."

"I don't know. I hope so. Seeing her body was one of the most awful experiences of my life."

Caroline held out her glass for me to pour. "Let's not talk about it anymore! It's been my life since Christmas. I'm

23

so very sorry about Whit. Can you bear to talk about him?"

"No," I admitted as I eased into the other chair. Across from us a gas fireplace flickered, offering illusory warmth. Next to the fireplace Caroline's Christmas tree still stood with a stack of unopened Christmas presents beneath it. I poured myself a serious glass of Gentleman Jack and made room on my lap for Caro's long-haired yellow cat. "Look Caroline, Darla's still missing," I said bluntly. "We need to talk about it. Then maybe we can get something to eat and go to bed."

Caroline tasted her single malt Scotch. "It's bad. She's more than just missing. Even if that poor girl in the morgue is not her, it's still bad."

The relief that made Caroline giddy was making me ill tempered. "Just spit it out, Caroline. It can't be worse than dead."

I swallowed some room-temperature Tennessee whiskey and waited. Finally she set down her glass and spoke. "It could be, Kate. It really could be. Darla had a baby."

"A baby! When?"

Caroline shrugged. "A few days before Christmas. And about two a.m. Christmas morning, she brought it to the emergency room at Highland Hospital."

"Oh, no!" I said. "Why?"

"This is where the really bad news kicks in," Caroline warned. "Her baby was suffering from malnutrition and dehydration. She abandoned it there. She told the intern she couldn't take care of the baby, and then she disappeared." Caroline paused before bitterly adding, "I didn't even know she was pregnant."

"Where's the baby now?"

"Still in the hospital. But they're saying just a few more days and the baby will be ready to come home. I've already talked to the case worker about bringing the baby here."

I was stunned. "Wait," I said. "Back up. Darla has a

scholarship at the University of Rochester. She's been right here in town all semester. You're telling me you had no inkling she was pregnant?"

Caroline pulled off her dark glasses and rubbed the scarred area around her eyes. "Darla wanted to go away to school, to really get away from home, but I told her if she stayed here at the U of R. and took the scholarship they were offering, I would leave her completely alone. And she promised to call once a week."

"Did she?"

Caroline shrugged. "At first."

"What a surprise," I said.

"It wasn't like you think," Caroline said, defending Darla as always. "Her scholarship meant I had some extra money to spend. Plus I had a ton of unused vacation. So after Darla settled down at school, I got in touch with some old nursing friends. We flew to Cambodia for old times' sake and then to Vietnam."

"And you didn't see Darla when you got back?"

"I didn't get back until after Thanksgiving. I phoned her a few times, but she didn't return my calls. Then, when I got the call from you saying Whit had been killed, I tried again to get in touch with Darla. I left her a ton of messages, but she never called and she didn't come home. Whit was my only brother, and you're her only aunt. It infuriated me that Darla could be so unfeeling! Finally I just stopped trying to reach her." Caroline sipped her drink and gestured dismissively at my silence. "Well, we both know Darla goes through these phases. But on Christmas Eve, when she didn't come home and I still had not heard from her, it dawned on me something might be wrong. So I called Joe Aguilar's sister, Rosa. We both attend Mass at Our Lady of Victory, and she's on the Rochester Police force. But officially, cops aren't very concerned when college kids don't show up for a holiday."

25

I picked at a frayed spot on the arm of the chair. "Caroline, could you just fast forward and tell me about this baby?"

"Yeah. In a nutshell, the baby was starved, dehydrated, and filthy. The diaper hadn't been changed for God knows how long and had caused a horrific staph infection."

"That's horrible! And Darla didn't say why?"

Caroline shook her head bleakly. "Darla didn't say much of anything. When the intern started asking questions about the baby's condition, Darla said she had to visit the restroom, and then she disappeared. It's almost as if she was re-enacting her own birth."

"You raised Darla to be a caring person. I just don't understand how she could deprive a baby of its basic needs, let it go hungry, not even keep it clean, and then desert it. It doesn't make any sense!"

"And it was Christmas! I was right here just three blocks away. Why the hell didn't she come here? She knows I would help her no matter what trouble she was in!" Caroline's hand dropped to Nomad's neck, her fingers twining in his pale golden coat. She paused long enough to sip her Scotch and run her hand along the table between us in search of her cigarettes. "I don't have any answers, Kate."

The Scotch in her glass disappeared. I got up and poured her more.

When I sat down again, I said, "How did you find out the baby was in the hospital?"

Caroline shook her head and gestured vaguely toward the unlit Christmas tree. "I can't begin to tell you what a bitch Christmas was. Even though Rosa wasn't particularly concerned when she stopped by on Christmas Eve, I was too worried to sleep. Nomad and the cat and I sat up all night by the tree waiting for Darla to phone. Sometime around six Christmas morning the doorbell rang. Rosa was at the door, and this time she had her partner with her...his name is Cisco, or something like that. They wanted to know if Darla was here.

"Then they started asking questions. Did I know where Darla was, had I known she was pregnant, could I tell them the names of her friends at school, did she have a boyfriend? I kept asking what was wrong. I guess I finally convinced them I didn't know any more than they did. So then they told me about the baby and made me promise to call them immediately if Darla showed up because she probably needed medical treatment."

"Why?"

"The baby's umbilical cord had not been cleanly cut, which means Darla didn't have the baby at a hospital. That's why I was so sure the girl they pulled out of the river was Darla. I just knew she had either killed herself or had become weak from hemorrhaging and fallen in."

"Why didn't you tell me all this on the phone?"

Tears were trickling down Caroline's face unheeded. "I guess I...just couldn't." She fumbled in the pocket of her slacks for a handkerchief. "So then Rosa and her partner drove me over to the hospital. Darla's baby was in the neonatal intensive care unit, just a week old, and crying with pitiful little mewling sounds. Did you know they put the IV in a baby's scalp? It's where the biggest veins are. I used to be a nurse, but I had a really hard time with that."

I shuddered. "It sounds frightful."

"I know."

We sat with our drinks for a few minutes. There were so many questions. I didn't know where to begin.

"Darla had to have been pregnant before school started. You didn't suspect anything?"

Caroline shook her head. "No. And when she called home before I left on my trip, she said she loved her classes, was studying really hard, going out with friends, blah, blah. She said she was glad I was going to take a vacation. And I was happy she was fitting in so well and had made some friends."

"Why would she let herself get pregnant? She had to know she wouldn't be able to take care of a child while she was in school."

Caroline turned to face me with a bitter and baffled look. "It's not as if she didn't get sex education from me. And she certainly knew how to get birth control pills if she wanted them." Caroline looked so sad my heart contracted at her pain. "Kate, she's had so much rejection in her life...."

"Oh, give me a break! You've devoted your life to that child!"

In point of fact, Caroline doted on Darla to an unhealthy extent. Over the years her indulgence and refusal to discipline the girl had frustrated Darla's teachers and a long line of therapists. So I wasn't surprised when Caroline shook her head and said, "You have to understand, Kate, Darla's never gotten over the fact that her father didn't know she existed and her mother wouldn't touch her when she saw her after her birth. You know what we've been through. When you're bi-racial, friends and dates are few and far between. Now my grandchild is another rejected child. It's like history repeating itself. Darla and her baby are all I have in this world. We've got to sort this out!"

I sighed. "We will, Caroline. We'll start first thing in the morning."

Caroline lit an unfiltered Lucky Strike, the only brand she would smoke, and offered me one. Like a fool I took it. The first drag clawed its way down my throat like the pot we used to smoke in college.

"I can't believe I just did that!" I choked. "I always think I'm tougher than I am."

28

We smoked together in silence. Then Caroline put her head back against the chair and closed her eyes. I unlaced my boots and eased back into my chair to put my feet on the communal ottoman. I had been wearing the same clothes for two days now, selected for warmth and comfort rather than style. Not Exactly Fifth Avenue, as Joe Aguilar had so rudely pointed out on the dock. The accuracy of his comment still rankled.

I glanced over at Caroline. The combination of single malt whiskey and exhaustion was taking its toll. I watched her face as she dozed and realized I had never even asked her if Darla's baby was a girl or a boy.

Chapter Five

At 4:30 in the morning I woke up in Caroline's tiny guest room in the throes of jet lag. After thrashing around in a futile effort to go back to sleep, I slid out of bed and went down to the kitchen.

Nomad was not in his bed, but the coffee pot mercifully held freshly made coffee. Evidently Caroline had also been unable to sleep and was out walking the dog. I rummaged through the secretary in the front hall for pen and paper to start a list of things I did not want to do. Then I sat and stared at the blank page until I heard Caroline stomping snow off her boots at the side door.

"Nomad and I walked over to the hospital to see the baby," she announced when I opened the door for her. "They let me drop in whenever I want." Caroline had worked at Highland Hospital as a social worker since Darla was two years old.

She disconnected the leash from Nomad's harness and shook snow out of her hair as she climbed the three steps into the kitchen. "They're moving the baby out of intensive care this morning. Get dressed, and after breakfast I'll take you over to the hospital. I have to be at work at eight, but it won't matter if I'm a little late. And wear something socially acceptable," she added, "in case we run into the cow from Child Protective Services."

Over breakfast Caroline gave me several suggestions for finding Darla. I wrote them all down. Darla was probably on a bus to nowhere with the baby's father, but the sooner I located her, the sooner I could return to England.

It was a cold three-block walk to Highland hospital, a sprawling, red brick affair that started out in the 1880s as Hahnemann Homeopathic Hospital. The hospital had a strong nursing tradition, its first graduates sallying forth before the turn of the last century wearing floor-length uniforms, stiff pinafores, and kick-ass expressions. In fact, until 1965 the school still served the nurses morning tea in the library. I knew Caroline harbored a secret dream that Darla would one day join Highland's nursing staff and become part of the tradition. It was a dream she should probably kiss good-bye.

Inside the hospital, the halls were warm and, surprisingly, offered no olfactory hints of unpleasant medical procedures. Even at this early hour, hospital staff was about and greeted Caroline by name.

Outside the Pediatric Intensive Care Unit, we ran into the first roadblock of the day in the form of a caseworker, Estelle Grayson, a.k.a. the cow from Monroe County Child Protective Services. She was a pallid young woman with wide hips and an unsmiling face. She wore a beige wool skirt and cream twin set with her ID clamped firmly over her meager bosom. When she addressed Caroline, it was loudly and in simple sentences as if she believed that Caroline's blindness also implied she was hard of hearing and somewhat witless.

"Ms. Scholfield, the baby is being moved from intensive care this morning. She will be released from the hospital in a matter of days. We will be placing her in foster care as soon as she is released."

Caroline looked stunned. "Foster care! You know I planned to take my grandchild."

"And you, Ms. Scholfield, know that is impossible. We have already discussed this. On more than one occasion. Without extensive preparation and support, we cannot place medically at-risk babies in homes where the primary caretaker is visually impaired. Even if you were, at one time, a nurse." She spoke the word *nurse* as if she doubted Caroline's qualifications.

"But," she continued brightly, "we are placing the baby with a very competent woman. She has three other foster children in her care right now. She's an admirable person. One of our best. I know you will like her immensely."

Caroline stood rigidly, her hand clenched in Nomad's fur. Her face flattened into stubborn lines indicating she would not like immensely any foster mother taking her grandchild.

Estelle Grayson looked me up and down, obviously not impressed by my frizzy hair and wrinkled attire. Rumpled was the best I had been able to do. Evidently, Caroline's iron and ironing board had gone off to school with Darla. "I don't believe I've had the pleasure of meeting you," she said to me.

The British are masters at rumpled hauteur. I gave it my best imitation. "Kate Scholfield, Caroline's sister-in-law. I've just flown in from London." I reached out to shake hands. Her hand was as cold as the proverbial mackerel. "But I do hope you will excuse us. I'm very anxious to meet the, ah, new baby before Caroline has to be at work."

Grasping Caroline by the arm, I firmly steered her into the Pediatric Intensive Care Unit. I am not a tough person. I get seasick standing on a dock, and medical situations leave me green around the gills. The thought of sick children makes me unbearably sad, but I knew I needed to separate Caroline and her arch nemesis before bridges became ashes. Neonatal ICU was the default option.

We traversed a brightly lit area full of medical equipment which I did not want to know about. As we walked through the unit, I cravenly avoided looking into any of the cribs, especially the ones with crying babies. In the far corner of the unit Caroline and Nomad stopped next to a frail, sleeping baby.

"Hello, Caroline," said the red-haired nurse on duty who was in the process of adjusting a beeping monitor behind the baby's crib. "Is this your sister-in-law from London?"

"Hi, Bea," answered Caroline. "Yes, this is Kate. She arrived late last night."

The nurse's smile was a warm greeting on a dark morning. She peered into the crib for a brief assessment of the baby and said, "Great. Then I'll leave you to the introductions."

Caroline reached into the crib and ran a loving hand over the frail baby until she found a tiny hand. "Meet little Katie," she said. "Darla named her baby after you."

Through a blur of tears I damned Darla and her sentimental trap. She had known all along I would come to her baby's aid. I stared at the baby's smooth, dusky skin, her black curly hair, tiny hands, and delicate shell nails. She was an utterly beautiful baby.

"Do you want to hold her?"

I shook my head. "No, I don't think so." I realized immediately it was the wrong answer. I hedged. "The IV... I mean, I don't want to hurt her."

"Just pick her up. She won't break."

It was like picking up a bird. Little Katie scrunched up her face and made a sucking motion with her mouth but didn't wake up. She arched her back and stuck out her butt which made it all but impossible to get a good purchase on her. She felt warm and slightly damp and smelled of baby powder. I awkwardly snuggled her down into the crook of my arm and was beset by an overwhelming sense of protectiveness.

Bea, the nurse, reappeared. "Diapers are on the table, Caroline," she said. "Go ahead and change her." Bea's beeper went off, and she hurried away.

"Kate will do it," Caroline called after her.

I glared at Caroline. "Caro, you know I don't know the first thing about babies!"

"What can be so hard about putting on a diaper? Just do it."

Furious at being backed into a corner by my sister-in-law and her wretched sentimental daughter, I lay the baby gingerly in the crib and pulled open the Velcro fasteners of her diaper. Her skinny little legs folded up, and her impossibly perfect little toes fanned out in protest. I picked up a fresh disposable diaper and put it on with the utmost care. The Velcro tabs could be readjusted, so I made them a little tighter. I did not want my first diaper falling off. I covered Katie carefully with a baby blanket and stood looking at her. *How could Darla have abandoned this lovely child? And even worse, how could she have mistreated her?*

The nurse came back and took the old diaper. "We weigh it so we can measure Katie's liquid in, liquid out," she told me cheerfully. She looked down at the baby and peeked under the blanket. "Oh, the diaper's on backward," she laughed.

With great proficiency and what seemed callous lack of consideration for the sleeping baby, she whipped off the diaper and put on a new one. "Picture goes in the front," she explained.

What could I say? That I hadn't been up close and personal with a diaper since the baby's now-missing mother arrived on a transport flight eighteen years ago? Back in the dark ages when they didn't have pictures on diapers?

Caroline's throaty, easy laugh saved me. "Kate has been overseas for centuries. She's way behind when it comes to American consumer goods."

The nurse smiled, "Well you two can just sit here and take turns rocking the baby for a while. I'll see you later."

34

After the nurse left, I hissed at Caroline, "We are not going to sit here and rock this baby. We're going to get a lawyer and find out what needs to be done so we're ready to take on Child Protective Services. Get your coat."

Chapter Six

We returned to Caroline's house. While Caroline arranged to take the morning off from work, I unpacked and threw a load of clothes in the washing machine. At nine I phoned Hardgrave, Tuttle and Walters, the Rochester law firm which handled Whit's affairs. After Whit died they sent me a request to contact them at my earliest convenience. I had ignored it. Now I needed them to keep Katie out of foster care. After that, they could start sorting out Whit's estate.

The Ellwanger and Barry Building sat across from the Crowne Plaza Hotel in the heart of downtown Rochester. Built in 1890, it had been designated a National Landmark building, but little of the original interior design remained. Michael Ferguson, one of Hardgrave, Tuttle, and Walters' junior partners, met us at the front desk. Ferguson's conservative navy suit was offset by tasseled loafers and an aggressive paisley tie. His bright blue eyes and wiry brown hair radiated energy and determination, the very assets we needed most.

Ferguson seated us around a table in a small conference room and offered us coffee which we declined. Then he offered us condolences over Whit's death. Finally, after hearing our concerns regarding Darla and her baby, he folded his hands on the table and collected his thoughts. "In placement issues," he began, "relatives normally trump foster care. Child Protective Services prefers to place a child with relatives. In this case, Child Protective Services may prefer to place the baby in foster care not just because you are blind,

Ms. Scholfield, but because Darla is a wild card. They don't know where she is. They also don't know how the two of you would respond if she showed up and demanded her baby."

Caroline's uncertain expression indicated she, herself, did not know how she would respond if Darla appeared and asked for her baby. "So having the baby in foster care gives them more protective control," she conceded.

Ferguson nodded. "And, with all due respect, their job is to oversee the welfare of the child. They will want to have the baby placed in a stable environment. Therefore, even if your sister-in-law were to stay for a while, CPS will probably not consent to place the baby with you, Caroline, because when Kate returns to London, there is still the issue of your sight. And no one knows at this point whether Darla will be able to take the baby. It's possible CPS would have to begin the placement process for the child all over again. Do you see where I'm going with this?"

Caroline pressed her hands together and said, "Do we have any hope at all?"

Ferguson was silent, his eyes roving around the room as he mentally assessed our options.

I turned to him. "Could Caroline and I have a few moments to discuss this?"

Ferguson pushed his chair away from the table and stood up. He tightened the knot on his paisley tie and said, "Certainly. Why don't you two sit here, and I'll have coffee sent in. Just let my secretary know when you're ready, and she'll find me."

When his secretary arrived with the coffee, its rich fragrance filled the room. Caroline felt carefully along the table to locate her cup. It rattled in its saucer as she shoved it aside. Her voice was bitter when she spoke. "Why did you ask Mr. Ferguson to leave? There's nothing to discuss. It's a nightmare. They're going to put Katie into foster care."

I pushed my cup aside, too, and leaned my elbows on the table. "Caro, we've been friends since freshman year of college. And we've been family ever since I married Whit...."

Caroline threw up a hand to interrupt me, yanked off her dark glasses in agitation, and pushed them onto her face again. "Look, I know this isn't the time or place to discuss this, and you aren't supposed to speak ill of the dead, but there have been times when I've been sorry I ever introduced you to Whit."

"Caro!"

"There! I know you're in mourning and you don't want to talk about him, but I've wanted to say that for a long time. It wasn't something I felt I could say while he was alive."

"Caro, for heaven's sake!"

"Well, it's true. He was an egotistical bastard, even if he was my brother. His career came before everything else. He had a one-track mind when it came to money and prestige and power. You know that as well as I do."

"So what? I had the opportunity to travel all over the world. It was a good life. I spent a lot of time alone, but I'm a solitary person. And I...loved him."

"But you always wanted children, and he didn't."

I felt a stab of betrayal. "Did he tell you that?"

"No. He never said a word to me about it. It probably was never important enough to him to mention. I could just tell by the way you were with Darla from the minute I brought her home, the way you cared for her while I was recovering. You would have been a wonderful mother. You should have had a whole tribe of kids."

I took a deep breath. "How about just one?" I said.

Caroline's face registered shock. "Good God! Are you *pregnant?*"

I laughed out loud in spite of everything. "Keep your voice down, you idiot!" I hissed. "They'll think we've lost our minds in here! Of course I'm not pregnant. I'm older than Methuselah!"

"Then what are you saying?"

I was silent for a moment, searching for the courage to say what needed to be said. "I'm going to ask if I can be Katie's foster mother."

Caroline shook her head, momentarily at a loss for words. It was an unusual state for her. Then she reached across the table searching for my hand. "Are you sure? Are you really sure you want to do this?"

"Caroline, I'm going to do this. You know and I know that putting that baby in the hands of stranger is not an acceptable option."

When Ferguson returned, Caroline did not even wait for him to be seated before she said, "Kate's going to move in with me and become the baby's foster mother."

Ferguson's expression was grave as he glanced at me to assess my reaction to her words. I gazed at him steadily but said nothing. His eyes shifted away from mine for an instant before he gave me a slight nod. "Right," he said briskly. "In that case, we should get started immediately. There will be a court hearing to determine the baby's placement. We want to demonstrate to the judge that we're committed to taking the baby and are working toward that end. The most important thing is to get our paperwork moving."

Several bureaucratic hours later, I was on my way to becoming a foster parent. It had been my own decision, but even so, I was numbed by the realization that I was losing everything that had been important to me. Whit was gone, but I would be granted no more time to mourn. Freedom to come and go as I pleased? Gone. Independence? I would be under the constant surveillance of people concerned with the baby's welfare. I would no longer be able to travel. I would have no time to write. And this could turn into a life sentence if I couldn't find Darla or if Darla proved unfit. There was no time for self-pity. Ferguson placed the last batch of paperwork in front of me. I signed it all.

"Your next hurdle," Ferguson warned us, "will be interviews and a home visit. Child Protective Services has to ascertain that you, Kate, will be an acceptable caregiver and that Caroline's house will be suitable for infant care. They'll call to make appointments, so you'll want to be ready."

Since Caroline was not a devoted housekeeper by anyone's standards, sighted or blind, she asked me to drive her home so she could start cleaning. Then I returned to the city through gently falling snow. My second meeting with Michael Ferguson regarded more personal matters and would be even less enjoyable. Little did I know.

Ferguson once again offered me his condolences over the death of my husband and more designer coffee which I declined. He pulled Whit's Last Will and Testament from a folder and placed it squarely on the table in front of him. He stared down at it for a moment and tapped it with the fingers of his right hand. The dark red stone in his school ring glittered in the overhead light. When he looked up, his expression was grave. There was, he explained, a serious issue regarding the estate.

A lawyer's profession is based upon the adroit use of words, but Ferguson seemed to be groping for a way to express himself. He took a deep breath. "Kate, the last time Whit was in Rochester, he added a codicil to his will. He left a...significant sum of money to a woman named Angela Brighton. Fifty thousand dollars, to be exact."

I felt the room shift. My voice when I spoke seemed far away. "Angela Brighton? The woman who died with Whit in the roadside bombing? She was his secretary. Why would he leave money to his secretary?" Suddenly my lungs stopped working. I felt as if I had to gasp each word. "According to the newspapers she...she was five months pregnant. The baby... was...the baby was a boy...."

Ferguson nodded. He paused and then said with reluctance, "Angela Brighton was carrying Whit's child. Of course, now that she is deceased, that money will revert to you."

I could literally feel the blood draining out of my face.

Ferguson rose abruptly to his feet. "Let me get you some water. Or perhaps a cup of tea?"

I could not even shake my head. My brain seemed to have dissociated from my body.

Ferguson poured a glass of water from a pitcher that was sitting on a sideboard and put it in my hand. As if from a distance, I heard ice clink. I lifted the glass to my face and pressed it against my cheek as if it could put out the fire in my face. Condensation from the glass trickled down my wrist. "Angela Brighton was carrying Whit's child? Are you sure?"

The lawyer nodded. "I'm very sure. Whit, himself, told me."

Devastation flooded every cell in my body.

Ferguson hammered home the details. "Before leaving for Iraq, Whit decided to amend his will so that, if anything happened to him, Miss Brighton and the unborn child would be adequately provided for."

"Fifty thousand dollars sounds adequate to me," I conceded bitterly. I stared across the room at the red drapes bracketing the late gray afternoon beyond the window. The room's dark paneling reminded me of a coffin. There had been no coffin for Whit. Instead there was a memorial bench on a wild and beautiful island, the antithesis of all that Iraq had been. Someday, when I was free again, I would return to that island and hack the bench into matchsticks.

Ferguson's voice brought me back to the present. "Whit was in a dangerous business in an even more dangerous part of the world. You know his company provided double indemnity life insurance if an employee died on the job?"

I nodded in mute response.

"Kate, because you were his legal wife at the time, the company life insurance policies come to you. As does the rest of his estate. You are going to be a wealthy woman. The figures are all here for you." He slid a stack of papers across the table to me. "There is just that one sum of money, fifty thousand dollars which...."

I stared down at the papers lying on the table. Tears slipped down my face and I wiped them away angrily.

"I know this is very difficult for you. Are you sure you wouldn't like something? Tea, perhaps?"

I shook my head. "Under the circumstances, hemlock would be more appropriate. Please go on. I'm sure there's more."

"There is one last matter to discuss."

"I can't wait to hear it."

Ferguson managed a small, rueful smile. "The last matter concerns Mylabelle Scholfield's estate."

I nodded. "Whit's aunt. I received your letter about her death right before Whit died, but I couldn't reach him, so...he never knew."

"She went quietly in her sleep. There was no indication she was even ill, although she was ninety-four. She divided her money between your sister-in-law, Caroline, and a small Pentecostal Church in Mendon, but, as you know, she left the rest of her estate to you and Whit.

"The rest of her estate being her old house in Mendon."

"Yes. Her Eastlake Victorian house, the outbuildings and all the contents. That is also yours now."

"I really liked Aunt Myla. I'm going to miss her. I guess

I'll have to arrange to put the house on the market and have some sort of estate sale. To be perfectly honest, I really don't want to think about it right now. I'll just sign whatever papers you need, and then I think I'll go...home. Well, not *home*. Back to Caroline's house. I guess it's going to be my home now." Tears ran down my face and dripped onto the papers in front of me. I blotted them ineffectually with my sleeve.

I drove back to Caro's house through two inches of fresh snow. Dusk was at hand and the sun was making a late debut. The beauty of the winter evening was wasted on me. As I drove past Highland Park, I glimpsed the snow-covered statue of Frederick Douglass. I recalled his statue had originally faced south, but Susan B. Anthony, never a woman to keep her mouth shut, said she thought he would have preferred to face north. The result was a 180-degree rotation of the stature. Perhaps I needed to take a few lessons in assertiveness from Susan B.

Five minutes later I slewed into the frozen ruts in Caroline's drive. As I walked in the unlocked side door, I called out to Caroline to announce my arrival. From his bed by the radiator, Nomad thumped his tail as if to apologize for the unwashed dishes still sitting in the sink and the vacuum cleaner idling in the middle of the kitchen floor.

Caroline, far from cleaning house, was sitting in her favorite chair with the yellow cat curled next to her. The phone was propped against her shoulder leaving her hands free for a mug of tea and a cigarette. Her used tea bag was sitting in her ashtray, and the acrid odor of wet cigarette butts filled the room.

"Absolutely not," she cried into the phone. "I don't want these people put in a shelter! They're going to need guidance. They've been living in mud huts for thirteen years. They've probably never seen a working toilet or an operational light switch. Let me call the rest of the committee. I'll get back to you." She slammed down the phone.

"There's been a slight glitch," she announced, flicking ashes carelessly toward the ashtray.

I crept into the chair next to hers and numbly waited for the next ax to fall.

Caroline took a drag on her cigarette and exhaled a series of perfect smoke rings. "It seems we have a refugee family arriving Thursday afternoon. We hoped to have more notice, but that's not always possible. The refugees are staying here until we can find them permanent housing."

"Caroline!"

"I'm the head of our church's Resettlement Team. No one else would agree to house the refugees, so I said I would. With Darla off to college, the house was pretty much empty. It seemed like a piece of cake at the time."

"Where are these refugees coming from?"

"Africa. Kenya, actually. They're Somali Bantus. It's a family of seven. I'm sure CPS will understand."

"Are you insane? CPS won't even begin to understand!" I pictured the triumphant look on Estelle Grayson's face as she trotted my namesake off to foster care. "You simply have to tell whoever is in charge of this refugee thing that you are in the middle of a family crisis."

"I can't, Kate. The family has clearance and is already on their way. They're arriving at the airport at four PM on Thursday."

"How long are these refugees going to be here with you...us? No, wait. Don't even answer that. The sun is over the yardarm, and my personal life took a real nosedive today. I'm damned if I'm going to postpone cocktail hour."

Over drinks, mine with ice, I repeated my question. "How long are these seven Bantu refugees who have no concept of modern plumbing or electricity going to be living with us?"

"Two or three weeks," said Caroline. "Maybe longer." I could tell, in spite of the impending catastrophe, she was enchanted with her mission project. "And, by the way, Church World Service does have a little training program at the camp in Kenya to teach them some of the basics."

"What an immense comfort."

"Of course, we had no idea we would be assigned such a large family. It won't be easy to find them a place to rent."

"That is probably the understatement of the century."

We sat drinking in silence. I stared at the unlit Christmas tree and the wrapped packages gathering dust beneath it. Caroline probably had visions of refugee resettlement dancing in her head. Every swear word I had ever heard swirled through mine. My grief was rapidly turning to fury at Whit and his entire wretched family. I knew I could never tell Caroline about Whit's infidelity. I was condemned to living with the shame and rage in silence. And now, thanks to Darla's baby and Caroline's refugees, there would be no time to deal with either the loss of my husband or the loss of the illusion that he had loved me.

From the glow of the table lamp, Caroline's small living room appeared warm and inviting. Original oak floors and gumwood trim, a gas fireplace framed on either side by leaded glass bookcases, and a stained glass window set in the landing of the stairs leading up to three tiny bedrooms, and a single black-and-white-tiled bathroom.

I pictured myself and Darla's baby crammed in this house with Caroline and seven African refugees. I envisioned frequent visits from a highly disapproving Child Protective Services caseworker. I had two choices. I could either take control of this situation or I could allow my life to spiral into chaos. I put down my drink. "Caroline, I have a solution to your resettlement problem. You know Aunt Myla left her house to Whit and me?"

Caroline brightened. "You think we could put the refugees there?"

"No. You're stuck with your refugees. I think I'll take the baby and go live there myself."

Caroline snatched up her pack of cigarettes. "You can't do that! Darla's baby needs to be here with me. She's my grandchild. You can't stash her out in that Victorian mausoleum where I'll never see her!"

The phone saved me from arguing with Caroline. It started to ring. It rang that night until after eleven. All the calls were concerning the imminent arrival of seven Somali Bantus.

Chapter Seven

Thoughts of Whit and Angela Brighton wracked me through the night. At 5 a.m. I acknowledged there was no sleep in the program, brushed my teeth, and headed over to the hospital. It was a clear, cold morning. Under the street lamps, ice glittered on uneven sidewalks and made walking hazardous. I was amazed Caroline made this trip five days a week, winter after winter, and never fell. Or maybe she did fall but never told anyone. That was more likely. Perhaps with the money left to her by Aunt Myla she could think about retiring.

Inside the hospital, there was an air of desultory activity as the night staff ended their shift. In Pediatric Intensive Care, the night nurse greeted me by name and told me Katie had been moved to the East Wing. She was improving rapidly. It was joyful news, but it meant she would be released soon, and we had so little time to get ready.

There was a merciful dearth of medical apparatus in Katie's new area where a nursery border of baby animals cavorted atop creamy yellow walls. Flowered curtains were pulled around most of the cribs. Behind her curtain, Katie was awake and squalling. I picked her up and began to rock her. Her face was red and wet, and she continued to scream in spite of my best efforts to comfort her.

"You're so beautiful. I simply don't understand how your mommy could abandon you," I whispered to her. "When she was little, she brought home anything that was hurt or lost – birds, turtles, snakes. Your grandma wouldn't let her keep them, so she brought them to your Uncle Whit and me. We had turtles and snakes in our guest shower, baby rabbits in laundry baskets, and birds in shoeboxes. What changed your mommy?" I feared I knew the answer, but I didn't want to say it aloud.

And where was mommy right now? In hiding? Shooting up in an alley? And what pretty story would we make up to tell Katie when she grew old enough to ask about her mother?

Morning's earliest hours catch us before we have our defenses mustered. Tears for Caroline and Darla and her baby ran down my face into the soft black curls that covered Katie's small, perspiring head. Holding her close, I offered a silent prayer to a God who seemed to callously relegate his own responsibilities to inept mortals. A harried nurse interrupted my matins. She pragmatically ignored my tears and handed me a bottle.

"What time does the doctor usually come in?" I asked, wiping my eyes.

"It varies," she answered. "Seven is a good bet." She dashed out, pulling the curtain closed behind her.

Katie sucked fitfully on the nipple, brown eyes open but unfocused. Milk ran out the corners of her mouth and into the creases of her neck. Soon her pink gown was saturated.

Caroline appeared with Nomad. "Kate, is that you?"

"Yeah, it's me."

"I smell milk. What the hell are you doing, soaking Katie in formula? Milk is not something babies absorb through their pores."

"Well, I got some of it down her throat. Most of it ran down her neck."

Caroline's gentle hands groped for the baby in my arms. "The doctor had an evaluation done before you arrived. Part of the problem is she's forgotten how to suck. But it may simply be nipple confusion."

"What's nipple confusion?"

"Darla probably started out nursing Katie. Now, of course, she's being bottle-fed. Did you burp her?"

"Oh, shit. I forgot babies need to be burped." I put Katie to my shoulder and gently patted her back.

Caroline said with ill-placed righteousness, "If you're going to be a foster mother, you'll have to give up swearing."

"Every word I know I learned from you," I replied. Katie lay limply against my shoulder. "I guess she didn't swallow enough milk to need to burp," I added.

"Put her across your knees and rub her back."

I followed orders. Katie squirmed and let out a belch that would have appalled a truck driver. Elated over my momentary triumph, I handed the soggy baby off to her grandmother. Then I got down to more serious matters.

"Caroline, we've got to be ready to take Katie home, and we don't have a lot of time. Could you call this morning to make sure the electricity and water are turned on in Aunt Myla's house?"

"So you're definitely going to stay out there?"

I nodded, remembered she couldn't see, and said, "Yes. I'm going to need every ounce of sanity I can muster. Your house will be a three-ring circus, and you know it."

She shrugged her defeat. "You're right. But...."

"Look, Caro, we can negotiate the terms of your visitation rights later. You know I'm going to be looking for all the help I can get with that baby. Right now we've got a million details to iron out. When you call about the electricity and water, could you also find out what kind of heat is in the house? If it's oil, we might need the oil company to come out and fill the tank. It would help if I knew which company Aunt Myla used."

"There's probably a sticker on the furnace," Caroline suggested.

49

"Right," I said. "Good thinking. I'll look when I go out there this morning. And could you see if the phone needs to be hooked up? Then start thinking about what colors you want for the nursery. Make one of your famous Braille lists of everything we need down to Q-tips and baby wipes."

"What fun!" said Caroline with enthusiasm.

"We'll go shopping this evening," I told her, "so everything can be delivered before the Child Protective Services people come to inspect the house. I'm going to stay here until the doctor makes his rounds, and then I'll pick up keys at the lawyer's office and drive out to Aunt Myla's."

"Good idea," said Caroline. "God only knows what it will take to put that place in livable order. And don't forget you promised to call Joe Aguilar and get me some goat meat for the refugees."

After Caroline and Nomad left for work, I settled down to wait. By seven there was still no sign of the doctor, and the same harried nurse's latest speculation was he would not be in until after Grand Rounds were over at midday. I waited half an hour longer, then gave up on the doctor and drove to the airport to trade in my mid-sized rental car for a four-wheel-drive SUV that drove like a tank. Since I was going to haul the baby around, I wanted lots of protection for her. Then I realized I would need a car seat for her. My empty stomach cramped with anxiety. There would be guidelines for car seats, but a lot of things about babies had no guidelines at all.

At the Sibley Building, Ferguson's gray-haired secretary flashed me a compassionate smile and handed over a new brass house key and a large manila envelope. In the envelope was a tangle of oversized old-fashioned keys. "We found all those keys in the pantry in a canning jar," she said. "None seemed to match the front door, back door, or any of the side doors. I don't think your husband's aunt ever locked her

50

doors. We had new locks installed. That new key fits all of them."

On the way out of the city, I passed a donut shop which reminded me I was starving and I had to call Aguilar. I hit the brakes on the SUV. They worked quite well.

It was warm inside the donut shop and aromatic with the fragrances of coffee and sugar. Customers in bulky coats sat on stools at a long pink counter with a view of coffee machines, racks of fresh donuts, and the blond who was dishing them up. I ordered coffee and a cinnamon roll the size of a dinner plate, and then I used the pay phone to dial Aguilar.

"Joe Aguilar? It's Kate Scholfield. From the Isles of Scilly...pronounced with the C silent."

"Why the hell haven't you called? My niece won't tell me a thing except the dead girl they pulled from the river isn't Caroline's daughter."

I briefly ran through the story up to the present, omitting only my afternoon visit to the lawyer.

"And now you're headed out to see this old house in Mendon? How about if I come along? Help you look the place over?"

"I thought you worked for the Department of Agriculture? Aren't you at work now?"

"Lady, I have to be in the plants by four or five in the morning. Normally I get off about one, but no one's going to squawk if I skip lunch and cut out a little early. It'll give 'em a chance to cut corners and make a few extra bucks."

Unaccountably my spirits lifted. "Okay," I said. "I'm at the Brighton Donut Shop on Monroe Avenue. Meet me here, and we can drive out together."

Fifteen minutes later, Joe Aguilar sauntered in, wide shoulders stuffed into the same leather jacket he'd been wearing when he found me in the pub on St. Mary's Isle.

"Still living on frosting, I see," he said caustically. He looked me up and down but diplomatically refrained from comment. I wasn't any closer to Fifth Avenue now than I had been on Saturday morning. If anything, I'd gone downhill. In addition to my usual flaws, I had haggard circles under my eyes.

From the donut shop, we headed south on Route 65. The winter landscape rapidly changed from suburbia to woodlands interspersed with gently rolling fields. A wedge of Canadian geese skimmed beneath the clouds in the brilliant blue sky. I rolled down my window and stuck out my head.

"What are you doing?" demanded Aguilar. 'You're supposed to be paying attention to the road!"

"I like to listen to the geese calling when they fly overhead. They mate for life, you know. I always count them and pray for an even number."

"Well, watch the goddamned road before we end up in a ditch."

Aunt Myla's Eastlake Victorian was located on the outskirts of Mendon, an area known for horse farms and historic cobblestone houses. I tested my four-wheel drive on the unplowed drive, and we slid to an erratic stop in front of a garaged designed to resemble a carriage house. I sat behind the wheel staring at the familiar view.

The house sat off to the right, festooned with porches, ornate woodwork, and an inordinate number of windows. Behind the house was a century-old, single-car garage, which Aunt Myla had used as her potting shed, and a two-storey barn covered with grapevines. The house, the garage, and the potting shed were all a dusty green with pale yellow and dark red trim. The barn was yellow in keeping with the tradition of all the old barns in the area.

When Whit and I visited Aunt Myla, it was like stepping back in time. We explored the old barn and walked down an overgrown path that meandered past the barn to a small pond, now ice-covered and ringed with frozen cattails. Beneath the black walnut trees and sugar maples that dotted the rest of the property, we drank lemonade and listened to Aunt Myla talk of times long gone.

Oh, Whit, a simple life just wasn't enough for you, was it? You were always happiest when we were on the go, when life was frenetic and novelty sparkled on the horizon.

Aguilar's voice shattered my reverie. "I thought you were in a hurry to get things done. Are you going to get out of the car or just sit here daydreaming?"

We trudged through snowdrifts to the front porch. The new key easily opened Aunt Myla's double front doors. When I hit the light switch in the two-storey entry hall, a grimy crystal chandelier glittered overhead. Aguilar and I sat on the steps of the curving staircase to take off our wet boots, then we stepped through a second set of tall oak doors into Aunt Myla's front parlor. It was a large dim room filled with musty Victorian furniture and an expanse of bay windows. The room was so cold I could see my breath.

"The place is a damned museum," said Aguilar in awe as he looked around. "There are what, six...seven doors in this room? Where do they all go?"

"Second parlor, library, porch, dining room...I can't remember them all. Excessive was never enough for the Victorians."

He laughed. "One drink too many and you'd never find your way to bed."

We walked through another set of paneled oak doors into the dining room. The chandelier over the mahogany dining room table had originally held candles and then been converted to gas. Now it was electric with a frayed wire that ran across the ceiling. I didn't turn it on. There were enough cobwebs hanging from it to start a conflagration.

I edged around the dusty mahogany table to turn up the thermostat on the far wall. Miraculously, the heat kicked on. Then I opened the door to the back stairs. In the dim light I could see a dead bat lying on the second step. I backed up and slammed the door. How was I going to get this place cleaned up in time to bring the baby here?

From the tiny powder room in the corner of the dining room I heard the toilet make alarming gurgling noises. Aguilar emerged with a sardonic grin. "Must be an original fixture," he said.

Aunt Myla's kitchen fixtures were also disastrously original. The huge black stove was filthy, and the oven door protested loudly when I opened it. Inside was a nest of mice. The refrigerator held a disgusting selection of old food, but the pantry shelves were bare. It struck me as odd that Aunt Myla had fresh food in her refrigerator when she died but almost no packaged food in her pantry. Especially in the winter.

Aguilar interrupted my thoughts. "I don't know how the hell you're going to cook anything in this kitchen. Even after it's cleaned up."

"Actually, I don't do much cooking."

"Well, what are you going to do when the baby starts eating solid food? Call Dominos?"

"Buy baby food in jars."

"Great. That and some instant frosting will fix her right up."

"Look, Aguilar, right now I'm more concerned about making this place livable by the end of the week. I can worry about the four food groups later."

"Don't worry, doll. I'll make a few calls when I get home. I've got contacts. I can have a crew of cleaners here first thing in the morning."

I picked up the phone on the counter and heard a dial

tone. Caroline had obviously been lighting fires under utility crews. I handed the phone to Aguilar. "Call them now. And tell them they can name their price. Child Protective Services will be coming out to determine if this place is suitable for a baby, and I'm sure they intend to arrive wearing white gloves."

"Why don't you rent an apartment in town? It's going to cost a fortune just to heat this joint."

"I've got money," I said. "And I don't want to be cooped up in an apartment. Besides, if Child Protective Services has to drive all the way out here on icy roads, they'll be much less likely to arrive unannounced."

"Well, while you're whipping this house into shape, maybe you should make an appointment at a beauty shop," Aguilar remarked callously.

When I opened my mouth to snarl a reply, he held up his hand. "If Child Protective Services is so concerned about the baby's welfare, you can be sure they're taking a good look at you. I know you lost your husband recently. It looks like you stopped caring for yourself about the time he went up in smoke. They'll say your physical appearance is a reflection of your mental health."

I turned and headed up the back stairs. Facing a dead bat was easier than facing the sting of Aguilar's words. Whatever had compelled me to invite him to come along? But, of course, I hadn't. He'd invited himself.

Upstairs, four bedrooms with tall windows and wide planked floors opened onto a long hall papered in caffeine-colored roses. I had to choose two bedrooms, one for Katie and one for me. I knew from previous visits I did not want to use the front bedroom. Its closet had always smelled as if mice were nesting behind the six-inch chestnut baseboards. I could just imagine Child Protective Services' opinion on that subject.

The bedroom at the back of the house was a dark, unappealing room with a scarred floor and a narrow door that led to the attic. I envisioned the dead bat's relatives hanging from eaves in the attic and crossed this room off the list, too. That left Aunt Myla's own bedroom for me and the smaller bedroom across the hall for Katie.

I opened the door to Aunt Myla's bedroom reluctantly. Rather than a residual odor of death, a faint hint of Crabtree and Evelyn's Lily of the Valley perfume greeted me. Family pictures and mementos littered every available surface. A pair of Aunt Myla's worn black shoes sat by her rocker, and her old raccoon coat lay where she had tossed it at the foot of her brass double bed. Her presence in this room was so immediate it was hard to believe she was gone. My eyes filled with tears, something which seemed to be happening on an hourly basis for one reason or another.

I crossed the hall to the room that would be Katie's nursery and opened the wooden shutters. This room was small and cozy and would be warmed by morning sun. There was an old treadle sewing machine by the window. Mismatched cabinets lined the walls. To make room for the baby, everything in here would have to be moved to the back bedroom or the attic.

Having this old house ready before Katie was sent home from the hospital would be next to impossible. A wave of stomach cramps hit me. I ran down the hall to the outmoded bathroom and threw up this morning's coffee and donut. Then I rinsed my face in the rusty sink and went downstairs to start making lists of all the things that had to be done.

A couple of hours later, I dropped Aguilar off in front of Brighton Donuts. As he headed across the ice-covered parking lot, I called out the window of the SUV, "By the way, I almost forgot. Caroline wants to know where she can get goat meat at a good price. Could you give her a call?"

"Goat? What the hell for?"

"She's planning dinner for seven Africans," I said. Then I drove off before he could ask more questions. Some things are better left undetailed.

Chapter Eight

Caroline was in her favorite chair fielding refugee-related phone calls when I returned. I made a cup of tea and drank it while listening to one-sided discussions involving appointments for TB checks and basic inoculations, screening for unsavory parasites, and temporary food stamp application forms. Piles of winter apparel in various sizes now covered all the furniture in the living room except our two chairs and the ottoman. Large plastic bags of bedding filled the unheated front entry.

Caroline hung up the phone, massaged the area around her eyes with the heel of her hand, and grinned at me. "Let's hit the baby store. I've been looking forward to this all day."

Over a quick dinner at the Highland Diner, Caroline and I discussed what we would buy.

"What color is Katie's room?" was her first question. Because of her lack of sight, she was acutely conscious of color.

"It has faded wallpaper, sort of beige with red flowers. Well not quite red, closer to rose."

"Then let's go with rose and beige and white," Caroline decided instantly. "I know Darla would love those colors." Intense sadness washed over her face.

"Damn it, Caroline..."

Caroline held up a hand to stop my protest. "Darla is the child of my heart. I love her and I believe in her. I just wish so much I could talk to her and be sure she's okay. She brought Katie to the hospital. I think that's a good sign. No matter what the police say, I'm not passing judgment until I hear the whole story. So when we shop for Darla's baby, we're going to buy things Darla would choose if she were with us."

At the largest baby store in town, we walked from display to display. We fingered everything and listened to the melodies of all the musical toys. Knowing how much Caroline loved the luxury of 'seeing,' I described everything in detail. After she came back from Cambodia, we used to stand together in greeting card shops. She would hold Darla, and I would read her card after card. Cards from Caroline never just said *Happy Birthday.*

We bought a maple crib and matching dressing table, a rocking chair, toys, diapers, bottles, and clothing. Monitors, shampoo, a baby bath tub, a bouncing chair, and a sizable book on childcare. Caroline's Braille list seemed endless, and my knees were threatening to buckle from exhaustion by the time we were done. I put it all on my credit card.

We arranged for everything to be delivered to Aunt Myla's gothic monstrosity. Everything, that is, except for a soft, yellow giraffe that played "Greensleeves" when its neck was stretched. Caroline would keep that with her for a while. "Katie," she assured me, "will recognize my scent on it and know her grandmother is not far away. And," she added, "I have an afghan from Darla's bed. You can take that and wrap Katie in it when you rock her. She mustn't forget the scent of her own mother."

"What color is it?"

"Orange. Why?"

"It won't match the décor."

"Don't be a smart ass."

Tuesday morning I arrived at the hospital at my usual predawn hour to spend time with Katie. We were dozing together in the rocking chair when the pediatrician arrived on his morning rounds.

"Dr. Stanford," he announced and held out his hand. He was in his mid-thirties, well over six feet, with a narrow frame and a gentle, compassionate smile. In the breast pocket of his white lab coat was a small, bright green bear.

"You must be Caroline's sister-in-law. You're taking the baby, right?"

"Yes, and I need to talk to you."

Dr. Stanford folded himself onto a rolling stool and said, "Shoot."

"First, tell me about Katie's medical condition, what happened to her, and what I will need to do to take proper care of her."

He extracted a couple of papers from Katie's file and scanned them briefly. "Darla Scholfield is listed as the mother. She's your niece, right?"

I nodded.

"According to the ER report, Darla said the baby was close to full term and delivered at home. There seems to have been no prenatal care except for some multivitamins which Darla said she took in the last trimester." He scanned the second page. "No father's name is given and no birth weight. Darla indicated she tried to breastfeed the baby but her milk never came in." Dr. Stanford shrugged. "She left before anyone could ask more questions. As for Katie's condition, to put it in lay terms, the baby was bruised, seriously dehydrated and malnourished. It's impossible to know what the circumstances were. Now it's simply a matter of bringing her up to a decent weight. We really don't expect any long term negative effects unless she stops sucking."

My stomach clenched. "How likely is that?"

"Since the baby nursed before whatever happened that led to her arrival in the OR, she has a memory of nursing to work from. I think she'll be fine." He smiled. "In fact, we'll probably release her in a few days."

"You can't release her too soon! My paperwork is still wending its way through the proper channels, and I haven't had a home visit from Child Protective Services yet."

"Unfortunately, it's against hospital regulations to delay discharge of a patient. There's nothing I can do about it."

"But they'll give her to a foster mother, and that woman already has three other kids to take care of."

Dr. Stanford shifted his angular frame and looked uncomfortable. I changed the subject.

"One more thing. I think I should take a class in baby care." I didn't want my lack of experience on record, so I added, "I want to be up on the latest information."

He scratched a number on a prescription pad and handed it to me. Then he unfolded his lanky frame and held out his arms for Katie.

Katie grunted and thrust out protesting arms and legs as the doctor went through a brief check-up routine. At the end of the exam her eyes opened and she squinted suspiciously. Dr. Stanford instantly produced a flashlight to shine into her eyes. Katie didn't like it at all, but he seemed satisfied with her reaction.

"She needs lots of loving," he said quietly as he handed her back to me. "The best way to avert failure to thrive is by giving her all the love and attention you can."

"I promise," I swore solemnly and hugged her close.

I was settling Katie back into her crib when Caroline arrived. I waited for her to feel her way into the rocking chair, and then I placed the baby in her lap.

"By the way," Caroline said once she was settled, "Rosa Aguilar's work number is in my coat pocket. I dug it out for you last night, but you had already fallen asleep in your chair. What time did you go to bed?"

"I didn't look at the clock," I said. "I just crawled up the stairs and under the covers."

I left Caroline holding Katie and went down to the cafeteria for scrambled eggs and coffee. Breakfast gave me the courage to phone Rosa at police headquarters, but she wasn't there. I searched through my purse for Aguilar's home number.

"Hello," he snapped. I could hear a TV news station in the background.

"Feeling crotchety this morning?" I said.

"I'm trying to catch the morning stock report before my father gets out of bed, lady. I hope this is important."

"I need to talk to your niece on the police force. I can't seem to catch her at work."

"She's usually out saving the world this time of day. She can't do it from a land line."

"Aguilar, ask her to call me. I just want one little family to have a happy ending."

"Meet me for lunch."

"No, thanks. I'm not interested in dating, even if I had the time. Which I don't."

"Don't flatter yourself. I only date good-looking chicks in high heels and the latest style. I'll ask my niece to lunch and you can talk to her then. I'll pick you up at your Mendon mansion at noon. Now can I go back to the stock report to find out if my investments have all gone down the toilet?"

I hung up the phone and climbed the stairs to the pediatric floor. Caroline was rocking Katie and singing her a lullaby about mockingbirds and diamond rings.

"Give me the name of your hair stylist," I demanded.

"Whatever for?"

"I have until noon to transform myself into a good looking chick in high heels and the latest style."

Caroline turned her face toward me as if she weren't sure what she was hearing. "What the hell did the cafeteria put in your eggs?"

"I need a new persona for dealing with Child Protective Services. Something that goes with a large estate in the country and a beautiful grand niece and her world class nursery."

Midmorning found me perched on an uncomfortable chair in a warehouse which had been converted to an exclusive salon called Indulgences. Its ultramodern lighting and mauve walls did nothing to enhance my appearance, and I wondered if Caroline would have patronized the place if she could have seen it.

"So, what would you like to do with your hair?" To her credit, Caroline's stylist seemed undismayed by my dreadlocks.

I straightened up and faced the mirror. Long frizzy brown hair going gray, cynical eyes the color of recycled glass, freckles splashed across a wan face, lines bracketing what had once been a wide grin. All this offset by a tired corduroy blazer and a pair of unwashed jeans.

"What do you think?" I knew I would be paying her an inordinate sum to sort out my appearance. Best to let her earn it.

She ran her fingers through my hair and eased it away from my face. "Put in highlights and then cut it really short?"

"Do it," I replied without an instant's hesitation. Who would resist convenience in the quest for beauty? "And while you're doing the highlights, can we get a cosmetics person over here and a manicurist, maybe? I'm in a bit of a hurry. I need to buy some new clothes before lunch."

She flashed me an entrepreneurial smile. "No problem!"

I returned to Aunt Myla's house with barely enough time to race upstairs to her bedroom. My new lizard-skin boots had three-inch heels and resounded smartly on the uncarpeted treads. I tossed shopping bags onto the bed and rummaged through Aunt Myla's dresser. From the top

63

drawer, I chose a pair of gaudy amethyst earrings. They complemented perfectly my new lavender sweater and sleek, gray wool skirt. I yanked a scarf out of another drawer. Filmy lilacs. The time-mottled mirror over the dresser reflected what a haircut, a little make-up, and a sack of new clothes could do.

Downstairs, the doorbell shrieked as if its wires had been fried. As a final impulse, I snatched Aunt Myla's old raccoon coat from the end of the bed and clattered down the back stairs, taking care to step over the bat's carcass. When I opened the door, I was gratified to see Aguilar rendered speechless for a change.

"You look like a million bucks," he conceded. He took my arm, but I yanked it away.

"Don't be so touchy," he said. "I was just going to help you down the steps in those boots."

"I'm quite capable of walking in heels."

"Fine, break your scrawny ass. It will save me the price of lunch."

Aguilar drove his black Lincoln like a maiden aunt. We crept down four miles of back roads to Route 65 and then turned left at the stop light and followed the road into the Village of Honeoye Falls. Before white settlers arrived in the area, the village had belonged to the Seneca Indians. It had been called Totiakton and was part of the Iroquois Six Nation League.

In 1789 Zebulon Norton bought up the land around the falls for twelve and a half cents an acre. By 1791 he had built himself a house, a gristmill, and a sawmill. As settlers moved to the land nearby, the village prospered.

Norton's two mills still stand. The Mendon Town Hall occupies the one overlooking the falls; the other houses art galleries and a restaurant called The Juniper Bean. It was here that Aguilar made a careful left turn into a freshly plowed parking lot. Rosa was waiting inside.

The Juniper Bean was a dimly lit tearoom filled with a mismatched collection of antique furniture. Judging from the number of people waiting for tables and the volume of conversation coming from the next room, it was a popular lunch destination even on a snowy winter day. Fortunately, Aguilar had made a reservation.

The harried hostess seated Aguilar, Rosa, and me at a corner table. From the wall over our table, a black-and-white cow in an idyllic pastoral painting gazed down benevolently upon our odd threesome. Aguilar had on his usual leather jacket and jeans. I was adorned in my new and borrowed finery. Aguilar's unsmiling niece, Rosa, wore the stern regalia of the Rochester Police Department. She had Aguilar's doleful eyes, dark brows, and dominant nose. They were family traits which were marginally more attractive in the male. Her dark hair was her finest feature. It was long and sleek, and she wore it pulled back in a thick braid.

We chatted inanely about long Rochester winters and record snowfalls until a frazzled waitress brought the day's special, lobster bisque and crusty French bread. The soup smelled delicious, but my stomach rebelled at the thought of actually swallowing it.

The hot soup fogged Aguilar's thick glasses. He took them off and scowled at me as he wiped them with his napkin. I picked up my spoon and forced down a few spoonfuls of the bisque. Then I asked Rosa if the police had any leads on where Darla might be, and it became immediately clear whatever compassion Rosa had for the case had been expended sending Aguilar haring off to the Isles of Scilly.

She stated starkly, "We don't have any idea where Darla is, but sooner or later she'll surface, and when she does, we'll arrest her." She glanced at Aguilar. Something in his face

65

must have made her realize how harsh her statement sounded. She shrugged and added, "I know your sister-in-law from church. She's a really compassionate person, and she never lets her blindness get her down. That's why I got in touch with Uncle Joe in Spain and asked him to find you. Caroline said you were the only family she had left."

"It was very kind of you to make the effort and very kind of your uncle to give up his vacation to track me down. Caroline and I are indebted to both of you." I stretched my face into a smile and made a mental note to make myself harder to find if I ever got out of Rochester again.

Rosa shook her head as if denying any softness on her part. "But that doesn't alter the facts of the case," she said doggedly. "Darla will have to face charges of neglect and abuse. She could go to prison."

I felt the blood drain out of my face. "Our lawyer said there was a law in New York which protects mothers who bring newborn babies to the hospital when they feel they can't take care of them. Won't the fact that Darla brought the baby to the hospital be a mitigating factor?"

Rosa nodded. "The Abandoned Infant Protection Act. It went into effect in 2000. An affirmative defense can be raised when a parent leaves a baby five days old or less in a suitable place with an appropriate person."

"Would you like to translate that into English?" demanded Aguilar.

An indulgent smile flickered across Rosa's face. "It means, Uncle Joe, if you have a baby and don't want it, you can leave it in a safe place and it will have mitigating circumstances in court. You don't even have to give your name. And you won't automatically surrender your future rights to your child."

"But Katie might have been more than five days old at the time. Will that matter?" I asked.

Rosa shrugged. "That's for the courts to decide. The hospital records show she was dehydrated and seriously underfed and battered. That's not abandonment. That's neglect and abuse."

For the second time in two days, shock brought on the sensation of being outside my body and of watching the room from a distance.

Aguilar glanced furtively around and hissed, "Rosa, what do you mean, *battered?*"

"Didn't you two know?" Rosa seemed surprised. "The intern in the ER noted bruise marks. He said the bruises were consistent with someone gripping the baby by her ankle and swinging her upside down."

I sat stunned. The perfume from Aunt Myla's scarf was suddenly overwhelming. The doctor in the hospital had said something about bruises but he had not elaborated. I reached for my teacup with a cold, shaking hand. *Tea, the British antidote to all crises until the cocktail hour.*

Aguilar leaned forward and shoved his soup bowl aside. "Isn't it possible someone else abused the baby and Darla was just seeking help for her?"

Rosa shrugged a second time. "Anything's possible, Uncle Joe. But when the intern talked to Darla, she insisted the baby was hers and no one else's."

Our blond hovered over our table for a second to see if we needed anything. Aguilar waved her away. She splashed fresh water in our glasses and disappeared.

"Did you personally talk with the intern who interviewed Darla?" Aguilar asked Rosa, his voice brusque.

"Yes, Uncle Joe. But it was a short interview. Darla didn't exactly stay around for a lot of questions."

I thought for a moment. "Did the intern mention what question triggered Darla's flight?"

Rosa wrinkled her brow as if trying to remember. "He

told us Darla clammed up when he started asking questions about what had happened to the baby. So he changed the subject and asked her where she had been living. On the admissions form Darla wrote she was homeless."

Aguilar looked appalled. "She and the baby were living on the streets in the middle of winter? That's unbelievable!"

Rosa folded her napkin into a neat square and set it by her plate. "Darla didn't stick around to give the intern any more answers. She clutched her stomach and said she was going to be sick. The intern gave her directions to a restroom right outside the ER. Darla never returned."

I shook my head. "I can't understand why Darla never contacted Caroline for help."

Rosa nodded in agreement. "I know. It doesn't make any sense. My partner and I were the ones who drove Caroline to the hospital the next morning. On the admissions form, Darla had listed her as the baby's grandmother, but it was pretty obvious Caroline had no idea her daughter had even had a baby."

I sat in silence. A glance at Aguilar's soup bowl confirmed his stock profits for the day had bought an unpalatable meal for both of us.

Rosa's appetite appeared unaffected by the conversation. She finished her soup and then spoke around a last bite of bread. "'We've been living in the wolf's den.' Does that mean anything to you?"

I set my delicate teacup back in its flowered saucer. "I beg your pardon?"

Rosa swallowed and replied, "As Darla left the cubicle, the intern heard her mutter under her breath, 'We weren't always homeless. For a while we were living in the wolf's den.' She was crying, and he wasn't positive he heard her correctly. But that's what it sounded like."

"She was crying?" I said.

"Not out loud. But tears were running down her face."

Chapter Nine

I glanced at my watch and jumped up from the lunch table. "Oh, no! I'm going to be late for the court hearing!"

Despite the urgency, Aguilar steadfastly refused to drive even one mile an hour over the speed limit on the way home. And to make matters worse, when we arrived back at Aunt Myla's house, the team of house cleaners was waiting patiently in the driveway.

I tossed a key onto the dashboard of Aguilar's car. "Here's a house key," I told him. "Just tell them to lock up when they're done. I have to leave right now!"

"I'll stay to see they do it right," he informed me. "You don't want those Child Protective Services people finding cobwebs in the corners. And drive carefully," he called after me. "Who's going to take that baby if something happens to you?"

I raced inside, ditched Aunt Myla's raccoon coat on a dining room chair and grabbed my more conservative London Fog. Then I ran into the kitchen and called Caroline at work. I got her voice mail which let me know she and Nomad were already standing outside the front entrance of the hospital waiting for me.

"Caro," I said when an automated voice told me to leave a message after the tone, "I know you'll never forgive me, but I can't get there to pick you up and still be on time for the hearing. I was meeting with Rosa Aguilar to talk about Darla, and I lost track of the time. I promise I'll call the minute the hearing is over." I slammed down the phone and raced out the door.

The Hall of Justice, a geometric stack of stone blocks set with windows lined up as precisely as grave markers in a military cemetery, was an unfortunate tribute to the architecture of the Sixties. Directly across the street was a convenient parking lot. The fee for convenience was seven dollars. I threw a ten-dollar bill at the attendant and did not wait for change.

Lines through security were backed up because it was the end of the lunch hour. I saw Ferguson breeze past in a parallel line for those of rank and privilege. He was impeccably dressed in a charcoal suit, blue shirt, red tie, and camel overcoat. Today he wore black loafers, no tassels. Perhaps tassels were too flamboyant for court appearances.

"Your hair looks great!" he said as he took my arm and rushed me onto an elevator. "We want to be on time. Judge Morrell is a real stickler for punctuality."

The elevator groaned as it crept from floor to floor, and I glanced around nervously.

"Don't be alarmed," Ferguson told me. "These elevators are just old."

Someone standing behind us added, "Yeah, they make a lotta noise, and they tend to catch on fire."

Fortunately, our elevator did not catch on fire. On the third floor, Ferguson ran off to shuffle last-minute papers and consult with court powers. I collapsed onto one of the benches that lined the marble-floored hall.

Seated around me were clusters of grim-faced petitioners flanked by lawyers and supportive family members. They were victims of abuse, fragments of newly shattered families, and single parents in desperate custody battles. They waited like ranks of penitents outside the gates of Hell, and I was appalled to find myself among them. My fury at Darla increased exponentially.

Across the hall was the Legal Aid office. The door was

propped open, and the room was filled with anxious women, their restless children, and one rabidly angry man. Two patient older women were trying to cope with all their needs.

Ferguson returned and saw me watching the panorama of human travail. He nodded toward the door. "In cases of neglect and abuse, Legal Aid provides a Court Appointed Special Advocate for children to represent their best interests in court. The Advocates are employed by Legal Aide and appointed by the Family Court judge. Don't be surprised if one is appointed for Katie."

I nodded mutely. Not much would surprise me at this point.

Ferguson continued. His tone was neutral but it held a carefully worded admonition. "The Special Advocate will visit you periodically once Katie is in your care. Katie's Special Advocate will be required to observe, take notes, and report back to the court."

I nodded again to let him know I understood what he was trying to tell me.

My canny lawyer checked his watch and perched on a chair across from me. He must have read the tension in my face because he smiled and changed the subject. "Did you know the Legal Aid Society traces its origin to Susan B. Anthony and the Women's Education and Industrial Union?"

I grimaced. "You'd have to be as tough as Susan B. Anthony to work in that office all day."

A few minutes later, a uniformed woman with a clipboard called my name.

I leapt to my feet. Ferguson murmured in my ear. "Relax. Once we're in the courtroom, just sit next to me and don't say anything unless the judge addresses you directly."

The courtroom was small, containing three rows of blond wooden benches, an American flag, and a desk on a raised dais for the judge. As we sat down, the bailiff called out, "All rise for the judge."

I stood up straight and made an effort to compose myself.

Judge Franklin Morrell was in his fifties. Years of witnessing the disasters people made of their lives had drawn his face into long, brooding lines. He sat down behind his desk, fiddled with his computer, and glanced at me over the top of his wire-rimmed glasses.

The bailiff murmured something incomprehensible, and a woman sitting at a small transcriber's desk at the edge of the platform started to type at a blistering speed. Everything said seemed to be in a legal jargon geared to confound the lay listener. I felt as if I were attending the mad court scene in *Alice in Wonderland*.

I wanted Ferguson to point out to the judge our monumental effort to be prepared for Katie's discharge from the hospital. I wanted the judge to know the CPS foster mother would not have time to give Katie the attention she needed. There were a lot of things I wanted the judge to know. Ferguson sensed my restlessness and kept a firm grip on my arm.

Finally, Judge Morrell addressed me. "Mrs. Scholfield, do you understand your commitment?"

I stood up. "Yes, your honor. I certainly do." I paused and then added grimly, "I will do my absolute best to take care of Katie."

The judge assessed me over the top of his glasses. "I'm sure you will, Mrs. Scholfield. Custody will be granted pending the completion of your paperwork. In the meantime, both you and the baby's grandmother, Caroline Scholfield, will continue to have visiting privileges."

I borrowed Michael Ferguson's cell phone to call Caroline, but she was not in her office. Nor were she and Nomad at home when I arrived to share the good news, so I got back in my car and drove over to the hospital. It was after five, and dusk was falling. There was no wind, but the temperature had plummeted, and I regretted trading Aunt Myla's raccoon coat for the London Fog. I all but froze on the short trip from my car to the hospital entrance. Whatever possessed the resettlement people to send refugees from Sub-Saharan Africa to Rochester, New York in the middle of winter? There would not be enough donated outerwear in upper New York State to convince Caroline's Bantus to emerge from the house before spring.

The hospital was once again in the throes of a shift change. Evening staff was clocking in, and a weary day shift was bracing to face rush hour traffic. I ran up the stairs to the pediatric floor. To celebrate the good news from court, Katie was about to make her fashion debut. In my purse were tiny pink overalls. The matching shirt was a soft, white fabric with little pink rabbits.

I loved the shape of Katie's dark Asian eyes. I loved her curly black hair and her smooth dusky skin. Soon she would smile, and I wondered if she would have the same dimple Darla had when she was a baby. Just a few more days and she would be ready to leave the hospital. I couldn't wait to put her in her new car seat and take her home with me! I would hold her on my lap and read her stories...

I turned into the pediatric ward and stopped dead. Estelle Grayson was putting an old blue snowsuit on Katie. Katie was crying. Caroline was standing helplessly next to the crib, and she was crying, too. Nomad wagged his tail weakly when he saw me.

"What's going on?" I demanded.

Estelle Grayson had her back to me. She answered before Caroline could.

"The baby is being discharged into the care of the foster mother." Grayson stuffed Katie's resisting arm into the sleeve

73

of the snowsuit. She glanced back at me, and I saw surprise register on her face. Clearly I was not the same disheveled person she had come to expect.

"But," I protested, "the house will be ready tomorrow, and I have everything I need to care for Katie. Caroline and I went shopping last night. We bought a crib, clothes, everything! And I've just come from court. The judge said I would have custody pending the completion of my paperwork."

Caroline's voice held a hopeless quality. "The hospital is discharging Katie now. I had no way to contact you. Ms. Grayson says your paperwork has not gone through all the channels yet, and Child Protective Services hasn't done the Home Study to determine if your house is suitable for the baby. The foster mother is on her way here."

Just then a short, plain woman of about forty walked in. She wore no make-up and did not smile or acknowledge us. She greeted Estelle Grayson as if they collaborated regularly.

"This is Loretta Whiting," said Grayson. She did not bother to introduce either Caroline or me by name. We were simply pointed out, in a rather stilted manner, as the baby's grandmother and great aunt.

Caroline's tears were contagious. I felt helpless against a tide of emotions.

Loretta Whiting looked discomfited. "I didn't know they would be here," she said to Estelle Grayson.

I snarled through my tears. "You two planned this so we would just arrive at the hospital and find the baby gone?"

"That's often what happens," said Estelle Grayson stiffly. She picked up a packet of discharge papers.

"Well, not this time," I retorted. "And what do we do about visiting rights?"

"After the week-end, once the baby has settled in, we can set up times which are convenient for Loretta," answered

74

the social worker.

Katie was screaming in her ugly blue snowsuit. Grayson said to Loretta, "It's best if we make this as brief as possible." She handed Katie to the foster mother, and they turned toward the door.

When they left, I glanced around the empty room. Katie's nightgown was in a heap on the floor. I picked it up and folded it. It was still warm and imprinted with her baby smell. Her crib looked abandoned and forlorn without her. I put my arm around Caroline. She was trembling. Not since Cambodia had life dealt her such a blow.

"Let's get out of here," I said. "I want to find a computer. I've got my laptop at your house, but I need a printer."

Caroline fished in her pocket and pulled out a crumpled handkerchief. She was the only person I knew who still carried lace handkerchiefs. She took off her glasses and mopped at her eyes. "There are computers in the library on the main floor by the Administrative offices. I can swipe you in on my pass. Why do you need a printer?"

"I'm going to write a letter to the judge."

"Right now?" Dismay sounded in her voice.

"Yes," I said. "Right now. It won't take long."

"You go ahead and write your letter. I'll go on home and start dinner. We have last minute grocery shopping for the refugees tonight. You didn't forget, did you?"

My heart sank. Of course I'd forgotten. Nor could I imagine what the refugees could possibly need that wasn't already waiting for them at her house.

We took the elevator down to the main floor, and Caroline and Nomad left me at the library door. On the wall outside the door were simply the words, *John R. Williams*. I could see where the letters, *Health Sciences Library*, had been removed. What could have happened to them? Surely

75

doctors did not steal that sort of thing.

The library was one large room with shelves for medical texts and journals. A medical student in a white lab coat was asleep in an overstuffed chair by the window. Her black hair was draped over the back of the chair, and her feet were propped on a coffee table littered with current issues of *The New England Journal of Medicine*.

I slid onto a chair in front of one of the available computers and jiggled the mouse. At the computer in the carrel next to mine, a kitchen worker wearing a blue hair net glanced up and then returned to his email.

It felt good to be in front of a computer. For a brief, illusory moment I felt as if I were in control of my life again.

I addressed a short, irate letter to Judge Morrell, sent it to the printer, and then took a few minutes to scan the BBC News website. There was a photo of a London bus with its windows blown out. Several bodies were laid out on the sidewalk. I leaned closer to determine where in London terrorists had struck.

The sleeping student's pager went off. She stood up, wound her hair into a bun, and headed for the door. I exited the website and followed her out of the library. I ached with homesickness, but London was far away, and, although I didn't realize it yet, I had terrorists here on the home front to combat.

Chapter Ten

It was dark by the time I extracted my car from the parking garage and headed for Caroline's house. Along the narrow residential streets which bordered the hospital, streetlights cast houses in deep shadow and caused patches of black ice on sidewalks to glisten malevolently. I regretted letting Caroline walk home alone.

As I turned the corner onto Caroline's street, I was confronted by the flashing lights of a pair of police cars. I braked, trying to make sense of what was going on, and saw Caroline huddled in the open door of one of the squad cars. Nomad was lying limply at her feet in a dark pool of blood. I could see his chest heaving as if he were struggling to breathe.

I slewed to the curb and ran over to Caroline. "Caro! What happened?"

Caroline was deathly pale. Her hands, when I grabbed them, were ice cold and shaking from shock.

"I'll tell you everything later," she said dully. "We've got to get Nomad to a vet."

One of the cops helped me lift Nomad into the back of my SUV. Nomad yelped in pain as we laid him down. Caroline awkwardly climbed in beside her dog, felt for his blood-soaked head, and pulled it gently onto her lap. Then she struggled out of her coat and laid it over him. The cop led the way to Animal Emergency Services on White Spruce Boulevard. He was easy to follow. He had his emergency lights flashing the entire way.

After the vet admitted Nomad, an attendant returned

Caroline to a seat in the waiting room, and the officer who had been waiting to question her walked over and sat down next to her. Caroline's clothes were soaked with blood and she was as white as the proverbial sheet, but she answered the officer's questions in a controlled, bitter voice.

"I'm sorry about your guide dog, Ma'am. Is he going to be all right?" the cop asked.

"He has broken ribs, internal injuries, and will probably lose sight in one eye," she said. "The vet says if he lives, he'll never be able to be a working dog again."

"A golden retriever is a pretty big dog. He didn't fight back? Bite the attacker or something?"

"Nomad didn't try to defend himself. He's a gentle dog, a guide dog. He's always worked in a safe environment. He thinks everyone loves him."

"I'm sorry, ma'am," the police officer said sincerely. "Really sorry. About your assailant, did you see, ah...hear...can you just tell me what happened?"

"I heard a car drive up and stop."

"Ma'am, could you tell if it was a car or a truck?"

Caroline shook her head. "It was loud. Maybe the muffler was bad. I don't know anything about cars."

"Right. What did you do when you heard the car stop?"

"Nothing. Nomad and I walk these streets daily. There's usually traffic. I heard a car door open and someone got out. He didn't turn off the motor. I heard footsteps approach. Heavy footsteps. I think he must have been a large man."

"So after you heard the footsteps, what happened?"

"The man walked up to me and asked if ...if I was...Caroline Scholfield. I said I was, and then something slammed Nomad. It was hard enough to wrench his harness right out of my hand. I heard him yelp in pain. Then I...I realized the bastard was kicking my dog. I must have yelled something like, 'Hey, what do you think you're doing?'"

The officer's radio rattled out a static-filled message. He fiddled with it for a second, looked up at Caroline and said, "Yes, ma'am. Then what did you do?"

"Somehow I managed to get hold of Nomad's harness again. I was going to run away. I felt the impact of more kicks through the handle of the harness and Nomad...was making horrible yelping sounds. I stupidly held onto him. He couldn't break away or defend himself."

"Did the assailant attack you also?"

"Not really. Nomad was cowering on the ground. I bent down to try to pick him up so we could escape, but the man grabbed me by the arms and yanked me up. I could smell alcohol on his breath. I screamed at him and struck out, but of course I was just flailing blindly." Caroline ripped off her dark glasses and turned her face toward the detective. "I think blindly sums it up accurately, don't you?"

The officer stared at her ashen, blood spattered face and unseeing eyes. "Yes, ma'am. I understand. Your assailant didn't say anything?"

"He said... something. I...I didn't really hear it. I was screaming bloody murder. Then he shoved me down on top of Nomad and I heard his footsteps going away. I heard the car door slam and his tires squeal as he drove off. I pulled off my gloves and tried to feel how bad Nomad was hurt. And then someone came out of their house and saw us, and I guess they called the police."

"You have no idea who would want to attack you? Maybe someone you've dealt with through the social work office at the hospital who might have a grudge?"

Caroline shook her head. "Sometimes patients are distraught about placement issues. It happens more than you would imagine. I can't pull any names out of a hat."

"Is there anything else you can tell me? Anything at all?"

Caroline threw up her hands in a gesture of despair.

"Why would someone attack my dog? Why didn't they just attack me?"

After the police officer left, she repeated her question. "Why didn't that bastard just go for me? Why did he have to hurt Nomad?"

"I don't know," I said. "It was a coldblooded, brutal act."

"That dog is like my best friend. I mean, he lies right by my bed at night. When I get up in the morning, my feet don't touch the floor. They touch his warm, furry body, and his tail thumps on the floor to let me know he's glad I'm awake. He's happy to go to work in the morning, and when we're home, he's happy just to follow me from room to room. Darla will be devastated. She adores him and he adores her. He always has, right from when we first got him."

"I know," I told her. "I remember."

Caroline brushed back her hair with a bloody hand. "And he's so gentle. The only time he ever harmed anything was when Darla had that little green turtle. Remember? She left that damned turtle's bowl on the floor, and Nomad just stuck his muzzle in the water and slurped it up."

I laughed because I remembered it well.

"It wasn't funny at the time," Caroline said sourly. "Darla was crying her eyes out, and I had to phone the vet to tell him what happened. I pictured Nomad dying from salmonella."

I concluded the reminiscence. "And after the vet stopped laughing, he said the acid in a dog's stomach was strong enough to deal with things like salmonella. So then Darla made you call back the vet and ask if he thought the turtle was still alive and crawling around in Nomad's gut."

Caroline grimaced. "And that made him laugh even harder." She laughed, just for a second, that deep throaty laugh that had been missing lately. "The vet said that turtle was dead long before it hit his gut, and that made Darla start crying all over again."

Caroline went into the restroom to wash up, and then we sat on the hard bench in the waiting room in silence. After a while she said she couldn't stand sitting there one more minute, so we went outside for a cigarette. We stood under the light outside the front doors, and I put my coat over her shoulders. Hers was in a plastic bag in the waiting room, soaked with Nomad's blood. The night was clear and bitterly cold, but I was grateful to be out of the waiting room even if it meant exposure to arctic temperatures and secondhand smoke.

Caroline lit one of her unfiltered cigarettes, inhaled once, and said, "There's something I didn't tell the cop, Kate."

"Do you want me to call him back? I've got his card."

"No. I deliberately didn't tell him."

"What was it?"

Caroline took another drag from her cigarette and rubbed her arm as if it pained her. "When that bastard came up to me, he didn't ask if I was Caroline Scholfield. He asked if I was Darla's mother. And after he kicked the shit out of Nomad, he twisted my arm and said, *Tell Darla to give back what's mine or next time it'll be you.*"

"Caroline! Why didn't you tell the officer?"

"Don't be stupid. We need to find that son of a bitch before the cops do. I don't know what Darla is tangled up in, but the last thing she needs is for the cops to make a connection between her and the scumbag who attacked me."

81

Chapter Eleven

Caroline and I returned to the waiting room and sat there for what seemed like hours. I was exhausted and so was she. I didn't think it was doing her any good to sit here, but she refused to go home.

"I love him," she said sadly. "He's the epitome of all that's good in the world. He's devoted his entire life to helping me. I can't just abandon him here."

We sat for a long time in silence. After a while she reached out and found my hand. "If we have to bury Nomad, can we put him out at Aunt Myla's?"

"Sure," I said. "But maybe he'll be okay. It's too soon to give up hope."

"I wish I believed that," she said. "I can't picture my life without him. I dread having to put him out to pasture. I mean, I could certainly work with another dog, and I would love that dog, but Nomad...would he understand why I was leaving him at home and going to work without him?" She shook her head and started to cry. "Ah, shit," she said. "All I do is cry these days. I've got to get a grip on myself. Let's go outside for another cigarette."

It was midnight before Caroline agreed to leave. Nomad was on an IV and well sedated. The vet told us to call at any hour for an update.

We drove home and went to bed, but sleep was, as usual, out of the question. Twice during the night I heard Caroline talking to the vet. I had no one to call for answers, even answers I didn't want to hear. All I could do was lie there and listen to the tick of the radiator, the tick of the old-fashioned alarm clock on the nightstand beside my bed, the tick of snow against the window. Unanswerable questions looped over and over through my mind.

...who could be so cruel as to attack a blind woman's guide dog...and who was this man who claimed Darla had something of his...what could it possibly be except drugs... or money...but if it was money, Darla could have used it to take better care of the baby...how could she have been stupid enough to get involved with someone like that...and where was she now...where was she...where was she...

...did that fellow use his feet and his fists on her, too...and what of little Katie...is he the one who left bruises on her...who would be cruel enough to hurt a newborn child...was she crying right now in a strange crib...would her foster mother pick her up and rock her in the middle of the night...or let her cry until she wore herself out...

...would it be safe to live by myself in that old house...how much effort would it take to make it habitable... mice in the oven...did the cleaners carry the nest outside or kill them...a dead bat on the stairs...were there more...would I be better off here...closer to Katie...

...when would they let us see her...that ugly snowsuit...should I give the foster mother some decent clothes for her...

... damn you, Whit...were you going to leave me...were you planning to move in with your new son and his mother...or just support them... keep them as a dark secret...how could you leave me...

...how am I supposed to handle all this by myself...

...Nomad...was he still be alive..suffering....

At six I staged a reenactment of my last morning on St. Mary's. I dragged myself out of bed and packed my suitcase. There would be no room for me here tonight. Caroline insisted she would be safe with a houseful of refugees, and arguing with her was an exercise in futility. I showered and went downstairs to make coffee.

Caroline's kitchen, with its red Formica table and black and white linoleum floor, was a warm family place. It should have been filled with the comforting smells of breakfast and the sound of the morning news. But today, the only sign of life was the yellow cat sleeping in Nomad's bed by the radiator.

Caroline appeared in the doorway. "I heard you get up," she said.

"How is Nomad? I heard you talking to the vet last night."

"Not good."

"Why don't you go back to bed for a while?" I said. It was impossible to keep concern out of my voice. "You look like five miles of bad road."

"No kidding. When I wasn't crying about Nomad and Katie and worrying myself sick over Darla, I was trying to anticipate what tonight's planeload of refugees would bring. I don't think I slept ten minutes."

"Take the day off and try to nap."

"Can't. My team at work needs me. We're short staffed. Two of our social workers are out on maternity leave. It's been just one baby shower after another." She walked over and poured dry food into the cat's bowl, fingering the bowl first, as she always did.

"Why do you always do that?"

"Do what?"

"Stick your fingers in the cat's food bowl."

"Because nothing screws up my day worse than pouring his food into his water dish."

I was setting a cup of coffee on the table for her when the phone rang.

Caroline snatched up the receiver, apprehension washing over her face. I watched her expression change to relief as she held out the phone for me.

"Where in God's name have you been?" demanded Joe Aguilar on the other end of the line. "I waited out at the house yesterday, but you never came back. And no one ever answers the phone at this number."

"If I told you, you would never believe me. Yesterday afternoon they placed the baby in foster care."

"Why? I thought you were going to take her."

"They said my paperwork wasn't ready. And last night someone attacked Caroline while she was walking home from the hospital."

"Is she okay?"

"Yes, but the assailant kicked Nomad almost to death. He's at the emergency vet."

"What kind of a son of a bitch would attack a guide dog? What's this world coming to!" He paused on the other end of the line. "Tell Caroline I hope her dog will be okay. In the meantime, what am I supposed to do with this goat?"

"Goat? Oh, right. The goat meat. Could you deliver it?"

"For you, doll, I'll deliver."

"If you brought it by about six thirty, you could personally give it to the refugees. No. Better yet, meet us at the airport at five o'clock. United Airlines, Flight 1967 out of Newark. You can help welcome them to the land of the free and the home of the brave."

"Some land they're coming to. They were probably better off in the refugee camp."

Chapter Twelve

After breakfast, I took my bags to the car, stripped my bed and put clean sheets on it. Caroline was in the kitchen listening to a classical music station on the radio and brewing a huge pot of barley beef soup. The smell of garlic, onions, and braising meat wafted through the house along with second hand smoke from her cigarette.

No one would be hungry for long in this house. The kitchen was overflowing with foods conforming to a Bantu diet. The contents of the refrigerator threatened to tumble out every time I opened its door. When I went down into the basement to wash my sheets, I half expected to find a crate of live chickens stashed in one of the dank, spidery corners.

In the front entry hall children's car seats had replaced bags of linens. Upstairs, the tiny bathroom was stocked with piles of towels, deodorant, and shampoo. Packages of diapers in varying sizes lined the hallway. In the bedrooms were mounds of blankets. Caroline's guest room and Darla's room each held a double bed. The overflow would sleep on the floor, but that would hardly dismay people who had been sharing a mud hut behind a barbed wire fence for thirteen years.

When I came up from the basement, I sat down at the kitchen table. I had learned from experience that Caroline did not want help in the kitchen, and she particularly did not want anyone under foot. The kitchen was warm and humid and fragrant from the soup simmering on the stove. I couldn't remember the last time I had sat in a kitchen and watched someone cook. Somehow, it seemed a far greater luxury than sitting in a fine restaurant. Caroline was rummaging around inside her pantry, no easy feat considering the amount of food stashed in there.

"I have to confess that I'm amazed at the resources your church has mustered," I said.

"It's not just a collection of goods," she said, disappearing into the back reaches of the pantry. She emerged moments later with two large cans of tomatoes. On each can was a small Braille label. From her earliest childhood Darla had helped Caroline label her groceries. I wondered who was doing it now.

Caroline set the cans on the counter. "As I was saying, it's not just a collection of goods, although I hear the collection of furnishings in my garage is growing daily. There are people lined up to take the family to the Health Department, register them with the Department of Social Services, enroll the kids in school, teach them to ride the bus, hunt for a suitable apartment, help find jobs, and sign up the adults for ESOL classes." She yanked open the drawer by the sink and felt around until she found her can opener. Then she slammed the drawer shut again.

"I've heard of ESL classes," I said. "English as a Second Language. What does ESOL stand for?"

"English for Speakers of Other Languages," she said. "A nicely turned phrase, don't you think? Classes are held during the day at the Family Learning Center down on Hart Street, but there are also informal tutoring sessions in the evenings."

"And you have people willing to drive into the city at night for that?"

"They probably would, but they don't have to. The tutoring sessions are held at local churches so the refugees can walk to them. For instance, that Greek Orthodox Church just down the street from Highland Hospital opens its doors every Thursday evening. And there are also classes in some

87

of the subsidized housing complexes. They're all run by volunteers from Saints Place. They started by collecting furniture for refugees. Now they do all kinds of things."

"Is there any way I can help? You haven't asked me to do anything except help take pictures at the airport tonight and help transport the family here."

"Your whole reason for being here is Darla and her baby. If you weren't here, I would...well, all I can say is I'll spend the rest of my life trying to find a way to repay you. As for the refugees, right now they're pretty well covered. Everyone at the church is really enthusiastic about this project. And why wouldn't they be enthusiastic? How often do people have an opportunity to personally, one on one, give a family a chance they otherwise would never have? A chance to get out of a refugee camp and have a future that doesn't involve violence and bloodshed? So we have lots of people lined up to teach them all the things they need to know."

"You told me they already had a crash course in the camp on American plumbing and electricity. What else could they possibly need to know?"

"You're such a smartass, Kate. They need to know how to run a washing machine, grocery shop, balance a check book, clean house...the list goes on and on."

Caroline paused long enough to open the two cans and dump the tomatoes into the soup pot. Then she said, "Believe it or not, we've even got two members of our church who not only want to drive the family to the mosque on Fridays, they want to go with them to see what it's like." She found her spoon and stirred the pot. Then she stuck her nose close to the soup and sniffed. "I believe it smells just about right. Now where did I put the lid?"

"On the counter to the right of the sink."

"Thanks." Caroline put the lid on the soup and tossed

the spoon in the sink. "You'll get to meet most of these people at the airport tonight. Try to smile sweetly and keep your cynical mouth shut."

I dropped Caroline off at work. She wouldn't let me walk her to the door, so I had to sit in the car and watch anxiously as she fumbled her way into the hospital without Nomad to guide her. Then I headed over to the University of Rochester Medical Center. A left turn onto South and a short jog down one narrow residential street took me took me past the high wrought iron fence enclosing Mount Hope Cemetery, its Victorian outbuildings and century-old landscaping a fitting resting place for Aunt Myla. Today every tree and gravestone glistened with a sparkling coat of fresh snow. I owed that lady a visit but it would have to wait.

Last night from the vet's office I called the university's School of Nursing and asked for the dormitory where Darla had been living. The girl who answered the dorm phone said she knew a first-year student who might be able to help me. Her name was Sonja Cohen. Her dorm room was next to Darla's, and they were in some of the same classes.

"Like, I'm happy to talk to you," Sonya cautioned when she came on the line, "but I didn't know Darla all that well? She was pretty much a loner. We hung together at lunch and stuff, but I don't think she told anyone she was going to drop out of school. She just skipped a bunch of classes and then stopped coming. We all thought maybe she had to stay home to, like, take care of her mother?"

Today Sonja's cluster of nursing students was in rotation on one of the surgical floors. She said she could meet me at nine in the small coffee shop on the first floor of the hospital near the bookstore. She didn't think her supervisor would mind if she used her break to talk to me about Darla.

I parked in a visitors' lot and steeled myself for a short, cold walk.

The Rochester Medical Center is an amalgam of brick structures old and new and incorporates Strong Memorial Hospital, the School of Medicine and Dentistry, the School of Nursing, and the Eastman Dental Center. It's an easy place to get lost if you don't know where you're going. Following the directions Sonja had given me, I crossed the street and turned up the sidewalk toward the Cancer Center. Smokers were huddled near the entrance, bracing the cold for a few puffs of nicotine. Signs indicated this would not be the case for long. The complex was going smoke free; classes and counseling were being offered. I tried to picture Caroline without her aura of smoke and failed.

Inside the building, medical students, interns, doctors, faculty, and patients crowded the halls. Fortunately, the coffee shop was not far from the entrance. It was small and noisy and fragrant with a variety of coffee blends and fresh baked muffins. Sonja was waiting at the door, easy to recognize in her nursing student uniform and winged nursing cap. She was a tall, plump girl with a beak of a nose and level brown eyes.

"Hi," she said, flashing a friendly smile as I approached. "Are you Darla's aunt?"

"I am," I said. "Can I buy you a cup of coffee? I certainly could use one."

"I don't drink coffee, but I would love some hot chocolate."

We settled at a ridiculously small table that wobbled and slopped our drinks when we leaned on it.

I handed Sonja an extra napkin and said, "Thanks very much for meeting me. I know you don't have a lot of time, but I really need to locate Darla, and I'm hoping you can help me."

"What do you want to know? Has something happened?" asked Sonja, wrapping her large, competent-looking hands around her mug of hot chocolate.

I did not want lurid details of Darla's current situation circulating around the nursing school, so I hedged. "I'm trying to help Darla's mother...you know she's blind."

"I know. She was working in Cambodia with Doctors without Borders and a land mine blew up in her face. Darla told me."

"Darla had her baby, but, as I told you last night, she's disappeared. Do you...have you any idea who the baby's father might be? I'm hoping Darla might be with him."

Sonja's face registered her astonishment. She pushed away her mug and stared at me.

"Darla was pregnant? I didn't even know!"

"The baby was born right before Christmas."

"Like, I can't believe it! I mean, she didn't even look pregnant!" She glanced down at her own figure. "Of course, Darla's really skinny. I know I'll look like a horse when I'm pregnant! Was it a boy or a girl?"

"A beautiful little girl. But Darla's gone, and we need to find her."

"Jeez, a baby girl. That's great. Darla loves kids! She's always wondering if she has brothers and sisters back in Cambodia. And she's planning to work in Pediatrics."

I persisted with my question. "Do you have any idea who she was dating? Or if she secretly got married?"

Sonja was silent for a moment. "Like, I really don't know how to say this? We sort of met these guys at a bar one night last fall. There was one guy named Wolf? He might, like, know where she is. I hope he's not the father!"

The short hairs on my neck bristled. According to Rosa, the intern heard Darla say something about living in a wolf's den. Could this be the wolf?

I leaned forward urgently and slopped our drinks. "Do you know how I can find this fellow?"

Sonja scowled and turned her mug in circles on her napkin, making a series of concentric brown smears. "I don't know why anyone would want to find him. He was one bad dude. One time Darla came to class with bruises on her arms and a black eye? Some of us tried to convince her to stop seeing him. But she just shrugged it off and wouldn't talk about it. Like, I really hope Darla's not still with *him*."

I shuddered and wondered what I could possibly tell Caroline. My coffee was growing cold on the table in front of me. "And you don't know this guy's last name or have any idea where he might hang out?"

"No, but the night we ran into him, we were all at the Canal Street Bar down on Main Street. Maybe he hangs out there?"

"Do you remember what he looked like?"

Sonja frowned. "Maybe five eight, shaved head, lots of muscles, tight t-shirt. Oh, yeah, and really pale blue eyes. I remember wondering if that's why he was called Wolf."

"What about other guys at the bar that night? Do you remember any other names?"

"Who would want to? They were, like, losers, into dope and stuff. We all said we had to get back to the dorm and study. Darla ran into some girl she knew from high school, so she stayed behind when we left."

Sonja gulped down the rest of her hot chocolate and said she had to get back to the floor. They were going to review the Crash Cart and she didn't want to miss it.

"I hope you find Darla. She'll be a really great nurse if she gets her degree," she told me as she looped her stethoscope around her neck and tried to repin her cap in her hair. "Like, she aces all the tests? And when you find her, tell her I would love to see her baby. What's the baby's name?"

I forced a smile. "Her name is Katie. Darla named her after me."

Chapter Thirteen

I spent the rest of the morning driving around downtown Rochester looking for Darla. The chances of spotting her on the streets were all but nil, but I did it for Caroline's sake and because I didn't want to drive out and sit alone in Aunt Myla's old house and because I couldn't think of anything better to do.

I started on Main Street at the Canal Street Bar. The bar was closed, so I drove up and down side streets off Main. I glanced into windows of seedy pawnshops and peered in doors of run-down minimarts which seemed to offer little except junk food and beer. I didn't bother with adult bookstores. Darla preferred fantasy of a different sort, Tolkien and Anne McCaffrey and Terry Brooks.

I drove briefly through the city's business district. Rochester had once been a thriving metropolis supported by dynamic enterprises like Kodak and Xerox and Midtown Plaza, the first urban enclosed shopping mall in America with Sibleys and McCurdys and the B. Forman Company as retail stars in its crown. Now Rochester was at a crossroads. Either it would evolve and revitalize or it would slowly decay. Caroline said Midtown was vacant now. The entire structure was scheduled for demolition, and it's Clock of the Nations was to have a new home at Golisano's Children's Hospital.

I had always loved downtown Rochester, and I had loved that clock. Everything I loved seemed to be vanishing in one form or another. Whit, illusions of a happily married life, my freedom, Darla, wherever the bloody hell she was, and now Midtown and its clock.

I headed for the main bus exchange, a place to which I had no emotional ties. Darla didn't have a car. If she went anywhere, she would have to use public transportation. I pulled over to the curb and wasted half an hour watching people get on and off buses. Darla wasn't among them, so I left the city center behind and searched through sleazier sections of the city, areas where derelict factories and warehouses were architectural specters of a bygone economy. On the periphery of these areas were dreary neighborhoods where single-family houses had been converted to multifamily use, boarded up windows and rusting fire escapes were commonplace, and broken chain link fences afforded access to vacant lots strewn with liquor bottles half buried in the snow.

For such a cold, windy day, Rochester's city streets were filled with a surprising number of people. The more enterprising toted briefcases and shopping bags. Those with fewer economic options pushed rusted shopping carts full of aluminum cans or loitered in doorways. I passed a woman with three small children huddled in the lee of a storefront for warmth. If that woman and her children were homeless, they could survive on the streets for a few hours, but sooner or later they would be forced to find shelter. Darla, too, would need a refuge, a place to get warm, the sort of place where it was acceptable for the public to walk in and stay a while.

I drove over to Court Street and parked around the corner from the Rundel Library. Arches beneath the library allow waters of the millrace to flow into the Genesee River. Today the water was swift and forbidding, and I shuddered as I realized I was staring down at the river very close to where the body of the girl who so closely resembled Darla had surfaced. How long had she been conscious in those turbulent waters before she succumbed to hypothermia or

94

drowned? My hands shook as I fumbled to put a quarter in the meter, and I felt a renewed urgency to find Darla before something equally sinister happened to her.

I went inside the library and traversed each floor, but Darla was nowhere to be seen. Nor did I find her at the YMCA after asking at the front desk if I could take a look at the facilities before deciding whether or not to join.

Next I tried rescue organizations. I went up Clinton Avenue to Catholic Family Services. A dark-skinned man with an accent I could not place stood at the front desk. He explained that, while they offered a variety of services for people in crisis, they could not divulge the names of their clientele.

"What about homeless shelters and missions? Would you have a list of them?"

"I'm not really sure," he said. "If we have one, I've never seen it."

I persisted. "Is there someone you could ask?"

While he went to ask about a list, I waited at the desk and read brochures detailing Catholic Family Services' outreach to the community. A few minutes later, the fellow returned and handed me a piece of paper.

"My supervisor said you could go around to all these places and show your niece's picture, but it probably won't get you anywhere. Agencies can't give out that kind of information anymore. He said your best bet is to fill out a missing person's report and let the police look for her. They've got the resources."

I smiled and nodded and thanked him. I did not tell him the police were already looking for Darla, and I needed to find her before they did.

Monroe County Department of Human Services was not far from Catholic Family Services. The large parking lot on St. Paul was crowded with cars, but I finally found a space between a van and a battered VW. It was hot inside the building and dense with people snaking through long lines. Overworked employees tried to herd me into various lines, but I waved them off and wandered around looking for a young woman who was nowhere to be found.

It was not yet lunchtime, but I was hungry and I had nothing to show for the morning except an empty gas tank and the name of a bar where Darla knew some exceedingly questionable people. I considered returning to Caroline's house for something to eat but decided instead to loop through the city and stop at Java Joe's by the Eastman School of Music. There was probably nothing in Caro's fridge I liked anyhow.

Java Joe's Cafe was a warm, dark place with stone floors and exposed pipes overhead, just the sort of place that would appeal to Darla back in the days when she was fancy free and had spending money in her pocket. There were bare plank tables, cushioned benches along the walls, and funky antiques scattered about. I ordered a turkey sandwich and the strongest coffee they had and chose a seat at a round table near a window. There was a large wooden blue and yellow shark with a mouthful of sharp teeth hanging over the table. Perhaps it was an omen.

Over lunch, in spite of my best intentions, I thought about Whit. It was inevitable. We had often eaten at this cafe before performances at the Eastman Theater. We had different taste in music, but Whit sat with me through the Rochester Philharmonic's classical performances, and I sat with him through their Pops concerts. I picked the bread off my sandwich and tried to make a mental list of things Whit and I had in common. I couldn't come up with much. London. We had both loved London. Cats, but we didn't own one. Children, but we never had any. Traveling, but we had seldom traveled together. Books. Yes we both had liked books. But, except for Tom Clancy, Whit exclusively read non-fiction, and I liked thrillers in which good guys triumphed over evil. That was about as far from non-fiction as one could get.

My thoughts drifted back to Darla. Keeping up with her had always been a challenge. As a child, she was bright, creative, and devious. Whit joked that instead of sleeping at night, she just plugged herself into an electrical outlet for recharging. When Darla started kindergarten, she was sent to the principal's office daily. Caroline finally took time off from her new job at the hospital to talk to the teacher. After Caroline pointed out Darla could already read on a second grade level and add single digits in her head, the teacher understood Darla expected more from school than ABCs and recess. She started giving her work that challenged her, and Darla's behavior improved.

In the third grade, Darla went through a phase of petty theft. Whenever she got caught, Darla said what she had stolen was for homeless people. Nothing Caroline said or did could stop her from stealing. As a last resort I went online and showed Darla pictures of prison cells. Then I told her I would miss her terribly if she had to go to jail. The pictures frightened her, but I think it was my words which changed her behavior. She cried and said she would stop stealing because I had no children of my own and she didn't want me to be lonely.

After that Caroline and I made a concerted effort to channel Darla's altruistic drive into socially acceptable methods of outreach. It meant hours and hours of volunteer work for all of us.

So what had gone wrong? What transformed Darla from a caring young woman who aspired to become a nurse into one who hung around bars, dropped out of school, and had a baby out of wedlock? How could the Darla I knew abandon her baby, a baby she had not even made an effort to properly care for? It had to be drugs. And now some hopped-up thug had mugged Caroline and her dog because Darla ran off with his money or his stash. Our only hope was to find her and get her off the streets and into a rehab program as fast as possible. We just had one problem. We had no idea where she was.

Chapter Fourteen

My first call was to Child Protective Services. I asked to speak to Estelle Grayson's supervisor. She was in a meeting but her secretary said she would call back.

I was in the basement folding my sheets when the phone rang. I raced up the stairs two at a time. The yellow cat, who had been sitting at the top of the stairs, abandoned his observation post and dove under the kitchen table as I ran past. I grabbed the phone.

"Kate Scholfield? This is Rhonda Wims. I'm Estelle's supervisor." Wims sounded older and more confident than Estelle Grayson.

"Thank you for returning my call, Ms. Wims. You know I have applied to be a foster mother for Katie Scholfield?"

"Yes, and I know the baby has been placed temporarily with a very good foster mother until all your paperwork is processed."

"And how long do you expect that to take?"

"It's hard to say. Are you in touch with Darla?"

"No, I am not. I wish I were," I said sourly.

"Is her mother?"

"No, and she wishes she were, too."

A long pause. "It's simply this. Darla harmed that baby. We are hesitant to place Katie with you as long as Darla is at large and might have access to her through one of you. We can reconsider once Darla is in custody."

There was an even longer silence on my end.

"So you are, in effect, holding Katie hostage to see if Caroline or I will turn in Darla? What about the court decision yesterday?"

Ms. Wims retorted in a voice that let me know I had broken through her defenses. "We are *not* holding the baby hostage. And we're in dialogue with the court now regarding this matter."

I did not try to keep the anger out of my voice. "Neither one of us knows where Darla is. I have put the welfare of that baby before all my personal considerations. I would never let Darla or anyone else jeopardize her. You must be aware I have gone to considerable trouble and expense to have everything ready when Katie was released from the hospital. And you also know what a good woman Caroline is. In spite of all her problems, she's heading Our Lady of Victory's resettlement program which is expecting a family of African refugees this afternoon. And she's a social worker at Highland Hospital. She would never do anything to put her grandchild or any baby at risk. Do you have any idea how hard on her this is? And, furthermore, in order to reside in England, I was vetted by Scotland Yard, fingerprints, background check with the FBI, the whole nine yards. It's standard operating procedure. There will be nothing in my background to prevent my having custody of Katie."

"I am sure there won't be, Mrs. Scholfield. When the time is right."

"And," I went on angrily, "I intend to do everything in my power to see that Katie has the best possible care. That includes a continuum of contact with both me and her grandmother so the bonding process is unbroken."

"You obviously do care very much about this baby. I am sure the foster mother will not be averse to having the two of you visit."

"Tomorrow?"

"Why don't we discuss it when we stop by your house for our Home Visit this afternoon? I know you're anxious to get things moving. Would three o'clock be convenient?"

"That would be fine," I said, wondering if she were trying to put me at a disadvantage by giving me so little notice. "Do you have directions?"

"It's out in Mendon. I'm sure Estelle has the directions. It would be much simpler for everyone if you arranged something closer to the city."

"Katie will be raised in my family's home. I don't believe it can be very good for children to put down roots and then have to move. I'll see you at one o'clock."

I glanced at my watch and dialed Ferguson. His secretary patched me through.

"What's up, Kate?"

"Call the judge and tell him Child Protective Services is trying to delay giving us custody of Katie. I'm sending him a letter to that effect this morning. I want visiting rights for me and Caroline confirmed today. Not at the foster mother's convenience and not after the week-end which would mean four days without seeing her."

"I thought that had already been ironed out."

"Well, there's a new wrinkle. They're thinking we might be in touch with Darla, so they're holding Katie hostage to force us to turn her in."

"You didn't use those words with CPS, did you?"

"Actually, I did."

Ferguson paused. "Well, let me just say I'm glad you are on our side. And Kate? There's another matter that we have to address."

I sighed. "What is it?"

"Your house in London. You realize you will have to reside here. You won't be allowed to take the baby out of New York, certainly not out of the country, even on a temporary basis."

"I know. And the house in London is sitting there

vacant and costing Whit's company a fortune."

Ferguson acknowledged that this was indeed the case. "With your permission, I can direct them to terminate the lease. But how will you find time to close up the house and supervise the packing and shipping of your things?"

I gripped the phone. The thought of going through Whit's things and possibly finding pictures or letters belonging to Angela Brighton was not something I could bear to face right now.

Ferguson's voice sounded hesitant. "Kate? Are you still there?"

"Yes," I said. "I wish I weren't, but I am." I cleared my throat to make my voice stronger. "Our landlord in London lives next door. His name is Nigel Weatherford. He's in his eighties, but he's very much with it. I'll send him a letter asking him to hire someone to go in and pack up everything I want to keep. I can make a specific list. I'll do it room by room. I'm sure I can do it from memory." *Especially during my sleepless nights.* "I'll instruct him to donate everything I don't want to Oxfam. One of their charity shops is on Putney High Street. Will that work?"

I could hear Ferguson breathe a sigh of relief. "Perfect," he said. "Fax me a copy of your letter. I'll take care of the rest."

I sat down at the kitchen table, put my face in my hands, and cried for Whit. I cried out of loneliness and sorrow, anger and grief, love and betrayal. I cried for the years we had together and the years we would never have. I cried because I had loved him and because there would never be an opportunity to know why he had betrayed me. I cried because his legacy was not the pure grief of a lost life, but the legacy of lost love.

When there were no more tears and my eyes were swollen and my throat was raw, I walked over to the cupboard and made myself a cup of tea. While it was brewing I went out to the car and got my laptop and began the list.

My tea grew cold. I got up and made more. The list grew incrementally. Few people are compelled to examine their memories, joyful and sorrowful, room by room, item by item. If you have limited space, what from your life do you take? I thought of the Bantu family Caroline's church was sponsoring. What had endless war and years in refugee camps left them to bring to their new country? And why was I sitting here weeping into my teacup?" When I compared my life to theirs, I was one of the most fortunate people on the planet. I shut down the computer, washed my mug, and returned the box of tea back to the same spot in the cupboard so Caroline would be able to find it. My old life was over, and there was no more time to indulge in retrospection. The present was hammering at my door with a heavy fist.

Chapter Fifteen

On the way out to Mendon, I stopped at Starbucks and dropped my list for Ferguson in a nearby mailbox. Next, I ran into Wegmans for some groceries. My last stop was for the purchase of a cell phone. As soon as it was activated, I switched it on and called Caroline.

"How is Nomad?" I asked.

"The vet says...he doesn't think he'll...make it. His chances of recovery are slim. And if he does recover, he'll be in constant pain. Maybe not even be able to walk. I...I'm going to have...to make a decision." Her voice broke.

"Oh, Caro. I'm so sorry."

Her voice quavered. "Look, one of my co-workers is going to take me over to see him at lunch time. I can't talk about it now."

"I understand. I was wishing so much for a miracle. Call me after you talk to the vet." I gave her the number of the cell phone.

By the time I got to Mendon there was little time to spare before Rhonda Wims and her entourage from the Child Protective Services arrived. I unloaded the groceries and began a hurried inspection of the house.

The kitchen was spotless, the mice in the oven had been evicted, and fresh flowers graced the kitchen table. Cobwebs no longer draped the light fixture in the dining room, and the faded oriental carpet was freshly vacuumed. In the front parlor, the lace curtains had been pulled back in the bay window to highlight a lamp only the Victorians could love. Faded red tassels dangled from the wrists of two disembodied brass hands. Each hand supported a branch of the lamp, and naked cherubs flitted across the lamp's twin globes. While I was debating whether or not to hide the atrocity in the coat closet, the doorbell shrilled. Rhonda Wims stood on the front steps flanked by Estelle Grayson and Leon Schwartz, the Court Appointed Special Advocate.

I invited them in and offered them seats in the parlor on the painfully uncomfortable Victorian loveseats. The loveseats, designed with the same soulless philosophy as the benches at London bus stops, were narrow and angled so one had to sit, back straight, with feet firmly braced on the floor to avoid sliding off the cushions.

I offered tea. The trio graciously declined, stating time constraints. The implication was clear. By locating myself in the wilds of Mendon, I had inconvenienced them. The thought gave me petty satisfaction.

Wims was a tall, graceful Afro-American. She wore her hair as short as mine and had intricate gold hoops in her ears. Her navy pantsuit, her manicure, her bearing were impeccable. Her speech held a gentle hint of a Southern city. Perhaps Charleston or Atlanta.

"I have to confess," said Wims as she glanced around the room, "I did not understand why you wanted to live so far out of the city. But this is a lovely house. And you say it belongs to your family?"

"I inherited it from my husband's aunt. As you know, my husband was recently killed in Iraq. His aunt died shortly before he did. The estate fell to me." Along with a lot of other equally bad news.

"We're sorry for your loss," said Wims kindly.

Silence filled the parlor. I had nothing more I wanted to say aloud on the subject of loss.

"How old is the house?" asked Estelle Grayson to fill in the silence. She was wearing black slacks today and a red sweater studded with pearls. Red was not her best color.

"It was built in 1887. With the will were papers from the Mendon Historic Preservation Commission. I think the Commission was trying to get Aunt Myla to declare the house an historic property. Doing so would put restrictions on the property, and I can't see Aunt Myla agreeing to that sort of thing. At any rate, she never signed the papers."

"Well," said Wims, dismissing further speculation about the historic merits of the house, "as you know, we're here to determine if the home will be suitable for Katie. I'm sure you understand this is required."

I picked up the cue. "Please, let me show the rest of the house."

I led them through the downstairs rooms and then back through the front parlor to the main staircase. My strategy was twofold. First, I was going for shock and awe. Second, the back stairs were narrow and dark, and I feared bats might be malingering in the stairwell.

I paused with my entourage at the top of the front stairs. "I'm sure you're concerned about the risk factor of the stairs in this house. As you may have noticed," I pointed out, "the double doors downstairs in the parlor and the door to the stairs in the dining room will prevent Katie from accessing the stairs from below. I have gates to place at both ends of this upstairs hall," I said.

The threesome nodded, their eyes traveling over dark chestnut woodwork, high ceilings, antique wallpaper, and the filigreed fixtures of old gas lamps.

I threw open the door to the front bedroom but did not pause. I did not want my visitors lingering there. No amount of cleaning would rid the closet of its unpleasant odor. On a hook in the closet I had found an old terrycloth bathrobe, its pockets stuffed with potpourri. It was Aunt Myla's rather creative approach to the problem and probably as good a solution as any.

The door to Katie's room was open, and the shutters had been folded back to let in afternoon light. I silently blessed Aguilar and the maids. They had assembled Katie's crib and put one of the new sheets on the mattress. A rose-colored blanket was folded over the crib's rail, and a brown bear with a quizzical expression sat in the rocker. The shelves of the dressing table were filled with baby supplies. What had once been Aunt Myla's wicker sewing basket now held an array of small plastic toys guaranteed to enhance the IQ of any baby. And Caroline's favorite purchase, a carousel music box, sat on the dresser.

I walked over to the dresser and switched on the music box.

The CPS contingent smiled politely and fanned out. Leon Schwartz walked over to the window and gazed out at the snow-covered fields beyond the driveway. Then he turned his back to the window and said to me, "You cannot leave bedding on the rails of the crib. It could fall over the baby's face and smother her."

I removed the offending blanket and remembered Michael Ferguson's veiled warning. What other failings would Leon Schwartz note in his report? The sweet sound of the music box trailed our footsteps down the hall.

"You've done a remarkable job," Wims conceded.

"Caroline helped choose everything," I said. "It took hours at the baby store."

A brief glance into my room revealed the maids had replaced Aunt Myla's worn chenille bedspread with a bright quilt and had carefully dusted all her bric-a-brac.

The bathroom had few redeeming features, but clean towels hung on the towel rack and a fresh bar of soap sat in the wire basket on the rim of tub. There was no medicine cabinet. Instead, a wide shelf held everything necessary for a little princess in her bath. On the cracked black and white floor tiles sat the yellow baby bathtub and a rubber duck awaiting the first incoming tide. I had not bathed a baby since Darla was little. I prayed my visitors would note only our careful preparations and not my trepidation and dismay.

We glanced through the door at the clutter in the back bedroom. I pointed out the door to the attic but did not offer to open it lest something rabid fly out.

We returned to the parlor.

"Visiting rights," I said firmly as I took my seat in the wingback chair.

Wims perched on the edge of the loveseat. She was a fast learner. She nodded. "Estelle will give you the details of the compromise we've ironed out. Please understand this was the best we could work out on such short notice. Judge Morrell phoned us and asked us to make every effort to allow you and the baby's grandmother visiting rights as soon as possible."

Wims nodded at Estelle who pulled printed papers from her briefcase.

Estelle scanned the first page and began to read the pertinent parts in a rather hectoring voice.

"Until you actually gain custody of Katie, you may pick her up from the foster mother on a daily basis. You may not bring her to your house or Caroline's house..."

I opened my mouth to protest. Wims held up a restraining hand.

Estelle continued. "Instead, you may take Katie to a mutually agreed upon place where you can spend supervised time with her. Two hours each day. Beginning tomorrow. At ten in the morning."

"What does supervised time mean?" I asked coldly.

Estelle had her answer ready. "It means a third party will be on hand. There is a Ronald McDonald House on

Westmoreland Drive. They often provide this sort of service for us."

My face must have reflected my opinion of the arrangements. Estelle Grayson flashed a look of concern at her supervisor.

Wims was undismayed by my hostility and interceded with equanimity. "The Ronald McDonald house is very nice, Mrs. Scholfield. And I personally believe you will make an excellent foster mother. However, legally we cannot hand over to you a baby in our custody until your paperwork is complete. Our commitment is to protect the children in our care."

I could not dispute her position. As for Estelle Grayson's lack of grace, she might be new at her job. On the other hand, she could simply be a cow.

"I understand," I conceded. "Your job is a difficult one, and God knows this world needs people like you on the front line."

Wims nodded. "I think you will be pleasantly surprised by the arrangements at the Ronald McDonald House. They are staffed by wonderful, committed volunteers.

"And Caroline is allowed the same visiting privileges?"

Estelle nodded as she riffled through her briefcase. "Here are directions to the foster mother's house. They are strictly confidential. You may reveal them to no one, not even Caroline. Caroline must wait at a separate location while you pick up and return the baby. You will have twenty minutes from the time you pick up the baby to reach the Ronald McDonald House. The same goes for the return trip."

My face mirrored my dismay. "That's ludicrous. Caroline is blind. She won't be able to see where we're driving. Why should she have to wait at a separate location? And what if the weather is bad? Do I reduce my speed to drive safely or do you prefer I jeopardize us all to meet your time constraints?"

"They are customary restrictions," snapped Estelle. "And you must sign in and out at the Ronald McDonald House."

Leon Schwartz, Katie's Advocate, changed the subject. I had the impression that while the two women were assessing the house, he had been looking for slight infractions to prove he was doing his job.

"Mrs. Scholfield, you do have a car seat for the baby?"

I nodded and struggled to maintain a modicum of poise. "It's already installed, facing backwards, in the back seat of my car. And, just to be safe, it's been inspected for proper installation by a member of the Rochester police department. Would you like her name and phone number?"

Chapter Sixteen

I turned the key in the lock after Rhonda Wims and her minions departed, and then I slumped against the wide doors in relief. The house had passed inspection. Tomorrow Caroline and I could visit Katie, actually have her to ourselves for two whole hours, hold her, rock her, show her some of her new toys.

The barometer was falling and so was the temperature. According to the radio in the kitchen, we were in for a storm. What a welcome for the Africans! I looked around for Aunt Myla's raccoon coat. Yesterday I had run into the house and had tossed it somewhere in my haste to get to the court hearing on time. Now it was nowhere to be found. There was no telling where Aguilar had stashed it in his quest to make the house presentable. My London Fog was not as warm, but it would have to suffice for the drive to the airport. Caroline's refugees would be shivering, so why should I be an exception?

At the barrier to the United Airlines gates Caroline stood in a throng of church people carrying balloons and small American flags. She was a picture of casual elegance in a dove-brown wool skirt, a pale russet sweater, tweed blazer and pearl earrings. She radiated energy and enthusiasm. No one would ever guess someone had attacked her last night and kicked her dog half to death and, behind her dark glasses, she was on the brink of collapse. She was deep in conversation with a middle-aged woman dressed in traditional African attire.

I walked up to Caroline and gently squeezed her arm.

"How are you doing?"

"I'm fine," she answered for the benefit of those around her. "And looking forward to finally meeting our refugees. Kate, this is Fatima, our Somali interpreter."

Fatima smiled. She had an incredibly kind face. I instantly felt I could tell this woman anything and she would understand.

"There are two families arriving this afternoon," Caroline rattled on. "So we've got two church groups here. The Lutherans are getting a family of five."

I gripped her arm and said, "Could I talk to you for just a minute?"

Caroline smiled graciously at Fatima and we stepped aside.

"The house passed muster and we can visit Katie tomorrow!" I told her in a low, jubilant voice.

Caroline reached out to hug me. "Oh, Kate, what a miracle. I can't wait to hold her. I've missed her so!"

I hugged her back. "You never called me from the vet's office. What did he say about Nomad?"

Caroline's face mirrored her devastation. "He's gone. I had to have him put down. I stayed with him and held him and cried like a baby."

The shock hit me in the pit of my stomach. "Caro, I'm so very sorry!" We stood together insulated from the crowd around us by our sorrow. As a guide dog Nomad had embodied love and devotion. But he had also been a part of the family, a furry, loving presence that had watched over Caroline and Darla for years. If I felt the loss this keenly, what must Caroline feel?

"Kate," Caroline whispered urgently, "You said this morning you were going to talk to one of the nursing students in Darla's class. Did you find out anything?"

I was saved from answering because just then Aguilar

saw us standing together and sauntered over. His concession to the weather was a red wool scarf draped under the collar of his leather jacket. "Ladies, I've got your goat in my car."

Caroline smiled brightly at him. "Wonderful!"

"And thank you for the flowers," I said.

"I thought they would make that old house look less like a haunted mansion when CPS came to inspect. And, in case you didn't notice, I also assembled the baby's furniture. It took me an hour and a half to figure out the damned instructions for that crib. Why didn't you have them deliver one already assembled?"

Before I could reply, someone shouted, "The plane's at the gate!" Everyone surged toward the observation area. Caroline clutched my arm. "Describe everything to me," she whispered. "I don't want to miss a thing."

We found a place in front. "A few people are disembarking. No refugees yet," I said to her.

We waited, and I readied my Nikon.

Caroline fidgeted with her lace handkerchief and said impatiently, "This is ridiculous! They must be deplaning the refugees last. Or they could have missed the flight. That's all we need."

"Relax," Aguilar told her. "If they get lost, Homeland Security will track them down."

Finally someone called, "Here they come!"

"They're straggling out of the gate now," I told Caroline. "They look dazed. Maybe numb would be a better word. They're just following the crowd. Do they know we're here to meet them?"

"I'm sure at some point someone told them their church sponsors would be at the airport to meet them. It could have been days ago. I'm not sure if it registered in all the confusion."

I continued talking while I snapped pictures. "The men

113

are wearing nothing but short sleeved shirts and slacks. They must have frozen on the international flight. International flights are always so cold."

"I know the airlines hand out blankets. I had one on my flight home in November."

"There are never enough to go around. You have to be smart enough to ask for one on the way to your seat."

Caroline frowned behind her dark glasses. "I'll write Church World Service a note. Keep telling me what you see."

"They're all trudging up the ramp. The women and girls have on bright African dresses and scarves covering their heads. And the children...Caroline, the children are so thin. Everyone looks exhausted."

Caroline nodded. "Their flight from Kenya landed in Newark at 5:43 this morning. They had to spend the entire day there. I don't even know if they got fed. I tried calling the airport, but I couldn't get through to anyone who could tell me anything."

Around us the crowd had fallen silent.

"What's going on?" Caroline demanded. "Why is everyone so quiet?"

It was hard to keep the emotion out of my voice. "All the refugees are walking in front of a huge American flag that's draped on the wall. Hold on...I have to stop talking for a minute and concentrate on getting this on film."

Behind us, I heard Aguilar mutter under his breath, "*Give me your tired, your poor, Your huddled masses yearning to breathe free...*"

Caroline turned around and gave him a beatific smile. "*I lift my lamp beside the golden door.* That's what we're doing right now, isn't it? Lifting a lamp beside the golden door."

People from the two churches started to cheer and wave. A few of the refugees glanced up. I squeezed Caroline's arm. "The tempest-tossed are beginning to realize all the cheering and balloons are for them. You should see their smiles!"

Fatima took Caroline's arm and drew her toward the arriving refugees. I followed, snapping pictures of Fatima as she greeted them. She spoke quietly in their native tongue and gestured toward Caroline as the head of their sponsoring team. I could tell by her gestures she was explaining that Caroline was blind. The men eyed Caroline gravely. The women stayed behind the men, their eyes cast downward. The children clung timidly to their skirts.

Church people came forward bearing armfuls of coats. There was a flurry of activity as sizes were sorted out. Our church came up one coat short. A man in our group whipped off his own winter jacket and handed it to a tall boy. The boy stared at him for a moment in surprise and then put on the coat. "Thank you," he said, awkwardly testing first words of a new language in a new land, not sure they would actually work.

Nobody had given footwear a thought. The men and children were wearing cheap white sneakers, probably issued upon departure from Nairobi. The women were wearing flip-flops. No one had socks.

Caroline was walking down the line of Bantus, touching each one, learning their names and the sound of their voices. Aguilar was behind her. "Didn't Kate tell me this was a family of seven?" I heard him say to her. "I only see six here. I think you got shorted."

Caroline turned and yelled in a clarion voice, "Tell the Lutherans not to leave. They've got one of ours. We've only got six here!"

Fatima said something to the mother of our family. She was a beautiful woman, straight and proud, with high cheekbones and eyes that seemed unafraid. She, as did all the women and young girls, wore a large yellow headscarf with the Church World Service logo stamped on it. She smiled at

Fatima's words. Turning around, she drew the edge of her yellow scarf aside. Asleep on her back was a baby. The seventh refugee had just been located.

In the car I turned the heat up to the maximum setting. The family, huddled in their new coats, stared out the windows to catch first glimpses of their new land. What, I wondered, did they make of the snow that was softly falling and blanketing the road, the city lights, and their church sponsor who was blind? There were endless adjustments ahead for these people. I wished them well with all my heart.

At Caroline's house, we unloaded everyone. Caroline took the mother of the family and the children upstairs to explain the shower and sleeping arrangements. Aguilar hauled a cooler into the kitchen and said formally to Fatima. "Please tell Mr. Mohamed this is goat meat to celebrate his arrival in America."

Mr. Mohamed listened gravely to Fatima. Then he nodded and beamed at Aguilar. "Ah," he said. "Thank you. Thank you."

I pulled Aguilar aside. "That was a really nice gesture. Are you up for further adventure?"

"Are you propositioning me?"

"Sort of. I need an escort."

"Where are we going?"

"To a bar. I have a lead on Darla's boyfriend. I think he might be the one who mugged Caroline last night."

A half an hour later, Aguilar pulled to a halt in front of the Canal Street Bar in an unsavory part of the city. His black Lincoln was grossly out of place among the huge, chrome-covered motorcycles. Neon lights flickered in the front windows of the bar and illuminated the ramshackle porch that fronted the building. Patrons with enough alcohol in their blood to make them oblivious to the cold were hanging out on the porch, grouped together, smoking and drinking and periodically tossing empty cans and cigarette butts over the porch rail. Through the bar's open door came the melancholy wail of Jerry Jeff Walker singing of desperadoes waiting for a train.

Aguilar did not bother to switch off the motor. "Are you out of your goddamned mind? You can't just walk into a place like this and start asking questions!"

"Why not?"

"Lady, they'll take one look at you and rip you to shreds. Then what will happen to the baby?" He mashed his foot down on the accelerator, causing the car to fishtail on the ice-slick macadam.

A muscular man with a shaved head was coming out of the bar. He paused in the doorway to light a cigarette.

I twisted in the seat and grabbed Aguilar's arm.

"Wait! I think that's him!"

The man on the porch exhaled and glanced up. For one second his pale eyes met mine. They glittered like shards of ice. Then Aguilar gunned the motor of the Lincoln and we sped off into the night.

"Lady, if you think that creep is the one who attacked Caroline, you need to get the police involved."

"You know Caroline can't identify her attacker. What exactly do you think the police can do without a description?"

"Well, what did you think you were going to do? Just saunter up to the bar and have a cozy little chat with a bunch of thugs?"

"We could have had a drink and maybe overheard something. Or followed that guy home to find out where he lives. Or maybe Darla was at the bar. You didn't even give me a chance to get out of the car!"

"You're damned right."

By the time Aguilar dropped me off at Caroline's house,

117

it was snowing in earnest. I unlocked my car and navigated slick roads into Mendon with the utmost care. When I reached the sanctuary of Aunt Myla's house, I made myself a quick snack. Upstairs, I climbed into bed and fell into a deep, dreamless sleep. I never heard the silent footsteps that passed through the house in the night.

Chapter Seventeen

The next morning, behind the bedroom's lace curtains which age had stained the color of tea, gusts of wind rattled the windows in their sashes and snow hissed against fogged panes of glass. The old house was creaking and groaning in the throes of a storm, but when I stepped out of bed, warm air rose reassuringly onto my bare feet through the ornate metal heat register in the floor.

In the kitchen I brewed a pot of French roast coffee in a battered percolator which I found under the sink and poured the coffee into a delicate blue and white tea cup from the cupboard. I took my coffee to the table, sat staring at Aguilar's flowers which were already beginning to drop their petals, then dialed Caroline on the cell phone. Through the window, I watched a relentless northwest wind contour the landscape with deepening drifts of snow. There were no horses in the nearby fields, no birds visible in the black walnut trees, and no sign a snow plow had been by.

A lilting African voice answered Caroline's phone.

"Good morning. Is Caroline there?" I said.

There was an incomprehensible reply followed by silence.

I could hear Caroline in the background. She was in full Peace Corps mode. "Right. Get your fork and test them. See? These yams are hard. They've been cooking in the oven for one hour. One hour. Now check the yams in the microwave. Already soft. Ten minutes! See how fast the microwave cooks?"

Whoever had answered the phone evidently had been

mesmerized by the cooking lesson and had forgotten I was on the line. I yelled into the receiver. "Caroline?"

Nothing. I hung up and dialed again. For the next ten minutes the line was busy. Then the same cheerful Bantu answered.

"Caroline!" I snapped. "I want to talk to her right now."

Caroline came on the line.

"How was your first night in the Gothic monstrosity?"

"Fine. I slept for the first time in a week. Did you get any sleep?"

"Yeah, some. Have you looked out the window?"

"Is it a blizzard?"

"Don't you have a radio?"

"I have a small Zenith, possibly a relic from the 1940s, here in the kitchen. It has two sticky knobs and a brown frayed electric cord. Every time I turn it on it makes a fizzy sound like it's going to short out. And, yes, I have my laptop, but I do not yet have internet access, something essential I seem to have overlooked."

"Well, according to my modern, functioning radio it's not a blizzard, but the roads are a royal mess. The official word is don't drive unless it's an emergency."

"That means we can't go get Katie," I said plaintively. "I'll have to call the foster mother."

"I know. I was looking forward to it so much! But it's only twelve degrees outside. That's too cold for salt to melt the ice on the roads. Driving would be a bitch."

"Should you be saying such things in front of the refugees?"

She laughed. "Piss off. I'll talk to you later."

At nine I phoned Loretta Whiting, the foster mother. Loretta maintained it would be extremely unwise to take Katie out in this weather. It was something she simply could not condone. I told her I had come to the same conclusion. I gripped the phone, my only connection to Katie. "How is Katie doing?"

"She's settling in."

That's it? Settling in? Am I the enemy? Can't you be a little more forthcoming? Did she sleep well? Is she eating? Have you bathed her? Do you have time to hold her and talk to her?

I strained to hear background noises but heard nothing but the rattle of dishes and sounds of children talking. No babies crying. I tried to take that as good news. I slumped at the table in my flannel pajamas drinking black coffee and watching it snow. Was Darla somewhere out in this storm worrying about her baby? I tried to think of Katie as her baby, not mine. I knew Katie was not mine. Yet when I held her in my arms, I felt a fierce protective love and a monumental tenderness. Those feelings were treacherous shoals for a foster parent. Until it was proven beyond a shadow of a doubt Darla had harmed her, Katie could never be mine. But a baby needed love like a daisy needed sunshine. I could not mitigate my love for Katie to protect myself. I would love Katie unconditionally and it would tear out my heart to give her back. I knew that intellectually when I signed the papers to become a foster parent. Now I knew it viscerally. *Live with it!* I told myself fiercely. *No one has a right to expect a life without pain.*

I put my coffee cup in the sink. The inclement weather was providing me with an unforeseen gift of time to get this house in working order before Katie became my primary responsibility. I decided to spend the morning moving Aunt Myla's things out of her bedroom. Upstairs, I paused in the doorway of the nursery. Everything in Katie's new room was perfectly placed. I walked over and picked up the rose-colored blanket and buried my face in its softness. How different the room would be with a baby in it. How different my life would be with a baby in it! I went into the bathroom

121

and invited the yellow rubber duck for a swim while I bathed in the claw footed bathtub. Then I got to work.

After boxing up Aunt Myla's treasures and carrying them up the narrow stairs to the cold attic, I folded all her clothes and put them in plastic bags to be donated to a charity. Caroline's refugees certainly didn't need them. Currently they had more clothing than I did. I put my meager belongings in the newly emptied dresser and closet and then headed down to wash the dirty clothes from my suitcase. On the way to the cellar, I stopped in the kitchen to rummage through the drawers for a flashlight. What I found was a battered chrome-plated prototype of the modern flashlight which seemed to work only when shaken. I stuck it in the pocket of my sweater.

When I opened the cellar door, dank musty air peculiar to old cellars rose to greet me. I made my way carefully down uneven wooden steps. At the base of the stairs, a low-watt bulb suspended from the rafters illuminated clothes lines running the length of the laundry room. A faded cloth bag filled with wooden clothes pins hung from one of the lines. Arrayed along the walls of the laundry room was a veritable graveyard of cleaning equipment - mops, frayed brooms, a yellow dust pan, feather dusters and what may have been an original Hoover vacuum cleaner with all of its attachments.

I threw my clothes into the washer along with some time-hardened detergent and turned on the machine. The sound of water rushing into the washing machine filled me with relief. If there was one mechanical item in the house that I really needed to work, it was the washing machine. I gazed with affection upon the dryer which stood next to the washing machine. I had never imagined household appliances could elicit such a feeling of well being.

Keeping a wary ear open for impending floods and related malfunctions, I wandered into the next room where the furnace was humming efficiently. It was a storage area for the old, the useless, and the worn out. In one corner was an antiquated wringer washer. Next to it stood a mangle. I ran my hand over its ungainly frame and tried to imagine a day spent in the cellar slogging clothes through the wringer washing machine, pinning everything on lines to dry, and then ironing it all on that mangle. It was a veritable glimpse into Purgatory.

Propped along the walls of the next room were broken window frames, screens, dilapidated shutters, and stacks of old doors. There was not a single room in this house lacking a door, so where had all these old doors come from and why had they been stashed down here? Aunt Myla had been the only one with the answer. Now it was simply another of the small mysteries surrounding her house that would never be answered.

I pushed my way past stacks of bushel baskets and crates to the huge cistern which had once provided water to the house. The cistern was bone dry and half-full of debris. Near the cistern was the object of my trek through the cellar, a small wooden door covered with old penciled notations of produce and costs of what had once been the working farm on this property.

I pulled on the door's rusty handle and flickered my antiquated flashlight over the primitive stone walls and dirt floor of Aunt Myla's root cellar. The root cellar gave off a dismal, sour odor from the area where the rock ceiling sloped beyond the perimeter of the flashlight's beam. In the past, Aunt Myla had apples, cabbages, and potatoes in here. Presently the root cellar contained nothing but more stacks of empty bushel baskets and crates. I backed out with a sigh of relief, pulled the door closed and hooked the rickety latch. I had not been looking forward to cleaning out long-decayed produce left to rot after Aunt Myla's demise.

The remainder of the morning I spent upstairs sorting through drawers, closets and cupboards. At noon I ate a Spartan lunch of cheese, olives and English water crackers and wished Aguilar were present to witness my foray into health food. Afterwards, seeing the roads were still unplowed, I crawled back into the unmade bed, which I now rightfully claimed as my own, for a long winter's nap. Little did I know how much I would need that nap to cope with the terrors of the coming night.

Chapter Eighteen

Late in the afternoon a crash from somewhere in the house startled me out of a sound slumber. I yanked on jeans and a sweater and clattered down the back stairs. Nervously, I peered outside each door. It had stopped snowing, but the evening was bitterly cold. The roads had not been plowed, there were no tire tracks in the driveway, and no footprints marred the crystalline snow that blanketed the yard. Whatever had made the noise, it had not been a visitor rapping on my chamber door.

In the kitchen, I poured a small glass of Gentleman Jack to dispel an unreasonable sense of unease. Then I walked through the house sipping the whiskey as I peered outside each window and then checked the old-fashioned window latches until I was certain every window in the house was securely locked. Finally, armed with a second glass of whiskey and the old flashlight as a makeshift weapon, I crept down the cellar stairs and made my way through all the rooms of the cellar, flashing the weak beams of the old flashlight into dark corners and behind the debris. I found only one thing out of order. The rusty latch on the root cellar door had popped loose, and the root cellar door was now standing ajar. How could that have happened?

Hair prickled along my neck. Here I was, alone out in the country, stranded by a snowstorm, and it was getting dark. Had Aunt Myla died peacefully in her bed as everyone had thought or could she have fallen victim to someone preying on the elderly inhabitant of an isolated farmhouse? Characters in horror stories die hideous deaths because they confront the forces of evil and do not have the good sense to either run or call for help. Here I was in this dark cellar, unequivocally alone. And that root cellar smelled like the lair of something evil.

I tried to pull myself together, but it was an uphill battle. I was a city dweller. Being alone out in the country seemed a lot scarier than being alone in a city. Phoning the police to say I was hearing mysterious noises would be the utmost folly. I would look like a fool, and, if word trickled down to Child Protective Services, I would be relocated by midweek to their choice of urban apartments. My only other option was to call Aguilar and tell him I was having a fit of the vapors. However, the way he drove, it would take him half the night to get here, and then I'd have the devil's own time getting rid of him again. That would put more stress on my nerves than a vampire lurking in the dim environs of this damned cellar.

Downing the last of the whiskey in one inelegant gulp, I returned to the kitchen, pulled half a rotisserie chicken and a prepackaged salad out the refrigerator, and forced myself to eat. Then, armed with a paperback mystery, my cell phone, the metal flashlight, and a box of Twinkies, I went back to bed. Somehow, near midnight, I managed to fall asleep.

It was barely three in the morning when I awoke with a start. From the nursery across the hall came the sound of the rocking chair gently rocking on the wooden floorboards. I tried to fight back the terror of being defenseless in the dark, of knowing someone was really, truly in the house.

Screaming for help would be futile. Besides, how can you scream when you are fighting for each panic-stricken breath? I fumbled for the cell phone on the table by the bed and punched in 911. "Help," I whispered. "There's an intruder in my house!"

After an eternity of waiting, a terminally calm dispatcher

extracted my name and address and then said, "There's a serious accident at the Victor exit on I-90. All available personnel are at the scene at the moment. It may be a while before a car can get to you. Where are you?"

Where am I? My hand was shaking so hard I could scarcely hold on to the cell phone. "I told you! I'm in my house!" I whispered.

"Where in the house are you?" came the relentlessly calm response.

"Oh...I'm in my bedroom. On the second floor. The one with the porch. Should I try to jump off the porch?"

"No. Does the door to the bedroom have a lock?"

"I...I don't know. I just moved in yesterday. You need to send someone out here now!"

"Someone will come as soon as possible. If you can lock your bedroom door, lock it. If it doesn't lock, shove something heavy in front of it. Or hide."

"Hide?"

"Yes. Hide. Don't come out until..."

The cell phone went dead. I shook it. Unlike the flashlight, shaking it did not help. I had forgotten to charge it. And now I could not explain to the 911 operator that the intruder was not just roaming somewhere in the house. The intruder was sitting in a rocking chair in the room across the hall!

I tried to stifle my ragged gasps as I slipped out of bed. Where was I supposed to hide? On a shelf in the closet? I grasped the flashlight in a death grip and tiptoed around the Twinkies wrappers to the bedroom door. I started to push the door closed. It creaked loud enough to raise the dead. I stared across the hall into the dark nursery, ready to bolt for the stairs if the intruder had heard the noise.

Moonlight reflecting off the snow outside the nursery window faintly illuminated a woman sitting in the rocking chair. She was wrapped in a raccoon coat.

"Aunt Myla?" I whispered. In the ghostly light the wraith slowly turned her head toward me. I could see tears glistening on her face.

"Hi, Aunt Kate," the wraith said softly.

"Darla! God damn it to hell! You scared the shit out of me!"

"Where's my baby?" Darla asked in a strange, listless voice. "Did she die?"

Chapter Nineteen

I turned on the light in the nursery. Darla sat huddled in the rocker wrapped in Aunt Myla's coat. She was filthy, and when I touched her forehead, I could tell she was burning with fever.

"Your baby is not dead," I snarled in fury. "She's with a foster mother."

"She's not...safe!"

"She's a lot safer with a foster mother than she was with you. Whatever were you thinking?"

"Aunt, Kate! You don't understand!" She started coughing, a dry, hacking cough that set off alarm bells in my head.

"I understand you left her starved and beat up on the doorstep of the hospital and then ran off. What more is there to understand?"

"I wanted you to come and take her."

I grabbed her arm in rage and yanked her out of the rocking chair. "She's not my baby. You're the one who got pregnant. She's *your* baby. An innocent. Why didn't *you* take care of her?" I realized I was screaming. I let go of her arm and watched her sink back into the rocker. I knelt in front of the rocker. "Why, Darla? Why didn't you tell your mother you were pregnant? Why did you risk that baby's life?"

Darla shrank back into the rocker. "Not safe...not safe."

She seemed to be drifting in and out of consciousness. I shook her. "Darla, you're sick. I thought you were an intruder. I called the police. When they get here they can call an ambulance and get you to a hospital."

Her fever-crazed eyes snapped open. She staggered up from the rocker. "Oh no, Aunt Kate! Why did you call the cops? I've got to get out of here before they arrive!"

"Darla, grow up. You have to stop thinking of yourself and start thinking of your mother and your baby."

Darla hissed in my face, her breath hot and so fetid it made me want to gag. "I *am* thinking of my mother and the baby. I'm the only one who can protect them. That's why I have to get out of here before the cops arrive. Don't you understand? Someone's after that baby. It's not safe for my mother to keep her. And I can't take care of a baby on the run!" She coughed raggedly as she shrugged out of the raccoon coat and shoved it at me. "Here. There are two kittens in one of the pockets. At least...take...care of them!"

For a moment I stood stunned as Darla lurched down the hall toward the back stairs.

I dropped the coat into the rocker and raced after her. "Darla, wait! If you leave the house, the police might see you. Besides, you're too sick to go out in this weather. Where have you been hiding?"

Darla's footsteps slowed. "In the root cellar. I was in there when you locked it. I pounded on the door when I realized it wouldn't open. I was terrified. But the latch wasn't very strong and I...managed to break out."

"Well, get back in the root cellar. I'll think of some way to get rid of the police."

I ran downstairs for the phone in the kitchen and dialed 911. The same dispassionate dispatcher came on the phone. I gave her my name and address and said, "I called earlier. I thought there was an intruder, but I just discovered it was someone, uh, someone abandoning kittens on my doorstep."

"I'll let the squad car know. It's already on the way. The officer will stop to check in on you just to confirm everything is all right."

130

Great.

I raced down the cellar stairs, ran through the cellar, and jerked open the door to the root cellar. Darla was curled up on the filthy floor, her eyes closed.

"Darla, get up. Give me your boots."

Darla sat up coughing violently. "Why?" she asked, gasping for breath. "You don't trust me? You think I'm still going to leave?"

"Just shut up and do it!"

I raced back up the cellar stairs and ran for the side door, pulling on Darla's boots over my bare feet. Then I stepped into virgin snow on the porch and tramped around before stepping down into the drifts that covered the steps and walk. Snow filled the unlaced boots as I struggled down the driveway to the edge of the road, stomped around to leave more footprints, then turned around, gasping for breath in the frigid air, and struggled back to the porch. Once inside, I pulled off the boots, hid them in the china closet, and stepped back outside onto the snowy porch, this time in my bare feet.

No sooner was I back inside than I heard the patrol car approaching.

I flew up the stairs and grabbed Aunt Myla's raccoon coat which now lay in a heap on the floor of the nursery. Out of one of the pockets I pulled two painfully thin, flea-ridden kittens. Their fur was spiked with filth, and their eyes were glued shut.

The doorbell shrilled, followed by loud pounding on the door. "Police! Please open the door!"

Clutching the two kittens, I ran down the stairs in my pajamas and bare feet. I opened the door and held up the mewling kittens. "Thank you so much for coming! I called back to say it was a false alarm. I heard someone outside, and I...guess I thought he was inside the house, but it must have

131

been someone abandoning these two kittens on my doorstep. The dispatcher said you were already on the way. I know how busy you are. I'm terribly sorry to have troubled you."

The cop stared at the kittens and then down at the boot prints and bare footprints on the porch. "Never mind," he said kindly. "No one takes responsibility any more. They just dump their own responsibilities on someone else and run."

Dump your responsibilities on someone else. What an enlightened concept, I thought as the cop pulled out of the drive. *I think I'll try it.*

I went into the kitchen, picked up the phone, and called Aguilar.

Chapter Twenty

"Are you nuts?" Aguilar yelled over the phone. "It's not even five in the morning. Would you like to tell me where I'm supposed to get cat food and a litter box at this hour?"

"These kittens are half-dead from starvation. They need food now."

"Don't you have milk in the house?"

"I don't think you can give newborn kittens milk. It gives them diarrhea. Get canned food, something that says it's a kitten diet. I'm sure there's a pharmacy or grocery store open. I'll have the coffee on when you get here."

"I can't leave until Pop gets up and I get him something to eat."

"That shouldn't pose a problem. Everyone enjoys an early breakfast once in a while. And by the way, get flea soap, too. You're an angel." I hung up before he could invent more excuses and ran down the cellar stairs.

Darla crawled weakly to the door of the root cellar. It was a monumental struggle to get her up the stairs.

"Can't," she kept mumbling. "Where's my baby?"

I dragged her into the bathroom where she sank to the tiled floor while I ran a hot bath. I stripped off her clothes and helped her into the old claw-footed bathtub.

Darla's body was emaciated. Her nails were broken from trying to force open the latched door of the root cellar. Her hair was matted, her body unwashed. She looked like the victim of a recent war.

"Wash!" I commanded her.

I left her in the tub shivering, eyes unfocused and

133

muttering, while I rummaged frantically through bags of Aunt Myla's clothes which, just this morning, I had carefully packed away. Darla and Aunt Myla were both petite women. I found a blue flannel nightgown and a pair of white wool socks.

I returned to the bathroom and threw them on the floor next to Katie's yellow bathtub. Darla made a feeble effort to sit up in the tub. In silence I scrubbed her and then washed her long, curly black hair. Once she was ensconced in the front bedroom, I said, "Stay there. Don't even think about leaving. We have a lot to talk about. I am your best hope right now. Piss me off, and I'll hand you over to the police."

Darla reached out a skeletal hand and managed three words.

"Thanks...Aunt Kate." She was asleep instantly.

I hurried down the hall and dug out my travel kit. It held every kind of medicine necessary to survive biological onslaught in places where no one spoke English. My limited medical knowledge told me high fever demanded antibiotics. Unless it was a virus, in which case we were up the proverbial creek. Because of her cough, I figured Darla had a respiratory infection, maybe even pneumonia. But she could also have an infection from giving birth in dire surroundings. I had two options in my kit, Cipro and Zithromycin. I seemed to recall Cipro covering a wider range of potential fever-related illnesses. I opted for the Cipro. And Tylenol. But not on an empty stomach.

I checked on Darla to make sure she hadn't run off, then ran downstairs, flailed around in the kitchen and returned to the guest room with scrambled eggs and buttered toast. Darla was asleep. I shook her. She cringed and whimpered.

"Darla, stop it. It's Aunt Kate. Wake up and eat this."

Her eyelids fluttered.

"Open your eyes. You know I hate to cook. Don't make

134

me throw this out."

Darla's eyes, when they opened, were glassy. She began to shiver although her thin body radiated heat. "Where's my baby?" she whispered and then started coughing.

I was frightened and desperately wished it was safe to take her to a hospital.

"Katie is fine. I promise. I'll tell you all about her if you will sit up and try to eat this. I've got antibiotics for you. You need to get well. Fast. Now stop slacking off and get these damned eggs down your throat."

Darla opened her mouth and let me spoon food into her. Just a little. I had no idea when she had last eaten. If she had last eaten when she had last bathed, she was lucky to be alive.

I taped a large note to the table by the side of her bed. *We are going to have company. Stay very quiet!!* I would let her sleep until Aguilar had come and gone. Then I would give her more antibiotics. And start asking questions.

Aguilar showed up at six-thirty. He stomped in with a disgusted look and set bags of kitten supplies on the dining room table. He had brought everything on my list and, in addition, catnip mice, two bowls, and tiny collars, one red and one blue.

"Want to see the kittens?" I asked, trying not to grin.

"Not particularly."

"One's black and white and one's a gray tiger." I opened the door to the powder room. The kittens were curled together in a basket filled with old towels.

Aguilar stood in the door looking down at the pathetic balls of filthy fur. "Very nice. What the hell are you going to do with two cats?"

"They're a gift for you."

"No thanks."

"Aguilar, you don't have any choice in the matter. It's

135

just short term. I can't have them here with Child Protective Services breathing down my neck. The last thing I need is two kittens sleeping in the baby's crib and dragging dead mice out for visitors to admire. These kittens have hung onto life against all odds. We can't dump them on the humane society and let them be euthanized."

"Give them to Caroline. She's a sucker for the needy."

"They wouldn't last a day with all the refugees. And she's mourning for Nomad."

"What am I going to do with two cats?"

"They would be good company for your father. Please, Aguilar. You're their only hope."

"All right, all right." He checked the Rolex on his wrist. "Gimme a cup of coffee and I'll run them over to the vet. Just to make sure they don't have rabies or some damn thing. You can brew coffee, can't you?" He shrugged out of his leather jacket and followed me into the kitchen.

I poured coffee into two of Aunt Myla's blue and white cups and set the cups on matching saucers. I put a cup in front of Aguilar who shrugged out of his leather jacket and hung it on the back of his chair.

"Aguilar, I need help."

"You just *got* help in the form of the adoption of two of the sorriest looking animals I've ever seen. And yesterday there was the small matter of an entire goat. Oh, yes. Let's not forget the trip downtown to a biker's bar. A real fun-filled evening."

"This help is in an entirely different league."

Aguilar sipped his coffee and winced at the taste. "What is it now?"

I leaned forward. "I want to preface this by telling you about my husband."

"What more do I need to know? He died and you put up a memorial bench overlooking that beach in the Isles of

Scilly. I still have the pictures I took of you sitting there."

"Yes. But when I got here and talked to the lawyer, I found out he'd been having an affair."

He shrugged. "Men do."

My eyes went flat with anger. I glanced down so he couldn't see my face. "He was having an affair, and the woman who died with him was carrying his baby."

Aguilar started to interrupt. I held up my hand to stay his words.

"And he left everything in his will that he possibly could to her. So, Aguilar, I don't have a lot of faith in people right now. But I desperately need to trust someone. And you're the only person who fits the bill."

Aguilar stretched out his legs, put down his cup, and sighed. "If I can help, I'll help. What do you need?"

"I need you to break the law."

"Most women just want a diamond ring and a promise that you'll love 'em forever. I should have known you'd be different." He shrugged, that particular Latin gesture that was becoming very familiar. "The nuns at my high school told me I'd never amount to much. But when I was in Vietnam, I swore to God if I got out alive, I'd live a straight life. I haven't done all that great, but I look after my family and, well, you know....When I go into a meat plant and see something wrong, sometimes the owners try to slip me a few bills. I don't take bribes because when I find something against the codes, I think of the people whose lives will be safe because I wouldn't look the other way. That's the best I can do."

I sat looking at him for a few minutes in silent admiration for someone who could express his code of ethics so clearly. "Aguilar, I need a save of my own. I need to save a baby," I said.

"I thought the baby was being kept by a foster mother

and you would have her soon. A week, maybe. That's why we were in such a rush to get the house ready and the nursery put together."

"There's been a complication." I hesitated for a second, then threw my cards on the table and gambled everything. "Darla's here. She's upstairs. Sick enough to be in a hospital."

"She's here? You want me to take her to a hospital?"

"No. She's terrified to turn herself in. She says she's running from someone to protect the baby, and...I think she's telling the truth. When the mugger attacked Caroline and her dog, there's information we didn't give to the police."

"Yeah? Why am I not surprised?"

"The attacker said, 'Tell Darla to give back what's mine.' Caroline and I thought he was talking about money or drugs. But what if it wasn't? What if it was the baby? Darla was hiding out on the streets, but she couldn't take care of a baby under those circumstances. So she took the baby where it could be cared for and no one would know where it was. Not to her mother's house but to the hospital. And she kept running so whoever was after the baby would think she still had it. And now she's here."

"How the hell did she get here?"

"I don't know how she got here, and I don't know how long she's been here. She's been hiding in the root cellar in the basement."

"You want me to round up a gang of Latinos and roust the creep at the bar? See what he has to say?"

"Could you?" I asked in amazement.

"Probably. I know a few guys."

"No. I want you to stay here and take care of Darla, make sure she doesn't try to leave. If she runs off again, she could die from exposure. I have to drive over to get Caroline and then pick up Katie from the foster mother's house. We get to spend two hours with her at the Ronald McDonald

House, and it's not something we can skip. I made a huge stink about not getting to see Katie. We have to show up."

"And it goes without saying you don't want me to turn Darla in to the cops."

"I especially don't want you to call your niece. It would take Rosa twenty seconds to haul Darla off to jail."

"Okay."

"Okay, you'll do it?" I could not keep the exhilaration out of my voice.

"Yeah." His mouth twisted into a wry smile. "I'm beginning to feel like someone Geraldo would pay a lot of money to have on his show, but yeah, I'll do it. Where's Darla? I guess you'd better introduce me before you leave."

Chapter Twenty-one

It was a clear morning, but a cruel west wind was whipping up last night's freshly fallen snow and driving it horizontally across the hood of my SUV. Even the snow fences which the towns erected every autumn along open stretches of highway failed to prevent drifts forming in the roads.

Caroline's driveway had not been plowed. Rather than get stuck, I parked along the curb. Fariq, the older of the Mohameds' grown sons, opened the front door for me. From the kitchen wafted the fragrant tang of tomato sauce simmering in a big iron pot. The living room was total chaos. Shoes, clothing, toys, the two little girls engaged in a game with a large, empty cardboard box, and the blare of the television which everyone was ignoring.

"How...are...you?" said Fariq, smiling conspiratorially as if his perfect English phrase was the day's best kept secret.

"Ah," I said as I tossed my coat on top of the jumble of clothing on the couch, "So you know English."

"I study. At Kakuma Camp."

Fariq's younger brother, Ahmed, sauntered into the living room, and Fariq cocked his chin in his direction. "Ahmed his English not so good. I am having first job."

"Your English will get no job," growled Ahmed. "I will have first job and buy cell phone to call Africa," he added, triumphantly upping the ante on the benefits his mastery of English would soon reap.

Halima, the mother of the family, appeared quietly in the doorway of the kitchen. She was holding her sleeping baby.

140

"Hi," I said to her.

Halima smiled shyly and shook her head as if to say that even the simplest phrase in English posed an insurmountable challenge for her.

Ahmed picked up a bundle of clothing from one of the chairs. "Sit down."

When I did so, he perched on the edge of the couch. "Do you know where I can buy cell phone?"

Caroline walked into the living room and groped among the clothing on the remaining chair for her coat. Fariq found it and put it in her hands. "We are being eyes for Caroline," he explained to me. "We will show her to work and to home."

Caroline said to me, "The guys are helping me since I don't have Nomad. It's good for me and good for them. And," she addressed the two grinning fellows, "any money you earn goes to the family for clothes and food and rent. I don't want to hear another word about cell phones."

"Caroline!" they cried in unison. "It is a trick!"

"A joke," corrected Caroline. "You say, 'It is a joke.' And it better be a joke!"

"How's the family doing?" I asked her as I guided her to the car, Nomad a melancholy ghost at her side.

"Great. They're the embodiment of positive thinking. I love having them here." She laughed. "They've already used up the phone cards we gave them the night they arrived. So now they're running up my phone bill calling everyone they know in the US. I've forbidden them to call Africa, but they really don't need to. They can find out everything from the Bantu grapevine here in the States."

"It sounds like a really close-knit community," I said. I was grateful to discuss any topic except Darla and her whereabouts.

"It is. But soon they'll be too busy for phone calls.

141

Monday they go to the Health Department, Tuesday it's food stamps, and Wednesday the kids start school. And the adults start English classes this week, too."

"Do they know how to get down to Hart Street on the bus?"

"Yeah. They can catch a bus in front of Highland Hospital. There will be other refugees at the bus stop who know where they're going. But our family is also going to evening classes at a low-rent housing complex on Mt. Hope, and we'll be driving them there. At least until the weather gets warmer. A lot of Somalis and Bantus live in that complex. We hoped to get our family into an apartment there, but there's a long wait for the three-bedroom units."

I dropped off Caroline at a nearby Wendy's while I went to pick up Katie at the undisclosed address of the foster mother's house. In contrast to the chaos of Caroline's small living room, Loretta's living room was spacious and tidy. Katie was lying on a blanket on the floor with a little gym of dangling toys set over her. Loretta was folding a mound of children's clothing. Two small boys were watching a cartoon featuring a penguin, a dinosaur and some other creature, possibly a pig. The boys looked clean and perfectly content.

I asked Loretta about Katie while she dressed her in the ugly blue snowsuit.

"She's doing as well as can be expected," Loretta told me.

"What does that mean? They wouldn't let her leave the hospital if she weren't doing well."

Loretta didn't reply. She simply wrapped Katie in a blanket and draped one corner of it over her face before putting the small, warm bundle into my arms. Then she held open the front door for me. "I'll see you in two and a half hours. You have the directions to the Ronald McDonald House?"

"Yes," I yelled over the wind. "And Caroline is sitting at the Wendy's down the road waiting for me to pick her up."

"It would probably be all right to bring her here. I know she's blind. But we have to follow the rules and play it safe. Not everyone is like you," she added kindly.

"I...appreciate that."

Katie lay limply in her car seat while I struggled to get the straps snug and fastened. It was nothing that a NASA engineer accustomed to operating in arctic conditions couldn't master. I backed carefully out of the driveway and crept down the street at a speed the British refer to as 'dead slow." In this weather, everyone and everything on the road presented a threat to the baby that was now my responsibility.

The Ronald McDonald House on Westmoreland Drive was a large, pale yellow building within easy walking distance to Strong Hospital. A whimsical statue of a giraffe gazed benignly over the parking area. There was a covered portico, but logistically, I did not feel comfortable dropping Caroline off to make her own way to the door, nor did I feel comfortable handing her Katie while I parked.

I found a space next to the handicapped parking, pulled Katie from her car seat and led Caroline up a ramp to a spacious porch set off by white pillars.

"This is delightful," I told Caroline. "There's a big giraffe overlooking the parking lot, a life-sized clown sitting on a bench here on the porch, and rocking chairs so people can sit outside when the weather is nice." I did not add that my fondest hope was that we would not be patronizing the Ronald McDonald House by the time the weather became decent enough to take advantage of the rocking chairs. We were buzzed in by a soft-spoken older woman with a warm smile. She told us we were welcome to use the living room which had a gas fireplace and several comfortable chairs, but one of the downstairs bedrooms might be quieter and a little more private. She pointed to a wide shelf in the dining area which held coffee and homemade cookies. Soup would be ready in the kitchen soon, she added. In the meantime, we should just let her know if we needed a bottle heated or a clean diaper. Then she quietly asked Caroline if she would like an arm to guide her to the bedroom since I had my hands full with the baby.

When she departed, leaving the bedroom door open, I said, "I was really apprehensive about coming here, but it's a wonderful place. I had no idea."

Caroline nodded. "Working at the hospital, I've arranged for out-of-town families who have children in the hospital to stay here, but I've never visited. The volunteers seem to know just what to say and do. It's a good place for us to be with Katie."

I breathed a sigh of relief and placed Darla's baby on the bed as gently as if she were made of spun glass. "I'll get her out of her snowsuit and give her to you. You can sit in the chair that's right behind you and hold her for approximately two minutes. Then it will be my turn."

"In a pig's eye." Caroline laughed as she pulled off her coat.

We took turns holding Katie, and we did our best to feed her the bottle which Loretta had packed. I watched anxiously as she swallowed a few times and then drifted off to sleep. Nothing would wake her.

I had packed my Nikon in the diaper bag. Now I pulled it out and began snapping pictures of the sleeping infant, her face in utter repose, her eyelashes fringing her delicate cheeks, her small, perfect mouth slightly open.

"Let's lie on the bed and put her between us," Caroline suggested when she heard me return the camera to its case. And that's what we did. We lay curled like large, warm

144

bookends protecting one small treasured volume, touching Katie's hands, moving her ever so gently to see if she would open her eyes to look at the toys we had brought, brushing our fingers through her curly hair. Caroline pulled the neck of the stuffed giraffe, and we listened over and over to "Greensleeves." When it was time to leave, I felt like crying.

After I dropped off Katie, I picked up Caroline from Wendy's again and drove her home. Ever since I'd found Darla in the nursery rocking chair, I had been racked by indecision as to what I should tell Caroline. Now that I had Katie, I understood much more poignantly how much Caroline needed to know her own child was safe.

On the other hand, Caroline had a track record of not listening to reason and making rash decisions without thinking through the consequences. With terrible regret, I decided that for the immediate future it would be safer for Darla and Katie if Caroline was out of the picture. The unspoken words of comfort I was withholding brewed a miasma that poisoned the air, but I bit my lips and kept silent. I could only pray that it was the right decision.

Chapter Twenty-two

When I returned to Mendon, Darla was curled up in the guest room bed sleeping as soundly as her child, black curls framing her wan face, purple lids shuttering her dark, almond-shaped eyes. Seeing her lying there young and defenseless, it was hard to imagine this picture of innocence had wrought such havoc upon the lives of those who loved her. Superimposed on the image of the young woman before me was the image of another young and defenseless woman lying unidentified in the city morgue, her life terminated and her corpse desecrated by an icy river death.

I felt Darla's forehead. Her fever was down, her breathing less labored.

Down the hall, Aguilar was camped in the nursery. He had pulled the rocker close to the door so he could watch all exits. "She only woke up once after you left. I gave her some soup and crackers. And some orange juice. She said my bedside manner was an improvement over yours."

"How lovely," I said. "Come on. I'm going to wake her up now and give her more antibiotics. Then I'm going to get some answers out of her."

Aguilar scowled.

"I'm sorry," I snapped, "but I have a problem with her lying in a nice warm bed and having food trotted up on trays while her mother is frantic to know what's happened to her. And, as for her baby...well, don't even get me started on that."

"Lady, she's pretty sick right now."

"I don't care if she's on her deathbed. She owes me an

explanation. Once I know what's going on, she can lie there recuperating while I straighten things out and get on with my life. This morning I wanted so badly to tell Caroline that Darla's here safe, but I couldn't. Maybe that's why I'm so angry." I stalked down the hall to the front bedroom.

Darla had heard me. She coughed hoarsely as she struggled to sit up. "Please...don't tell Mom. She'll do something crazy. And you don't know what...how dangerous it could be. If Wolf finds her, he'll do anything to make her tell him where I am." Her eyes grew wide and frightened when she realized she had slipped information she shouldn't have.

I knelt by the bed and brushed back her hair. "Darla, I think your friend, Wolf, already got to your mother."

Darla bolted upright, convulsed in another paroxysm of coughing, and then wiped her streaming, panic-stricken eyes.

"Someone attacked your mother on her way home from the hospital Wednesday night. The attacker mauled Nomad and then gave your mother a message for you."

"Oh, no! What was the message?" Darla asked fearfully.

"He said, 'Tell Darla to give back what's mine.'"

Darla closed her eyes and moaned softly. After a minute she asked, "Are they all right? Mom and Nomad?"

"No, they're not. Nomad had to be put down. His injuries were too severe. Your mother wasn't hurt but she's devastated."

"Oh, no! I can't believe it! I can't believe anyone would be cruel enough to hurt poor Nomad! But if Wolf found Mom and knows where she lives, she's still in danger! He'll come back. And Nomad...he was part of our family!" Darla sat on the edge of the bed and looked frantically around. "Give me my clothes. I'm going to go find that son of a bitch! I'm not going to let him get away with hurting my Mom, and he's not getting his filthy hands on Katie!" She bent over, racked by another fit of coughing.

"Darla," said Aguilar in a gruff voice, "My niece is on the police force. She's a good woman. I'm going to call her."

"Can the cops prove Wolf is the one who attacked my mom? Because, if they can't and they let him go, he'll do it again and it'll be worse the second time. Believe me! He's after Katie, and he'll do anything to get her!"

Aguilar shrugged and glanced at me.

"He won't be able to find Katie," I told her. "I'm the only one who knows the foster mother's address."

Darla looked horrified. "And you think you're safe? You have no idea what you're dealing with."

"That's why we should go to the police," Aguilar persisted.

"No! You don't understand! There's more at stake! He's Katie's father. He can legally take her...and then he'll..." Darla coughed and shook her head futilely. "Just...just give me some time. I'll think of a way to deal with this. So no one gets hurt. Please! Please, Aunt Kate! Please!"

"Darla, for heaven's sake! If nothing else, we can contact a battered women's shelter. They deal with abusive relationships. They've got safe houses, lawyers, whatever you need. They can take out a restraining order against him."

Darla started to cry. Aguilar glowered at me. "Look, there's no reason to make her so upset. I don't see why we can't wait a couple of days. No one's going anywhere. The baby is at an undisclosed location. Caroline isn't going to be alone. She's got a houseful of refugees, and they're tougher than they look or they wouldn't have survived thirteen years in refugee camps. Those places aren't exactly resorts."

"True," I said, "and at least one of them is going to be with her whenever she leaves the house. The two older boys are taking her to and from the hospital in lieu of a guide dog. But..."

"But what, Aunt Kate! It sounds okay. It really does!"

"It may sound okay to you, but your mother has been through the fires of hell. Do you realize the reason she called me and asked me to fly here was to identify a dead girl who had recently given birth? She thought the dead girl was you! Can you imagine what that was like for her? And now you want her to just carry on wondering where you are and if you're okay?"

Darla's face had gone pale. "What do you mean she called you to identify a dead girl?"

"About the time you ran off from the hospital, a dead girl was found in the river near the Dinosaur BBQ Pit and Grill. Your mother heard the description of the girl on the news. She was terrified it was you, so she called the police. They asked Father Donnelly to identify the body since your mother couldn't. But the girl looked enough like you that even he couldn't make a positive ID. That's why I had to fly here."

"Did you see her? Did she really look like me, Aunt Kate?" Darla whispered. Her dusky completion turned gray green as if every drop of blood had drained from her thin face.

"She did look like you," I told her. "I saw her in the morgue. She even had the same long curly black hair. But her navel wasn't pierced." I smiled gently at her, expecting her to smile back at our old secret. Instead, she pushed aside the covers and ran down the hall.

She slammed the door behind her, but Aguilar and I could hear her in the bathroom vomiting.

Chapter Twenty-three

Aguilar picked up the tray he had brought Darla earlier and glared at me. "Now look what you've done. You need to lay off the inquisition."

I snatched the tray out of his hands and stomped down the back stairs. Aguilar wisely departed, muttering about taking care of things at home. I went into the kitchen for something to eat. Afterward I cleaned up the kitchen and started straightening up the rest of house, all the while worrying about Darla, worrying about Caroline's safety, worrying about the wretched kittens, and most of all, worrying that I would never be able to properly care for Katie once I was allowed to bring her home.

It was such a frightful risk. Suppose she choked or I was in an accident or I dropped her? Would I be hauled before the courts of justice for child abuse? How would I prove I loved the baby and had only her best interest at heart? And what was her best interest? Me, an inept foster mother beleaguered by constant intervention from Child Protective Services and Caroline, the doting grandmother? Or was Katie's best interest her real mother, an intelligent young woman with a promising future who had turned into the village idiot and dropped out of school to shack up with a rabid punk and get herself pregnant. And now we had the added risk of that punk coming after Katie.

Tragically, the only way to protect Katie was to leave her in the custody of CPS or somehow prove her father had attacked Caroline. Check and checkmate. In the meantime, all I wanted to do was sit with that baby and rock her and promise her no one would ever hurt her. It was the one thing beyond my ability to do. She was with Loretta Whiting, the foster mother, and I could not see her again until my allotted two hours tomorrow. In the meantime, Katie's father was dangerous, on the loose, and beyond the reach of the legal system.

I ate lunch and went upstairs to check on Darla. I felt as if I had come to the limits of my endurance. She was asleep, so instead of making my bed, I crawled into it. When I woke up hours later, I showered and dressed. Feeling remarkably better, I brought two cups of tea and some cookies upstairs on a tray and pulled up a chair so I could sit and talk with Darla.

Her face was wan. She had dark circles under her eyes, and when she coughed, it was in horrible, wracking spasms. She pushed herself up against the pillows, her eyes filling with tears. "Aunt Kate, I'm so sorry for all the trouble I'm causing. I know you'll never believe me, but I started out trying to do the right thing. It all just got away from me."

"Don't think about it right now. Drink your tea and I'll tell you about Katie."

"Did you get to hold her this morning?" Her face was wistful. What must it be like to give birth and then leave your baby and hear nothing more? I couldn't imagine.

"Yes, we did get to hold her. Your mother and I went to the R..." I stopped, suddenly realizing how easy it would be to let slip information that might jeopardize the baby and my chance to be her foster mother. "We spent two hours with her this morning, but I'm not allowed to disclose her location. She was sound asleep the whole time. We were really disappointed. We'd been looking forward to holding her and playing with her, but Katie slept right through our visit."

"Is she warm and snuggly when you hold her?"

I smiled. "Warm and very snuggly. In fact it's like holding a little heater. She cuddles up under your chin, and you can feel her hair infinitely soft against your cheek. And she seems to be eating well, although the bottle we were going to give her went to waste except for about two swallows."

Darla stared out the window, her face a mirror of despair.

I tried to change the subject. "Did you see the nursery? Your mom and I picked out everything together. Your mom said rose and white are colors you would like, and this morning when we went to see Katie, we brought along a throw from your bed. They say babies know the smell of their mother."

Darla continued to stare out the window, tears slipping down her face. I stared out the window, too. The sky was intensely blue. The snow-covered yard glittered in the sunlight. A chickadee flew past, and I envied its freedom. I suddenly wished I could go for a walk. Not just a trip to the mailbox where there would be no mail. A long, solitary, peaceful walk, unencumbered by care, to enjoy all the wondrous details of a winter day.

Darla seemed to read my mind. "Aunt Kate, do you remember when I was little and you and I used to go for walks together? Walking with you was so special. You seemed to see everything. Spiders carrying their egg sacs, pieces of a robin's egg, a hummingbird's nest...."

I smiled. "You still remember that hummingbird's nest?"

"Of course I remember it. You said we couldn't take it until after the hummingbirds were finished using it. So you and I went back to the tree right before Christmas, and it was still there. You told me to take off my shoes and socks and climb on the roof of Uncle Whit's brand new Mercedes to reach it."

"Your uncle always wondered how those dents got in the roof of his car."

Darla blinked her eyes and put on the sleepy, innocent look I knew so well. "Mom and I put the nest in our Christmas tree that year. You said in some countries it's considered good luck to have a bird's nest in your Christmas tree." Darla's eyes filled with tears again. "This was a terrible Christmas for Mom. Someday I hope I can make it up to her. I wonder if she put up our tree. And I wonder if she found the hummingbird's nest to put in it. It's wrapped in cotton in the plastic crate with all our ornaments."

I remembered Caroline describing her Christmas Eve sitting by the Christmas tree with the cat and the dog, waiting all night for Darla to come home. My voice took on a sharp note. "She put up the tree," I told Darla, "and she still has all your presents wrapped and waiting for you. She loves you as much as any mother could. And she believes in you with all her heart."

I didn't add that I often wondered why, but Darla was smart enough to know what I was thinking. Her mouth trembled. "I know, Aunt Kate. I'm so very sorry. And I'm sorry about Uncle Whit, too. I'm sorry he died, and I'm sorry I never even sent you a note."

"Let's just talk about happy things," I said, "or we'll both be crying."

Darla coughed harshly and wiped her eyes on the sleeve of Aunt Myla's flannel gown. "Like what?" she asked bitterly.

It was a good question.

"I took some pictures of Katie this morning," I told her. "Later, I'll get my camera and show them to you. Right now I'd like to just sit here and rest. We could talk about Aunt Myla. She left her house to me and Uncle Whit. It will be fun to explore. I already have, a little."

"I loved Aunt Myla. She was so eccentric. I'm going to

miss her so much! While I was hiding here, I kept expecting her to walk through the kitchen door in that old flowered apron she used to wear. The one with the yellow-striped pockets. It was so sad."

Obviously I had no talent for comforting the bedridden and the forlorn. I stood up and picked up the tray. "When this mess gets straightened out, are you going back to nursing school?"

"I hope so. I hope they'll take me back. I really want to be a nurse, and I'll need a good job so I can support Katie. I want her to have a good life, Aunt Kate. I want her to grow up with my mom and you and me as her family. I want her to have pets, and be a Girl Scout, and have vacations at the sea shore, and be around people who love her, and have all the things I had when I was little."

I said gruffly. "We all do, Darla. Now why don't you try to rest? It's time for your antibiotic. Eat the cookies on the tray. You're not supposed to take antibiotics on an empty stomach."

"Aren't there any more Twinkies? Joe Aguilar said there were some in the pantry." She tried on the pitiful look she used when she wanted something I had.

"I ate them for lunch."

Darla laughed and then coughed. For one brief minute she looked and sounded like herself. "Is that all you ate for lunch, Aunt Kate?"

I flashed her a disgusted look, wondering exactly how she had managed to turn the tables on me yet again.

"You eat more junk food than anyone I ever knew," she needled.

"Well, keep your mouth shut about it. I'm tired of having Aguilar on my case, and I don't want my namesake to get the wrong idea about me."

"Take good care of her, Aunt Kate. No one knows

where she is. Right? No one but you?"

"Not even your mother knows," I assured her. "Just me and the Child Protection people, and they're real dragons."

"So are you, Aunt Kate. But a good dragon."

I left with the tea tray before I exhaled and set her sheets on fire.

Chapter Twenty-four

Late in the afternoon the phone rang. As usual, it was Aguilar. "I've cooked a standing rib roast. I'm dropping by with dinner for you and Darla. She needs something more substantial than that crap you're feeding her."

I gritted my teeth. "I wouldn't want you to come all the way out here just to deliver food. I've got plenty of stuff in the pantry." In truth, in spite of all my worrying about coping, I had given no thought to dinner. I thought wistfully of London where I could walk to any number of restaurants or simply ring up a black cab for take-out.

Aguilar wasn't giving in. "I saw what you had in your pantry when I was making soup for Darla. You both need some meat on your bones. I'll be there in about forty-five minutes. Turn on the oven and open one of those bottles of Merlot you've got stashed under the sink. You gotta give red wine some time to breathe."

"Darla can't have wine while she's taking those antibiotics. Besides, she's under-age."

"Well, I'm not," Aguilar said and hung up.

The roast was medium rare, there were scalloped potatoes and fresh asparagus to go with it, dinner rolls, and, of course, the wine, of which I drank more than my fair share. Darla murmured pitifully that she felt too weak to come downstairs, so Aguilar heaped up a plate on a tray for her and carried it up to her bedroom. He came down looking smug. "She said it all looked delicious. Poor girl. I told you she just needed a decent meal to get back on her feet."

"Did you tell her you're adopting her kittens?"

"Yeah. She's really happy about it. She told me that it was good Pop was holding them a lot."

I wondered how Aguilar and his father would feel about Darla and her rescue project when his furniture began to look like Shredded Wheat from the kittens' claws. With sudden insight I realized that the real pro at dumping her responsibilities on others was Darla. I could only pray it was not a genetic flaw she had passed on to Katie.

After dinner, avoiding the risk of having Aguilar plant himself next to me on one of the Victorian loveseats in the front parlor, I suggested taking a second bottle of Merlot and moving to the library.

I never knew Aunt Myla's husband. He died before Whit and I were married. The dark-paneled library must have been his retreat. A World War I campaign desk sat against one wall. Glass-fronted lawyer's bookcases filled the adjacent wall. Framed photographs hung randomly about the room.

Aguilar stood looking at them. "You know," he said, tapping one of the photos, "this is a picture of a group of Teddy Roosevelt's Rough Riders. You ought to have an appraiser come in and look at this stuff. You might be sitting on a goldmine." He walked over to one of the bookcases and peered through the glass. The bookcase was crammed with books. "You should have these books appraised, too. They look old enough to be first editions."

"I sort of like it all just as it is without knowing if it's valuable. It's comforting to have all of Aunt Myla's things around. It makes this place feel like a home. A real home. I don't want to do anything with her possessions right now. I just want to live here, and enjoy them, and be part of the ongoing history of this old house. I think it's what she'd like me to do."

We settled near the windows on the worn leather cushions of a pair of Mission Oak armchairs. For the first time since I left the Isles of Scilly, I felt mellow and relaxed.

"There's not a single damned fireplace in this house," Aguilar commented. "How do you suppose they kept warm before central heating?"

"I think there used to be a fireplace in the front parlor. Aunt Myla said they boarded it up when they put in central heating. And they no doubt had a wood-burning stove in the kitchen."

We sat peacefully and talked about the house and what it must have been like to live a hundred years ago when this house was first built. Then we talked about the refugees and what a monumental adjustment it must be for them to transition from life in Africa to a new life in modern America.

Aguilar shook his head. "Caroline told me the mother of the family gave birth when they were running from the fighting in Somalia. She lost that one and another child that became ill. Both boys. But they had to keep running if they wanted to stay alive."

"How unspeakably sad," I said. "No wonder she always has her children in her arms and the littlest one in a sling on her back. Darla should spend some time with her. She'd learn a few things." I suddenly felt like crying and groped for a lighter subject. I asked how the kittens were doing.

Aguilar grinned. "Pop spent the day in front of the television with both of them in a towel on his lap."

I grinned back. In a very short time, Aguilar was becoming more involved with the fabric of my existence than Whit had ever been

I was pouring the last of the wine when I heard a car in the driveway. "Damn!" I said. "Ferguson warned me the legal guardian makes random visits. This is a fine time for him to show up!"

I jumped up and pulled open the shutters. In the

moonlight on the new fallen snow, I saw it was not the court-appointed advocate paying us an unexpected house call. It was Darla. She was backing down the drive in Aguilar's Lincoln.

I slammed the shutters closed. "Well, that's the end of that chapter."

"What are you talking about? Is someone here?"

"No. That was just the poor invalid departing in your Lincoln."

Chapter Twenty-five

Aguilar leapt to his feet. "How the hell did she get my keys?"

"How do you think? She waited until we opened a second bottle of wine, and then she slipped down the back stairs."

He ran into the kitchen and glanced around. "My jacket's gone! It was right here on the back of the kitchen chair. Where the hell did it go?"

"Check with the invalid. If you'll remember, the last time a coat went missing Darla was in it."

"She took my car *and* my jacket?"

Darla had planned her departure well. While Aguilar and I were sitting all cozy in the library, Darla had decamped with the cash in my purse, my new cell phone, the antibiotics, and a shelf's-worth of cookies and crackers from the pantry.

"I told you she couldn't be trusted!" I yelled as Aguilar bemoaned the plight of his Lincoln. "Poor little Darla. Now she's vanished again!"

"Does she even know how to drive a car?"

"How do I know? She had Driver's Ed in school, but, of course, Caroline doesn't own a car."

"Great. Just great." Aguilar reached for the cell phone clipped to his belt. "I'm calling Rosa."

"Wait, Aguilar. We've got to think this through."

While Aguilar stormed around the kitchen in a black rage, I tried calling my cell phone. Darla didn't answer. I left her an angry plea to call.

"There are only two places Darla would be headed," I

told Aguilar. "To see her mother or to find Wolf."

"Yeah? And what if she finds that punk? She must weigh ninety pounds soaking wet. She's gonna get seriously hurt."

"You're right," I sighed. "The guy has a history of violence. Call your sister. But there goes any chance Darla has of turning herself in and getting her baby back. She's up for child abuse and auto theft now."

"We can at least tell the cops to put out an APB on this bastard she's gone looking for."

"Aguilar, how can they do that? We have a minimal description, no address, and no last name of a guy we saw one time outside a downtown bar. We can't prove he attacked Caroline. In fact, we don't even know if his name is really Wolf."

"Fine, do nothing. But what am I supposed to do about my car? I need to get home. I need to check on Pop, and I gotta get some sleep. I have to be at work at five in the morning."

"I'll drive you home. On the way we can drive to Caroline's house to see if Darla is there. Just let me get my boots."

Of course, Darla had not been able to find her own boots so she had taken mine. Aguilar stood watching as I pulled Darla's soggy boots out of the china closet where I had thrown them during the kitten episode. His expression said he was convinced I was madder than a hatter, but, for once, he was blessedly silent.

We drove to Caroline's. Lights were on all over her house even at this late hour, but Aguilar's precious Lincoln was not in the driveway. He gave me directions to his house, and I listened to him rant and rave all the way there.

The Park Avenue neighborhood reminded me of a European neighborhood with turn-of-the-century houses and apartment buildings on tree-lined streets. It was an area where residents could walk to shops and to an endless variety of cafes and restaurants. In the summer Park Avenue came alive. Small tables sprang up outside the cafes, shoppers strolled the sidewalks, and a street fair drew huge crowds. Tonight it was cold and dark. The sidewalks were deserted, and most of the eateries were closed.

Aguilar directed me down one of the side streets off Park Avenue. His two-story white house was small but well maintained. A porch light was on, and upstairs a light glowed behind the curtains of a dormer window. The house seemed like a safe harbor, and for a brief moment, I wondered what it would be like to live there with a man who would be intensely involved in my life, a father-in-law who sat before a fireplace with cats on his lap, and a kitchen brimming with home cooking.

"If you find out anything, call me on my cell phone," Aguilar instructed. "I can't wait to hear the next chapter in this saga." He slammed the car door, effectively destroying my vision of a tranquil lifestyle, and disappeared inside the house. The porch light went off, and I sat alone in the driveway with only despair for company. What I was about to learn is that there are far worse companions than despair.

Chapter Twenty-six

I drove slowly back to Caroline's house, steeling myself to confess Darla had been with me and I had kept it a secret. Caroline would consider it the ultimate betrayal. She was my only real friend. I wondered if our friendship could survive such a blow.

At least I would not be waking anyone up. Every light in the house was still on. I rang the bell at the side door a number of times, worrying if someone in the refugee family was sick. Finally one of the little Bantu girls opened the door. Her eyes were frightened, and when I smiled and asked why she was up so late, she turned and ran.

I followed her into the living room. The only space in the room which was not splattered with blood was the couch where Halima sat, protectively cradling her baby. Her daughters were next to her on the couch, clinging to her long, brightly colored dress, their face mirroring their fright.

I stood stunned. "What happened in here? Who got hurt?"

Halima shook her head grimly.

"What happened in here?" I repeated. "Where's Caroline?"

Halima gestured towards the front door. One of her daughters piped up. "Go hospital," she said, proud of her English.

"What happened?" I demanded a third time.

An ominous silence filled the room.

I ran for my car, tore out of the driveway, and headed for the hospital.

When the woman at the reception desk in the ER waiting room learned I was looking for Caroline, she wordlessly escorted me down several hallways to a hot, airless room with institution green walls and overhead florescent lighting. Two unsmiling police officers stood just inside the door. Neither of them was Rosa. At a rectangular cafeteria table, Fatima, the Somali interpreter, was sitting with Fariq, Ahmed, and their father on orange plastic chairs. The three Bantu men wore tight, impassive expressions. In the stark overhead light, it was impossible to miss the bloodstains on the hands and clothing of all three men.

I glanced in panic at Fatima and then the officers. "What's going on? Where's Caroline!"

Once the officers ascertained I was Caroline's sister-in-law, they informed me Caroline was in surgery. *Ribs, spleen...kidneys, concussion,* they said.

I felt as if the room were tilting. Fatima said something to Ahmed, and he stood up and gave me his orange plastic chair. I sank into it. Someone handed me black coffee in a Styrofoam cup. I drank the coffee, needing both hands to steady the cup.

With Fatima as interpreter, the three refugees repeated for me what they had already told the police. A man with strange blue eyes and a shaved head had come to Caroline's house. There was a lot of shouting. They believed the man was the husband of Caroline's daughter. He wanted Caroline to tell him where her daughter was and where his child was. He began to hit Caroline with his fists. They wanted to help Caroline, but the man yelled at them and told them to keep out of it. They did not know the laws of this new country. In Africa men often beat women.

Caroline would tell the man nothing. He beat and kicked her until she was unconscious. Then he told the Africans to keep their mouths shut or he would come back and do the same to them. Yes, after the man left, they called 911 as they had been taught, but they did not know what to say. They tried to tell the person on the phone the address of Caroline's house as they had been told to do if there was trouble. But the person on the phone could not understand them, and the police did not come. They knew people at the hospital would help Caroline. So they wiped the blood off Caroline's face, wrapped her in sheets, and between them, they had carried her through the dark, ice-covered streets to the hospital.

Caroline was a good woman, they said. They hoped she would not die. The resignation on their faces said they were familiar with death's indifference to hope.

The room fell silent except for the static of the police radios on the belts of the two officers.

It was 2:47 in the morning. Protecting Darla was no longer an option. I told the officers I believed the man responsible for beating Caroline was a man named Wolf. I had no address for him, but I knew he hung out downtown at the Canal Street Bar. Then I told them I thought Caroline's daughter, Darla, might be looking for Wolf. I said I feared for her safety.

The officers said the bars in town were closed now, but they would check it out tomorrow as soon as the bar opened. In the meantime they would put out an APB with the man's description. One of the officers handed me his card. I glanced down at it. Edwin Jones. Then I glanced up at him. "Is that all you intend to do?"

"Don't worry, Ms. Scholfield. We're on this. In the meantime, you're all free to go. We'll keep you posted."

I tossed his card in my purse and drove the refugees back to Caroline's house.

Halima had put the children to bed and was trying to clean up the bloodstains in the living room with one of Caroline's dishtowels. I hugged her and thanked her and

165

found detergent and a bucket and some rags for her to use.

Next I called Our Lady of Victory, got a recording with an emergency number for Father Donnelly, and called him. Then I returned once again to sit in Highland Hospital's Intensive Care Unit. Practice did not make it easier, and Caroline had a lot more tubes in her than her granddaughter had. The astringent odor of Betadine overlaid the coppery smell of blood, and the numerous beeping monitors did nothing to reassure me Caroline was going to pull through this horrific assault.

Chapter Twenty-seven

As the first glow of the new day brightened the east window of her hospital room, Caroline briefly regained consciousness. I took her hand. Her eyes were mere slits in her swollen, battered face, and her blonde hair was glued with dried blood.

"I didn't tell the bastard where Darla was." Caroline's hoarse words were barely decipherable around the tube in her bruised mouth.

"Oh, Caro, you couldn't tell him! You didn't know!"

"I...knew. You have her...at Aunt Myla's."

Her reply left me speechless. "How did you know?" I stammered, unwilling, unable to tell her that I had let Darla slip through my fingers.

"I...just...knew. Take...care of her and...her baby. For me." Caroline's swollen eyes flickered closed. She slid her hand out of mine and then off the bed, groping for Nomad so she could curl her fingers in his fur for comfort. I pulled my chair closer to her bed and took her hand again lest she remember he was gone.

When morning rays of sunshine began to fill the room, I tucked her hand gently under the covers. I didn't close the curtain. I hoped she would wake to the warmth of the sun and just for a minute find the day good. Then I went down to the cafeteria to turn up the heat on her daughter.

When I called the number of my new cell phone, Darla answered. She was crying.

"Aunt Kate? Oh, thank heavens! I thought you would never call! My mother! It's all my fault!"

167

"Darla! Where are you? Your mother is...."

"I know. And it's all my fault! I went to our house, but the guys had already taken Mom to the hospital. I saw...the... blood. I couldn't go to the hospital because I knew the police would be there. And when I called the hospital, they wouldn't tell me anything because of the HIPAA regulations. Do you...do you know how...? Oh, Aunt Kate! Is she going to *die*?"

I stood in the cafeteria listening to Darla's sobs as I told her what little I knew. Then I said firmly, "Darla, stop crying. It's time to go to the police and tell them everything you know. The most important thing now is to help them find Wolf and lock him up. You've caused enough damage trying to protect yourself."

"Aunt Kate, I keep telling you! It's not me I'm trying to protect. It's Katie."

I snarled into the phone. "You are being stupid and arrogant. And look what it's done to your mother."

"Wait, Aunt Kate. Just listen." There was a long silence and then Darla said, "See, I...I think I know who the dead girl is," she said.

"You knew her?" *Was Darla going to tell me she was involved in murder, too?*

"Her name is Aleisha Guthrie, right?"

"The people at the morgue didn't tell us her name. We all thought the dead girl was you."

"I'm sure it's Aleisha. She's...she was... my friend from high school. People always thought we were sisters because we looked so much alike. Her mother was Vietnamese."

I glanced nervously around the deserted cafeteria. "Why would you think your friend is the dead girl?" I hissed into the receiver.

"Being around Wolf has that effect on people," Darla answered bitterly. "But it's a long story. See, Aleisha's mother

168

works the welfare system. Over the winter, she dumps all her kids into foster homes and goes off to Florida to the racetracks. She comes back in the fall and gets them all back so she can collect more welfare...."

"Get to the point, Darla. I don't have unlimited quarters for this pay phone."

"I *am* getting to the point, Aunt Kate. See, after graduation, Aleisha aged out of foster care, and when her mother left for Florida, she had nowhere to go. So she got a job in a bar. And then she met Wolf and moved in with him."

"She worked at the Canal Street Bar. Right?"

Darla's voice quavered. "How do you know about the Canal Street Bar?"

"I got a lead from one of the nursing students in your class. Aguilar and I drove down there one night. He wouldn't let me get out of the car, but I saw Wolf standing in the doorway."

"Aunt Kate! Stay away from him! You have no idea how dangerous he is!"

"I think I'm beginning to get the picture. If you recall, I'm here at the hospital with your mother in the ICU. And then there's Nomad. I saw firsthand what Wolf did to him."

"I could kill Wolf for hurting my family," whispered Darla. "And maybe I'll have to."

"Darla, he's after *you*! And you have your baby to think of. You're already on the run for child abuse and car theft. Do you want to go up for murder, too?"

She's not mine," Darla said, her voice so low I could barely hear it over the background noise in the cafeteria.

"Who's not yours?"

"Katie. She's not my baby."

My stress level shot through the roof. I flashed back to Darla's emaciated body in the bathtub, her tiny breasts and

169

flat stomach. She had not looked like she had given birth a month earlier, but what did I know about giving birth? I had chalked up her appearance to starvation. As usual, when dealing with Darla, it was never wise to assume anything.

"Then whose baby is she?"

"She's Aleisha's baby. And Wolf is her father."

I was too stunned to speak. Finally I choked out, "You kidnapped her?"

"Aunt Kate, are you still there? I'm hanging up. I'm sorry, but there's something I have to do."

"Wait! Darla, don't hang up..."

The phone went dead. I tried calling back, but there was no answer. I slammed the phone onto its receiver. Darla didn't mind telling me what had already happened. But she wasn't about to share what the future held. She would simply call again as soon as she set the next crisis in motion. Darla was going after Wolf, no matter what the cost. The only way to keep her out of worse trouble than she was already in was to get to him first.

Chapter Twenty-eight

I searched through my purse for the card Edwin Jones handed me last night. When I dialed the number on the card, a recording said he was not available to take calls, but please leave a message. *What message? Thanks to Darla, I didn't even have a cell phone so I could leave a contact number.* I tried calling Rosa and received a similar recording.

In frustration, I called Directory Assistance for the non-emergency number for the Rochester Police Department. I dialed it and asked if there was any way I could contact Rosa or her partner or one of the cops who had been in the ER last night. I spelled their names. I was told the officers were currently off duty. *Was this an emergency?*

What could I say? I knew Darla was going to do something stupid, but I didn't know what or where or when. It wasn't an emergency yet, but it was going to be. Frustrated, I hung up the phone.

Tantalizing odors of breakfast filled the noisy cafeteria, and I realized I was hungry. I bought coffee and a plate of eggs and grits and carried the tray to a table in the corner of the room. I stared at my plate, struggling to absorb Darla's latest serving of bad news. She had taken Katie from her birth mother. That was kidnapping, a federal offense. Since I was not related to Katie, my qualification as her foster mother was in jeopardy. That put Katie indefinitely in the care of Loretta Whiting. If Katie was lucky, she might be adopted by strangers. If she was not lucky, she would be returned to her psychotic father. Either way, she would be a child adrift and at risk. Long ago I had wanted a baby, but it had never happened. Now it seemed my destiny was to battle for children who were not mine. I would battle for Darla, because I understood now what Caroline meant when she called Darla the child of her heart. And I would battle for Katie because she was the child of my heart.

I forced myself to eat, and while I ate, I idly watched hospital life ebb and flow through breakfast lines. Doctors, technicians, and specialists. Kitchen workers and maintenance staff. Volunteers, administration, and IT gurus. Family and friends of patients looking as tired and anxious as I was. Even some patients, riding in wheelchairs garbed in faded hospital-issue gowns, casts, braces, trailing IV poles.

There were very few nurses and very few interns. Interns and nurses rarely merit leisurely breaks. Caroline said interns grab a quick bite whenever they have a chance, and nurses are lucky to find time for their mandatory thirty-minute lunch break. Up on the floors they pour coffee that grows cold and snack on whatever gifts family and friends of patients bring in supplication and gratitude. For the foreseeable future I, too, would bring offerings in gratitude for the care of someone I loved.

God, please, don't let Caroline die. Don't let her be crippled for life. Don't let her lose what little sense of light and shadow remains of her vision. And most of all, please don't make me have to tell Caroline that Darla and Katie are lost to her.

I swallowed the last of my coffee and went back through the cashier's line for more quarters. Then I returned to the pay phone and riffled through the tattered pages of the phone book. I found a number for the Canal Street Bar, dialed it, listened to the recording on the other end of the line, and then called Aguilar on his cell phone.

"Did you find Darla?" he demanded without even saying hello.

"No..."

172

"Well, what is it, doll. I'm at work."

"It's Caroline..."

"Now what's happened!"

I filled him in about Caroline's condition and my conversation with Darla.

"Hold on," he said. "I need to get someplace where I can talk." I heard footsteps and a heavy door slam. Then he came back on the line.

"Lemme get this straight. Darla said the girl they pulled from the river was her friend? And the baby belonged to her? What the hell's the matter with Darla? She just ran off with her friend's baby? Doesn't she know they put you in jail for that?"

"I know," I said tiredly into the phone. "I know. And if I don't find Darla soon, she might go down for murder, too. She's after Wolf for what he did to her mother and Nomad. I'm afraid she thinks the only way she can protect Katie is by putting him permanently out of commission. I have to find her, Aguilar. I need you to meet me at the Canal Street Bar."

"Lady, we've already been through this. That place is a dive. If we go down there again, we're bringing back up. I'll see if I can round up a few guys. In the meantime, you need to call the cops. Call Rosa."

"I did, Aguilar. I called her partner, too. Neither one of them is on duty. Then I tried calling the cop who promised me he would check out the bar today, but he's not on duty either. So I need you to meet me there."

"The bar isn't going to be open at this hour."

"I know that," I snapped. "I just called the bar and got a recorded message. They open at eleven-thirty for lunch trade. Someone will have to show up soon to start cleaning up, or get food ready, or whatever. We have to find out where Wolf lives. It's the only way to find Darla. I'm afraid to wait for the cops to get to work on it. It didn't sound like a priority for

173

them last night, and now they're off duty. I don't need your drinking buddies for back up. I need your badge."

"My badge!"

"I want you to flash it to get whoever is working in the bar to tell us what we need to know. We'll catch him unaware. The lighting in bars is never very good. He won't be able to see the fine print on the badge. He'll think you're a cop."

"Impersonate a police officer? Sorry, doll. No way. There's nothing you can do now except wait for Rosa or the other cop to return your call. That's really sad about the baby, though. And I feel terrible about Caroline. She's a beautiful lady and doesn't deserve this. That daughter of hers needs to get her head on straight. But this is a job for the cops. So you're going to have to wait until they call you back or you can call 911. I gotta get back to work. Keep me posted."

"Aguilar," I said dully, "I can't keep you posted. I don't have a cell phone anymore. Remember? But, never mind. I'll go to the bar alone."

Aguilar swore and then said, "Okay, you win. I'll call Rosa at home and tell her to get her ass down to the bar. But would you at least wait until she gets there before you do anything idiotic? That psycho chasing Darla put Caroline in the hospital and killed her dog. And, for all I know, he threw the baby's mother in the river. What do you think he'll do to you if he finds out you know where his baby is?"

Chapter Twenty-nine

As was typical for January in Rochester, the weather had taken a sudden nosedive. Ominous, low hanging clouds now obscured the sun that was shining so brightly through Caroline's hospital room window just a short while ago. A cruel west wind raked the deserted parking lot of the Canal Street Bar where I sat shivering in my rented SUV and praying Aguilar had managed to contact Rosa. If she didn't show up soon, I was out of options. It was always my untested belief that in arctic conditions, you could sit in a running car only so long before you asphyxiate or freeze. Since landing in Rochester, there were times when either option held a certain appeal for me.

A battered white pickup truck rattled into the parking lot, its tires crunching over ice-filled ruts. My windows were steamed over. I could not see the driver. It's hard to shiver from fear if your body is already shaking from cold, but I somehow managed it. I did not even have a can of Mace to protect myself. I locked the doors of the SUV, slid further down into the seat, and waited to see who would emerge from the vehicle.

It was Aguilar. He stormed up to my SUV wearing a white shirt, a navy tie, and a picture ID clipped to his white lab coat. It was the first time I had ever seen him in anything other than jeans and a leather jacket. The cold didn't seem to faze him. I wiped my running nose on the sleeve of my trench coat and rolled down the car window.

"I can't believe the things you get up to," he yelled over the wind. "Prime time television can't hold a candle to you."

"Where's Rosa?" In my own ears, my voice sounded as if it were coming from a tunnel. Maybe it was shock. Shock and despair. Would shock and despair generate greater firepower than shock and awe in the upcoming battle? I would know soon enough.

"I tried calling her," Aguilar yelled into the window, "but she's gone off to Buffalo for some damned law enforcement seminar. My aunt said she won't be back 'til after lunch. And her partner doesn't answer his phone."

"Then we'll have to deal with this ourselves."

"Let's get this straight, lady. *We* is not an option. I am not going to impersonate a police officer for you or anyone else."

I climbed out of the car and yelled into the wind. "No problem. I have a better idea."

"Yeah, I bet," he hollered, but he followed me as I ran for the porch of the bar.

I pointed at the emergency phone number taped in the window of the locked door. "This is what we do. We call this number, tell them we had a complaint last night about the...I don't know...whatever someone would complain about to get you people out. Tell them they need to come down here right now and open up the place for inspection."

"My people don't inspect restaurants. That's the Health Department."

"I don't care, Aguilar! Just wear your white coat and flash your badge. They're not going to know the difference. We go in. You get them into the kitchen and find infringements. I'll look around the bar for phone numbers or something."

"Are you kidding? That's your plan?"

"It will work. Just swagger in there. It's something you do well."

Aguilar started to laugh. "You are a piece of work! What

176

if this Wolf creep's phone number is not just lying on the counter in clear sight like a clue in some B-grade movie? We tie 'em up and waterboard 'em until they cough it up?"

"Then we play bad inspector, good inspector. And you get to play bad inspector. You're probably rather talented in that department, too."

Aguilar mouth twisted into a sarcastic smile. "Is that so?"

"So you stomp all over them. I'll be the nice guy and offer to let them off the hook if they can give us Wolf's address. As long as they keep their mouths shut and don't alert him. They don't have to know why we want him. They'll just be glad to get you off their case so they can open for lunch."

Aguilar wore the cynical expression of a New Yorker who has just received his latest property tax assessment.

I held out my hand, willing it not to shake. "Give me your cell phone. Trust me, this will work."

Aguilar flashed me a disgusted look. He reached inside his lab coat and unclipped his cell phone from his belt. Then went to his car and came back with a clipboard.

When I saw his clipboard, I couldn't help grinning. "Hey, look on the bright side. If we're armed with government forms, we probably won't even need to use your badge!"

And it worked. It took Aguilar about five minutes to spot enough offenses to close the place down. I heard him pointing out roaches, rat droppings, and related infringements that would keep me out of restaurants for the rest of my life.

The interior of the bar was sparsely lit. Someone had stacked chairs on tables but had not yet washed the scarred plank floor. Realizing I had very little time, I headed for a narrow hall leading to the restrooms, hoping to find an office. A mop stood propped against the wall next to a pay

177

phone. The phone had been made obsolete by the advent of cell phones. The mop had been made obsolete by lack of use. I shuddered at the thought of what I would find in the restrooms. One whiff of the odor of beer mingled with urine emanating from the partially open doors convinced me that unless someone had scrawled Wolf's phone number on the wall of one of the stalls, there was no reason for me to explore either the Ladies or the Gents.

The only one other door in the hall was an emergency exit, so I returned to the bar and began a frenzied search through papers lying around the cash register and behind the bar.

As Aguilar had predicted, I found nothing related to the whereabouts of Wolf or any other customer. However, when I went into the kitchen where Aguilar was browbeating the help, my most compassionate smile and a promise to let them off the hook elicited an address for Wolf on D Street in one of the more unsavory neighborhoods of the inner city.

I rode with Aguilar who had borrowed the old white Ford truck from one of his nephews until the Lincoln turned up. He headed up North Clinton toward Clifford Avenue while I used his cell phone to try to reach Darla.

"Ask her where the hell my car is," Aguilar yelled at me over the growl of the truck's diesel engine. But the whereabouts of his precious Lincoln remained a mystery because Darla did not answer the phone. I left her an urgent voice mail saying we were on our way to Wolf's house and not to do anything stupid at least until we got there.

Wolf's house was a dilapidated clapboard affair with cracked windows, torn screens, and weeds poking through the snow along the crumbling foundation. There was no garage and no sign of a car, although there were recent tire tracks in the frozen ruts which served as a driveway. The house looked uninhabited. On the snow-covered porch, we pounded on the door to no avail.

"Give it up, lady," said Aguilar. "There's no one here. There's no telling when this punk might come back. You don't know if he's armed, has a gang of hoods living with him...."

I ignored his dire scenarios and kicked my way through mounds of trash to peer in the front windows. Aguilar cursed and followed suit. Through the tattered drapes on the front windows it was possible to see a broken down sofa surrounded by empty pizza boxes and crushed Coors cans. We trudged around the back of the house. Windows in the kitchen revealed nothing other than a filthy Formica table, a kitchen sink piled high with unwashed dishes, and a refrigerator whose door gaped open on its hinges leaving the sordid contents available for roaches that were scuttling around. I was horrified to think Katie would ever know this man as her father.

Aguilar summed it up eloquently. "This place ought to be torched," he said. "And we are leaving right goddamned now. Get in the truck."

Chapter Thirty

By the time we returned to the Canal Street Bar for my car, I barely had enough time to make it to Loretta Whiting's house to pick up Katie for my allotted two hours at the Ronald McDonald House. I dared not speed. Like tardy behavior, Child Protective Services frowned on traffic infractions. If I turned up late, I could not even plead poor driving conditions. The morning wind had piled the storm clouds along the eastern horizon, leaving the remainder of the sky relentlessly blue.

The Ronald MacDonald House and its welcoming staff beckoned like a sanctuary in the current madness of my life. To cuddle on a bed with a warm, sleeping baby was a thing devoutly to be wished for, a transitory joy of motherhood no one could take from me, and a chance to shut my desperately tired eyes.

I should have consulted my horoscope before indulging in such flights of optimism.

Katie screamed from the minute I tucked her into her ugly blue snowsuit until I returned her to it two eternal hours later. And as frosting on my personal cake, Leon Schwartz, the Court Appointed Special Advocate, showed up at the Ronald McDonald House to observe my ineptitude.

I did not rest on a bed in a peaceful, well-appointed bedroom cuddling a sweet baby. I sat wedged defensively into a wing chair in the living room by the gas fireplace, struggling with Katie and parrying what Leon thought were discreet probes into the private lives of Caroline, Darla, and myself. I had to admire Katie's intractability. Not only did she scream bloody murder for me. She arched her back, wailed bitterly, and turned red and sweaty in the hands of both Leon and the two grandmotherly types who were staffing the Ronald McDonald house that day.

"Way to go, girl!" I said as I stashed her into her car seat at the end of the visit. "You'll fit right into this family. *Take no prisoners* is our family motto. Are you sure Darla isn't your mommy?" I started the car, and Katie's' puffy little eyes shuttered closed. Within seconds, she was fast asleep.

Back in Mendon, I had just sunk up to my neck in a bathtub full of hot water and jasmine bubble bath when I heard the phone in the kitchen ringing. Draped in one of Aunt Myla's threadbare towels, I swore all the way down the back stairs and stood dripping on the kitchen floor as Darla coughed and wheezed and wept into the phone.

"ICU finally agreed to talk to me, even without a pin number. Mom is going back into surgery, Aunt Kate," she said. "Can you please be there? Please!"

"If it weren't for you, she wouldn't be going into surgery," I pointed out cruelly.

"I know. But I'm going to fix it all. I promise."

"I'll go to the hospital as soon as I can dry off and get dressed. But first we are going to have a conversation. Now, *do not* under any circumstances hang up this phone. I'll be right back. I need to find something more than a wet towel to keep warm."

I glanced around, but the rack by the back door offered nothing except Aunt Myla's raccoon coat which smelled of cat urine and Darla's filthy body. I shrugged into its hairy, stinking depths and snatched up the receiver. "Darla? Are you still there?"

"Yes, Aunt Kate." Her tone was uncharacteristically meek.

"Aguilar and I wasted the morning trying to track down

181

Wolf. His house is deserted..."

"He's not there anymore, Aunt..."

"Do *not* interrupt me. Thanks to you I have once again gone all night without sleep, and, impossible as it may seem, my day has been even worse."

"Okay, Aunt Kate. Sorry."

I continued grimly. "After I ditched Aguilar in the parking lot of the Canal Street Bar, I went to pick up Katie at the foster mother's house – risking both our lives on the icy roads – and she screamed for two straight hours at the Ronald McDonald House."

Darla started to make sympathetic sounds.

"Shut up," I said. "She would not have been out in this weather if it weren't for you. I'll go to the hospital to be with your mother until she comes out of surgery, and then I am going to buy a one-way ticket back to London. And when I get there I will drop so far off the face of the earth even Interpol won't be able to track me down."

"Aunt Kate, you can't!"

"I can and I will. The only way I will change my mind is if you call Rosa right now and turn yourself in. Hold on. I'll get her number for you."

"I have it, Aunt Kate. It's here on your cell phone."

"Right. *My* cell phone. *My* boots, *Aguilar's* jacket. *His* car. *Our* sanity and physical well-being. Is there anything else you would like us to sacrifice for your cause?"

Darla screamed into the phone. "Don't you understand? I have to make sure Wolf never gets his hands on Katie! Whatever it takes!"

"Darla!"

"No, listen. Let me tell you about the day I kidnapped Katie. And then you can decide if you want to help me or go back to London."

"Is my cell phone charged?" I asked.

"Wha...?"

"Is the cell phone charged? This is one conversation I do not want cut off before we finish it."

Darla coughed and retched. Then she said, "Yes, Aunt Kate. Do you think I'm dumb enough to steal your cell phone and not take the charger, too?"

"Right. Tell me about the day you kidnapped Katie."

"Remember, Aunt Kate, when I told you about Aleisha? How she shacked up with Wolf because she had no place to go? I mean, that was really stupid because he is a mean, vicious man. But what was even more stupid was she let herself get pregnant. She said she was looking for security. Can you believe it? Why should anyone have to get pregnant for security? So I was staying with her at Wolf's place..."

"You mean that filthy dump on D Street?"

"No. That filthy dump is his personal space. He keeps his women in subsidized housing units over by the river. They collect money and food stamps from Social Services each month, and then he makes the rounds and takes the lion's share of it."

"The housing unit is by the river? Is that why you think Aleisha is the girl who drowned?"

"Or got thrown in. Yes."

"And you were staying in one of those apartments with Aleisha."

"Off and on. I didn't have any choice. Aleisha was having trouble with her pregnancy. I needed to be on hand when the baby came, especially if it came early."

"And that's why you were skipping your classes?"

"Yeah. I was afraid to leave her alone. Wolf wouldn't let her go to a doctor or the hospital. He didn't want a record of the pregnancy. He was going to sell her."

I gasped. "Sell Aleisha!"

"No, Aunt Kate, he was going to sell *the baby*. Do you

have any idea how much you can get for a baby on the black market?

"How would he know he wasn't selling her to some sort of pedophile?" I asked in horror.

"Don't you get it? He didn't care. Aleisha's baby was a commodity, a little cash cow he intended to turn into revenue. Considerable revenue. But Aleisha wouldn't hear any of that. She was convinced Wolf loved her. She said if I went to the cops or Social Services, she'd swear I was making it all up."

"So what did you do?" I whispered into the phone.

"I did what Aleisha wanted me to do. I stayed with her and delivered her baby. But once Katie was born and Aleisha held her for the first time, she realized she didn't want Wolf to sell her baby after all. The baby finally became... real for her."

There was a long silence.

"Darla?" I said into the phone. "Are you still there?"

"Yeah," she said, her voice bleak. "I'm still here."

"Where was Wolf all this time?"

"He was hanging around, drinking, and threatening what he would do to me if anything happened to the baby. While Aleisha was in labor he popped in and out of the apartment. He never stayed long because he didn't want to hear her crying. When he was in the room, he made her muffle her screams with a pillow. The minute the baby was born and he saw she was okay, he went off to call the buyer and celebrate his newfound wealth. And that's when Aleisha told me to take the baby and run. Right then before Wolf came back or she had a change of heart."

"I don't want her to end up like me,'" she said over and over. "I don't want my baby to end up like me."

"What a heartbreaking decision to have to make!"

"I know. She was barely conscious, and she was in a lot

184

of pain. But she was right, Aunt Kate. We couldn't let Wolf sell the baby."

"So what did you do?"

Darla sighed. "I agreed to take the baby. I told Aleisha that when Wolf came back and found the baby gone, she should say she'd been too weak to stop me. I wanted to call the police, anybody that might help us. But Aleisha was convinced Wolf loved her, and she was determined to protect him. At any cost."

"What do you mean 'at any cost'?"

Darla paused. "Aleisha threatened me. She said if I called for help, even after I left the apartment, she would say I'd been hanging around all this time because I wanted the baby for my own. And when I realized I couldn't have her, I called the cops out of spite. She told me she would let me take the baby, but she wouldn't let me do anything that might get Wolf in trouble."

I felt an overwhelming sense of sorrow. For Aleisha, for Darla, and for little Katie. And for the first time I realized why the Child Protective People were as tough as they were. The real question is how they managed to deal with the dark side of humanity and still see the good in people.

"So you took Aleisha's baby and ran," I said.

"What choice did I have?" Darla demanded. "I didn't have time to take proper care of Aleisha, and I didn't have time to clean up the baby. I just wrapped the poor little thing in a blanket and hid her under my coat. And then I got out of there. Down the elevator, through the lobby, and out the double doors, terrified every second that Wolf would see me. I saw a bus coming, and I ran across the street as fast as I could. And that's how she got those horrible bruises on her leg. The sidewalk was a sheet of ice, and I slipped and almost dropped her. Do...did... the cops...did they say Aleisha died from childbirth? Or...was she...alive when she went into the

185

water?"

"I don't know, Darla," I said as gently as I could. "They didn't say. And, besides, you don't know for sure the woman they pulled from the river was Aleisha." I paused for a second and then said, "Tell me where you are, honey, and I'll come get you."

"No. I have something I need to do. I have a plan. I'm going to set up Wolf. I'm going to get him to meet me, and as soon as I know when and where, I'll call you. I know the dead girl is Aleisha, and I know she didn't commit suicide. I don't want there to be any doubt Wolf is the one who pitched her in the river. Once he's locked up, then Katie and my mom will be safe, and you can go back to London."

Chapter Thirty-one

I raced over to the hospital, grabbed a ticket at the tollbooth on my way into the parking garage, and waved at the guard on duty. I left the SUV at the first non-handicapped parking slot I found and headed up to West 6. Caroline was already on a gurney in the hall waiting to be wheeled down to the OR when I arrived.

"Hi, Caro," I said. I took her hand and tried to smooth her matted hair.

She turned her head in my direction. Her face was black and blue from the beating, but it was the swelling around her left eye that made my stomach churn. Before the attack Caroline could discern shadow. What would a head trauma do to that limited ability which meant so much to her independence?

"Hey, Kate," she said in a hoarse whisper. "Glad you're here...." She licked her battered lips and tugged on my hand to pull me closer. She smelled of blood and perspiration and antiseptic. Her hand fumbled for a sheaf of papers lying next to her on the bed. "Here," she said. "Sign these. It gives you power of attorney. It says DNR, DNI. If I conk out, make sure some gung-ho intern doesn't revive me. I'm not living the rest of my life as a vegetable." She blindly held out the papers and I signed them, calling a nearby nurse to act as a witness.

As soon as the nurse departed, Caroline said, "Now tell me what's happening before they start pumping me full of stuff. I don't want to...go into surgery without knowing."

I hesitated. How could I tell her what I knew without

sending her blood pressure over the moon?

Caroline's hand squeezed mine with a grip surprising in strength for a woman in her condition. "And don't try making up something rosy," she warned. "I may be flat on my back, but I want the unvarnished truth."

I laughed in spite of everything, the hospital smells, the sight of Caroline looking like road kill on her hospital bed, the sound of a man coughing up his lungs in a nearby room. Caroline made a wheezing sound, and I realized she was laughing, too. An aide coming down the hall with her arms full of linens looked startled. In her experience people probably did not enjoy their hospital stay quite so fully.

"Okay," I said. "They're going to give you enough anesthetic to make even you tranquil. You might as well get your money's worth. I talked to Darla. She knows you're here, and she knows who put you here. She's decided to take on Wolf by herself. She has a plan."

"Watch out for her...plans," Caroline whispered hoarsely. "Darla has an overdeveloped sense of justice. She could hack out that bastard's heart and end up behind bars for life."

Two transporters walked up and started checking the ID on Caroline's wrist and the IV drip in her arm. "Caroline Scholfield?" one of them asked to confirm her identity.

Caroline waved them off. "Give me five minutes," she said. "This is urgent."

"Caroline, the doc's waiting for you."

"Let him wait, Carlos. I'll sort it out with him later. Take a little walk up the hall."

"Hey, Caroline," Carlos grinned. "You know me, huh?"

Caroline said, "Carlos, I'd know your sexy voice anywhere. Now back off."

Carlos cocked his chin at the other transporter. "Let's take a little walk," he said for Caroline's benefit. "We can give the lady a few minutes. We know she can't outrun us."

188

Caroline waited until she heard the squeak of their rubber-soled shoes recede down the hall. "Quick!" she commanded.

"Okay," I said in a voice barely above a whisper. "Darla believes the dead girl in the morgue is Aleisha, her friend from high school."

"Oh, no!"

"That's not the worst of it, Caro. There's more. Wolf is Katie's father, but her mother isn't Darla. It's Aleisha. You wanted it straight," I told her when she gasped. "Darla dropped out of nursing school to stay with Aleisha until the baby was born because Wolf wouldn't let Aleisha go to a doctor for maternity care or to a hospital to deliver her baby."

Caroline tried to push herself up against her pillow, and I had to grab the IV line running into her arm to prevent her from pulling it out. "Why the hell not?" she demanded.

I carefully set the IV line back on the thin white blanket that draped Caroline's body. "Because Wolf was going to sell the baby. He didn't want an official record of her birth."

Caroline struggled to sit up. "*What!*" she shrilled. *"Sell the baby!"*

I glanced furtively around. "Caroline! Keep your voice down. You're out in the hall!"

She shrank back against her pillow and hissed, "That son of a bitch was going to sell *my* grandchild?"

"Well, under the circumstances, Katie's not really your grandchild. But yes, Darla said that was his plan. As soon as the baby was born, I guess Wolf went off to celebrate. Aleisha realized it was the only chance they would have to thwart his plan, so she told Darla to take the baby and run. And that's what Darla did."

Caroline stared into darkness. "Darla should have called 911."

189

"Darla didn't have any choice. Aleisha told her if cops showed up, she would say Darla had been planning to kidnap the baby. Or words to that effect. It's hard to know what really transpired. Everything I'm telling you is third hand. But, according to Darla, right up to the end Aleisha tried to protect Wolf. She believed he loved her."

Caroline put her hand to her face and ever so lightly touched the swollen area around her eye as if my words had shattered the narcotic barrier which kept the pain at bay. "And then Aleisha turned up in the morgue," she whispered. "My God! Does Darla know if she...if Wolf murdered her?"

I shrugged and said, "Darla has asked me twice if the police know if it was murder or suicide. So my guess is she doesn't know. I don't even know if the police are sure how Aleisha died. And to be perfectly honest, we have no way of knowing if the girl in the morgue is really Aleisha."

The transporters returned. "Time's up, Caroline," said Carlos. "We gotta roll." He went to the head of the gurney and started wheeling her down the corridor.

"Katie *is* my grandchild," Caroline told me grimly as she let go of my hand. "And don't you forget it."

I walked beside her gurney until they put her on the elevator. Then I went into the lady's room. When I came out, I asked at the nurses' station where I should wait while Caroline was in surgery. Father Donnelly, the priest from Caroline's church, was standing nearby talking to a man in a bulky jacket, dark glasses, and a red-and-black knit hat which was pulled low over his brow.

Father Donnelly called to me, and the man he'd been talking with turned and started toward the elevators.

Kate," the priest said, "I've been trying to reach you to find out how you're managing with Darla's baby." The man in the knit hat stopped and glanced back at us. When he saw me watching him, he turned and continued down the hall.

"Who is that man?" I asked Father Donnelly.

"One of the maintenance staff. He knows Caroline. I rode up in the elevator with him. He just got off duty and was coming to see her. I guess we both missed her."

I nodded, and, to my chagrin, I began to cry. "They just took her down to surgery," I told him through my tears.

"Oh, my dear..." said Father Donnelly.

"I'm so afraid she'll die!"

Chapter Thirty-two

Hours later, one of the surgeons found me slumped in a sparsely cushioned armchair in a small, stuffy waiting room. He had iron-gray hair and a face eroded by fine lines. He looked as tired as I felt, but he sat down to offer reassuring words. I later wondered if he had any idea how important those few minutes were to me.

Stuffing his scrub cap into a pocket, he began to recite a litany of the procedures they had performed. When he saw my face growing paler by the second, he smiled. "Let me put it this way," he said. "I've known Caroline for twenty years or more. The woman is virtually indestructible. There's no reason we can't anticipate a full recovery. She could pull through on will power alone, but we're giving her some pain medication and antibiotics just so it looks like we're doing our part. She'll be fine. I guarantee it."

When they transferred Caroline from Recovery to the post surgical floor, I trailed behind and settled by her bed intending to whisper comforting words to her in her unconscious state. I folded my arms on the edge of her bed, put my head down for just a second, and instantly fell asleep.

I awoke with a feeling of dread and glanced at my watch. It was almost six in the evening. Under the lingering effects of the anesthesia, Caroline was breathing regularly around the tubing, and when I reached for her hand, it was cool and dry. A male nurse with a diamond stud in one ear came in to reset one of her monitors.

"You must be exhausted, honey. We've been in several times to check on her, and you haven't stirred. Go home and get some rest. And don't worry about a thing," he said. "We're not going to let anything happen to this lady. She's one of our favorite social workers."

I took the elevator to the lobby and turned down the empty corridor leading to the parking garage. As I pushed through the doors leading to the main level of the garage, I realized I had no idea where I had parked my car. A quick check of my ticket yielded no clue.

The garage was deserted. Visitors had already gone home for dinner, and the hospital would not change shifts again until eleven that night. The high-pressure system which had ushered in clear skies this morning had caused the thermometer to hit single digits. I shivered uncontrollably as I made my way around treacherous patches of ice and trudged up the ramp to the next parking level.

On the level below, I heard the hospital's electronic doors wheeze open as someone entered the garage with a quick, measured tread. I turned to call out a warning about the ice, but my feet suddenly went out from under me. My sharp cry startled a flock of pigeons that had been pecking through discarded food wrappers, and they launched themselves into clumsy flight.

I lay stunned by the sudden pain, feeling the oily sludge that coated the cement soak through my jeans.

"Watch out," I called out to the other person walking through the garage. "It's really icy up here. They need to get more salt on these ramps before someone breaks their neck."

There was no reply, but I heard heavy footsteps coming my way. I forced myself to my feet and glanced down the ramp, thinking someone had heard my cry and was coming to my aid. Over the roofs of the vehicles parked along the ramp, I caught sight of a red-and-black hat. A red-and-black hat coming my way....

I was not accustomed to being preyed upon. I lost

critical seconds standing and staring even after the hat vanished from view. It took my brain far too long to process the warning. *Red-and-black hat.* It had been a bright day, and sun reflecting on snow created a hazardous glare for drivers. Dark glasses hadn't seemed all that incongruous inside the hospital if a worker were on his way home for the day. I remembered how the heavyset man wearing the dark glasses had turned away as I approached Father Donnelly. And I remembered how, as he was heading toward the elevators, he glanced back when the priest mentioned Darla's baby.

Wolf had been in the hospital because he was staking out Caroline's room, hoping Darla would show up to see her mother. He was wearing a knit hat to cover his shaved head and dark glasses to conceal his pale blue eyes. And now he was coming after me because he knew I was the one who had the baby. His baby!

I knew better than to scream for help. In the empty parking garage, no one would hear me. And even if someone did hear me, Wolf already had a good idea where I was because I had called out a warning about the ice. Either way, he was going to get to me long before hospital security arrived. Memories of Nomad's bloody fur and Caroline's battered body sent me hobbling away from the ramp as fast as I could.

It was too late.

I heard Wolf's heavy boots behind me and then his labored breath. I felt his hand grab the back of my coat and let out a pitiful cry.

"You bitch," he hissed. "I want my baby!"

He jerked my coat, and I stumbled. I flung my purse in a backhanded swing which caught him in the head. Adrenaline and fear gave me the edge. That and the fact that I had bottled water and three paperbacks in my purse. I whirled and saw the malevolent twist of his thin lips and the fury

194

glittering in his baleful blue eyes. In blind panic, I thrust my hands out and shoved him. He was on ice, and he went down heavily. I grabbed my purse and ran for my life.

The first large vehicle I came to was a maroon van parked nose to the wall. I slipped behind it and clambered onto the salt-encrusted bumper so my feet were not visible to anyone glancing under the car. Then I cowered down with my back braced against the cold cement wall and hoped that in the poor lighting I would be invisible.

A few moments later, I heard Wolf lumber past the van. "You fucking bitch! I'll find you," he muttered. "And when I do, you're gonna be one very sorry woman."

For a long time I remained where I was, shaking with fear, my muscles screaming as I forced them to maintain the awkward position. By the time Wolf's footsteps receded down the ramp, I could barely move. I limped out of my hiding place to peer through the girders to the floor below. I heard a car door slam, and as I watched, a black Camaro sped into view on squealing tires. The driver was wearing a red-and-black knit hat.

Fear made me indecisive. Was Wolf giving up? Or was he coming up the ramp to find me and run me down. I peered through the girders again and realized he was doing neither.

He was backing into a handicapped parking space, positioning his car so he could simultaneously monitor the hall leading from the parking garage to the lobby, the bank of elevators, the stairs, and the exit. As I watched, he rolled down his window and pulled out a pack of cigarettes. He shook a cigarette out of the pack and stuck it between his lips. His lighter flared.

He had effectively trapped me. All he had to do was sit there like a cat at the entrance to a mouse's hole and wait for me to make a move.

I stood there and tried to think. I could wait up here in the freezing garage until someone drove by, or I could keep searching until I found my car. Either way I still had to pass right in front of Wolf to make my escape. And I knew without a shadow of a doubt that witnesses or innocent bystanders would not deter him from coming after me.

My only option was to somehow get past him with enough headway to reach the tollbooth and yell for the guard on duty to call Security. Moving as silently as I could, I began circling the outer wall until I located the elevators and the stairs next to them. The elevators debouched just outside the doors leading to the hospital lobby. Wolf's position enabled him to see anyone getting on or off the elevators, but I had a plan. It was a risky plan, but it was better than playing cat and mouse in a deserted parking garage, especially since I was the mouse. A very cold, very frightened mouse.

I pushed the button that summoned the elevator. When the first one arrived, I propped the door open with my purse. Then I summoned the second elevator. It arrived moments later. I got on the first elevator just long enough to press the down button sending it to ground level. Then I counted slowly to ten, sent down the second elevator, and began to creep down the stairs, taking care to prevent Darla's boots from clattering on the metal treads. I paused at the point where I, too, had a view of the elevators arriving at ground level.

As the first elevator arrived and the doors opened, Wolf tossed his cigarette out the window and jumped out of his car. He swore when he saw the elevator was empty and positioned himself directly in front of the second elevator. He could hear it descending, and it was obvious his intent was to grab me the minute I emerged.

Using those few seconds when Wolf's attention was focused on the elevators, I ran down the remaining stairs and bolted for the tollbooth. My hip hurt like hell from the fall, but I was motivated by the knowledge that if Wolf glanced up and saw me, my current pain would be nothing compared to what he would inflict.

I almost made it.

I ran down the remaining stair and stopped, stunned. There was no one on duty in the tollbooth, no one to summon Security. Like Lot's wife, I glanced back. I did not vaporize in a pillar of salt, but when I saw Wolf following me on foot, I panicked. I bolted, not for the hospital entrance which I might have reached before he caught me, but for the deserted sidewalk that led down the hill and into the night.

The thud of Wolf's heavy footsteps behind me was terrifying. The sidewalk, which sloped downhill, was slushy from salt put down to prevent pedestrians from breaking their necks on hospital grounds. I slipped and slid until I reached the bus stop fronting the hospital on South Avenue. Then I hit ice again. Flailing my arms and clutching madly at the rock wall that bordered the sidewalk in front of the hospital, I somehow managed to stay on my feet.

Wolf was not so lucky.

He was right behind me, close enough that I could hear him panting, but when he hit the ice, his feet flew out from under him a second time. He hit the sidewalk hard. I heard the breath go out of him on impact.

A black man wearing a long coat over blue scrubs was waiting at the bus stop. When Wolf got up on all fours, cursing foully and whipping his head around to see where I was, the man must have seen the look of fear on my face. He pointed at a city bus lumbering to a stop. "Quick!" he yelled to me. "Get on that bus!"

The door of the bus opened, and I leaped on, not even waiting to see if anyone wanted to get off. The black man was right behind me.

"I saw that dude runnin' down the hill after you," he said. "I thought you was runnin' to catch a bus. You okay?"

I nodded and turned around to offer him a weak smile. "Yes. Thanks to you. That was fast thinking!"

"You want me to call the cops? I got my cell phone here."

I shook my head. "I'll get off and find a phone as soon as my knees stop shaking." I intended to call hospital security, but I didn't want anyone overhearing my conversation.

The bus picked up speed, and I bent down to peer out the window. Wolf was still standing on the sidewalk staring after our bus. As I watched, he turned back towards the hospital, then stopped, bent down, and picked up something that had been lying on the sidewalk.

"Oh, shit!" I yelled in despair. "I dropped my purse back there!"

The bus driver eased his foot off the gas pedal. "You wanna get out here?"

I shook my head. I didn't want to get off until I put some distance between Wolf and myself. I pointed to the large, medieval-looking church further down the street. The parking lot was full of cars, and there were lights glowing behind the stained glass windows. "Can you let me off there?"

I fished in the pocket of my jeans and handed the bus driver what few coins I had for the fare. Then I perched on the edge of a seat close to the door. Wolf had only to open my purse to find my name on my British driver's license and my credit cards, but at least there was nothing in the wallet that had Aunt Myla's address on it.

I glanced down at the keys in my hand. They were all I had left to show for a close encounter with a man Aguilar called a punk. But Wolf was more than a punk. He was a

198

predator, and he would be coming after me. It was just a matter of time.

Chapter Thirty-three

The street was dark. Overhead, stars that glittered like shards of glass surrounded a razor-sharp sliver of moon. Reaction set in. I became aware of my shaking limbs, the bitter cold, the pain radiating from my hip. I slipped behind a tall hedge and watched the road. Sure enough, about five minutes later a black Camaro came speeding along South Avenue, slowing at bus stops and intersections. As it crept past the spot where I was hiding, a bus passed in the other direction, hurling filth slush from under its wheels. Its headlights illuminated the man in the driver's seat just enough for me to see his shaved skull. It was Wolf, his rear license plate obscured by the grunge that corrodes cars over the course of Rochester's winters.

Across South, The Holy Spirit Greek Orthodox Church was holding a preliminary planning session for their spring festival. An elderly gentleman who wore his thick glasses and fringe of white hair with quiet dignity stood up and greeted me when I appeared in the doorway. His eyes roved over my white face and dirty trench coat. When I asked if I could use the phone, he led me to the church office without comment. I was frightened enough to wish I could hide there until morning. Instead I called the Highland Hospital switchboard and was eventually transferred to a security officer who identified himself as Charles Vancouver. He suggested I ask someone at the church to drive me to the emergency entrance of the hospital. He said he would meet me there.

Luckily, the church meeting was breaking up. When I emerged from the church office, the same elderly man kindly agreed to drive me to the hospital. Then he offered me a handful of chocolate chip cookies and a cup of coffee while he and his wife put on their coats and gathered up their papers.

His wife was a large woman with steel-gray hair cut in a bob. She looped her arm through mine on the way out the door. Her face was furrowed with concern. "You're shivering," she said in heavily accented English.

I nodded. "A man tried to mug me in the parking garage of Highland Hospital. I got away from him and jumped on a bus, but he has my purse."

"That's terrible," she said, "but at least he didn't harm you. Hurry and get into the car. Ianos can turn up the heater to make you warm."

Her husband unlocked a rusted Volvo. "Don't worry, my dear. We'll drive you right to the door of the hospital and wait to make sure you get inside safely."

I slid onto the littered backseat. Their kindness made me feel like crying.

At the hospital, lights from an idling ambulance bathed the Emergency entrance in streaks of red. For some reason, even that brought tears. I wiped my eyes, thanked the couple, and limped up to the security officer standing just outside the double doors. He was a tall, lean fellow with enough equipment on his belt to fend off an Al Qaeda offensive. As I approached, I heard the ambulance driver say something to him about multiple stab wounds, and I realized how lucky I was that Wolf had not come after me with a knife. Or a gun.

I waved to the couple in their car as they pulled away. The Security officer led me inside.

"You're limping," he said. "Are you hurt?"

I shook my head. "No, I'll be okay. I slipped on ice."

"Just now?"

"No. Earlier. In the parking garage before I..," I

shrugged. It was a long story.

The security office was a claustrophobic room, small, cluttered and hot. There was barely space for a desk and a few chairs. A window overlooking the Emergency waiting room provided a view of sick and anxious people waiting for treatment or news. It also provided a view of the double doors leading to the parking area outside the ER. I turned my chair so I could watch the doors. If Wolf walked through them, I wanted to be the first to know it.

Vancouver poured coffee from a coffee maker on a shelf near the desk and put it in front of me along with packets of sugar and powdered creamer. "So," he began, "you said on the phone you were accosted by a man in our parking garage this evening, but you first saw him earlier today up on West 6."

I nodded and fiddled with my coffee cup. What I really needed was a stiff drink.

He scribbled something on a pad on his desk. "Did you get a good look at him up on West 6?"

"No. He had on a red and black knit hat that covered his head. And he was wearing sun glasses."

"Inside the hospital in the middle of the day?"

I shrugged. "He was talking to Father Donnelly. According to Father Donnelly, he said he was a maintenance worker at the hospital and was on his way home. It was a bright day. Sunglasses didn't seem all that incongruous. Besides, I was upset because my sister-in-law had just gone for surgery. I didn't give it much thought. But now I'm afraid he might be the man who attacked her. According to witnesses, her attacker had a shaved head and blue eyes. I think he was wearing the hat and sunglasses to disguise his appearance."

Vancouver stared out the window as he thought. "Heavy set fellow with blue eyes and a shaved head. Doesn't sound like anyone on our maintenance staff, but I'll get hold of the head of Maintenance and check. Are you sure this guy said he worked here at the hospital?"

"Evidently that's what he told Father Donnelly."

"And this same man chased you in the parking garage this evening?"

I nodded and told him what happened. "And I dropped my purse running from him," I added. "He picked it up. It has my British driver's license and my credit cards in it."

Vancouver took my name and contact information. Then he made a few phone calls. I listened in, understanding that once again the good guys had not a whit of tangible evidence. Security could write up a report that I had lost my purse, and I could foster the unlikely hope someone would find my purse and turn it in. But no one witnessed Wolf attacking me in parking garage, and the man at the bus stop who followed me onto the bus had not called in what he had seen.

My hip hurt. I shifted in my chair. "Just in case this fellow is Caroline's assailant, I think you should move her to a different room. I don't want him to be able to come back to the hospital and find her."

Vancouver nodded. "We can do that, just to play it safe. I'll call West 6. We can put her on a different floor and set it up in the computer so if anyone calls or asks for her except you or Father Donnelly, the caller will be informed there's no record of a patient by that name in the hospital. We have to do that more often than you would think." He stood up to indicate the interview was over. "I'll make sure this guy's description is circulated. And if someone turns in your purse, we'll let you know."

Vancouver waited while I visited the ladies room. I made the mistake of glancing in the mirror and saw the image of a victim, pale and defenseless and scared. No wonder people were propping me up and offering me drinks laced with caffeine. I straightened my shoulders and raked my fingers angrily through my hair. It was all I could manage. Not only did Wolf have my credit cards, phone, and driver's license. That bastard also had my comb, my lip gloss, and three paperback books I had not yet read.

When I emerged, Vancouver drove me through the parking garage until I found my vehicle and was safely inside it, doors locked and motor running. He waved me through the tollbooth since I had no money to pay, and then followed me until I turned onto South Avenue. There was no sign of Wolf with or without a red-and-black knit cap.

As I headed toward Mendon, I sighed in relief. For the moment, Caroline was safe, Katie was safe, and I was safe. Darla, as usual, was a wild card. All I could reasonably hope was she was taking the antibiotics and using the money she had filched from my purse to find food and shelter. I decided to say nothing more about the mugging. Once again I feared that if the police did not believe me, they would label me an alarmist. If they did believe me, Child Protective Services would hear of it, move Katie to a new, undisclosed location, and terminate my visiting rights. If I told Aguilar what happened, I would have to listen to him rant and rave and threaten to call Rosa. Darla had a plan to put Wolf behind bars. As reluctant as I was to side with her, she looked like the only game in town.

The house in Mendon was dark and silent. In one of the sugar maples an owl hooted, and another answered. I thought of a book I had read years ago, *I Heard the Owl Call My Name*. In some cultures an owl was a sign not of wisdom but of death. A ripple of unreasoning fear ran up my spine as I made my way up the snow-covered steps of the side porch.

Once I was inside the house, I slammed the door and locked it. Then I went from room to room turning on lights and checking the locks on windows and doors. Finally, I settled in the kitchen. I pulled a bottle of red wine out from under the sink, but an extensive search of Aunt Myla's drawers confirmed my worst fears. That God-fearing woman had not owned a corkscrew. Aguilar must have brought his own when he came to dinner. I poured myself a generous portion of Gentleman Jack and picked up the phone.

Caroline had been moved to a new room. She was awake, grateful to still be in possession of her spleen, and ready to tackle preliminary sips of a clear liquid diet. Next I phoned Darla.

"How's Mom?" she said the minute she answered. "I've been trying to call you for hours, Aunt Kate. How come you don't answer your phone?"

"I'll tell you in a minute," I snapped. "First things first. Your mother is okay. Out of surgery. They didn't have to remove her spleen. Now she just needs plenty of bed rest."

Darla said, "They'll have to tie her down for that."

"Or take away her pain pills," I added.

"Yeah, that would work. Although she has a tremendous tolerance for pain."

I didn't reply. Now that I was safe at home, anger was replacing fear, and that made it hard to remember all this had come about because Darla had been trying to help her friend. She should have gone to the authorities long before Katie was born, but at least she had shown compassion and a brave heart. I reined in my temper and told her about Wolf's latest foray.

"I hate it that you're out there in Aunt Myla's house alone. Be sure all the doors are locked. He's crafty and mean. Don't take any risks."

"How can you sit on the other end of this phone and say that? I know you're plotting some sort of harebrained scheme."

205

"Aunt Kate, the only way to make the world safe for Aleisha's baby and you and my mom and me is to put Wolf out of commission. So drop the subject. I can do this. But...."

"But what?"

"But if...well, if anything happens to me, I want you to adopt Aleisha's baby."

I silently shook my head. What blind trust Darla had in those she loved. "Darla, I'm old enough to be Katie's grandmother."

"You're not too old to adopt, Aunt Kate. How old are you anyhow?"

"Forty-two."

"See? That's not too old. You'd only be sixty-four or sixty-five when she's ready to graduate from college. Women still bear children in their forties."

"I'm in no position to test that theory."

"But if I can put Wolf out of commission, I'm going to try to adopt Katie myself. Before I stopped going to my classes, I spent time in Miner Library at the U. of R. reading *Danforth's Obstetrics and Gynecology*. I copied everything about delivering babies, and I memorized as much as I could. All the while Aleisha was in labor, I prayed for her and the baby. And when Katie was born, it was so incredible. It's like she's already mine. I held her for just one moment before I put her in Aleisha's arms. At least Aleisha got to hold her before...before...."

"Darla, let's just go to the police with this."

"No, Aunt Kate," Darla said sadly. "It won't work. They have no evidence that Aleisha was murdered or they would be looking for her killer. They have nothing to tie Wolf to Aleisha. His name isn't on the apartment lease, and no one there is going to say they ever saw him coming and going at that building."

"But...."

"And there's nothing in the newspapers, Aunt Kate. I've been to the public library. I read every back issue of the *Democrat and Chronicle* since the day Katie was born. There's nothing other than that first article about that businessman spotting Aleisha's body in the river. I'm the only one who can do this."

"At least tell me where you are, then," I pleaded.

As Darla always did when I brought up either the subject of the police or her location, she hung up and refused to answer further calls. I felt like throwing the phone across the room. Thanks to Darla, the only phone I had to throw was a plastic princess-style phone, sunshine yellow and firmly attached to the kitchen wall.

Chapter Thirty-four

It was a rough night. Every sound brought me upright in bed, mouth dry, and heart pounding. About four in the morning I finally fell asleep. It was after eight before I awoke. I showered, ate breakfast, and then called Caroline. She swore she was doing fine.

I told her she had been moved at my request and to give out her new room number to no one. "And I'm not coming to visit you for the next few days," I said. Then I told her why.

"Well, shit," she said. "Now who's going to pop in with flowers and balloons and get well cards?" The weakness in her voice in no way mitigated her ability to make me smile.

"If I pass a florist on my way to the Driver's License Bureau and the cell phone store, I'll arrange for a delivery."

"There's no sense going to the DMV," she said. "You don't have ID for a new license."

"Sure I do," I answered. "My passport is here in my computer case. And I have proof of my address because I have copies of all the legal papers I signed to become a foster parent. So stop worrying. I have things under control."

It was bravado. I didn't have anything under control, but Caroline was still under the influence of powerful drugs, and she believed me. "Watch your back," she admonished just before she hung up. I could hear the fear in her voice. Even powerful drugs could not offset the memory of the beating she had taken or the memory of having to put down her dog thanks to a man whose brutality seemed to know no bounds.

I alerted the credit card companies that my wallet had

been stolen. Then I dug through Aunt Myla's boxes until I found a purse, a bright, hand-woven bag I had sent her from Lisbon. It still had the store tag on it in Portuguese.

I stopped at the bank and the cell phone store. It took an interminable amount of time to select a new phone and fill out the paperwork for the wretched thing, but I had no choice. I had to have another cell phone, for my safety and for Katie's. From now on I would be carrying it, not in my purse, but in my pocket.

On impulse, I also stopped at the Black Sheep, a children's shop in Pittsford Village where I found a mobile of clowns with bright faces and silly smiles. Then, even though time was short, I ran across the street to Pittsford Florist to arrange for balloons and flowers to be delivered to Caroline. She would enjoy the attention. She claimed flowers from a florist smelled like luxury.

I arrived fifteen minutes late to pick up Katie for our morning trip to the Ronald McDonald House. Loretta had her bundled in her blue snowsuit when I walked in. It was obvious there was no time for conversation this morning, but I didn't care. I was going to have Katie to myself for two entire hours.

Her eyes opened when I slipped her into her car seat.

"Hi, baby," I said softly. "Want to go for a ride in my big red car?"

She blinked. I was thrilled that she was awake. "Okay," I told her and gave her a nervous little pat. "We can sing songs all the way to the Ronald McDonald House. Do you happen to know *The Wheels on the Bus*? It was one of your mommy's...I mean Darla's favorites."

I sang her every verse as I navigated late morning traffic on Mount Hope. The day was overcast, but warm enough to melt the ice on the road, so I added another verse, *The wheels on the car go slush, slush, slush.* It made me smile, but only for a moment, because then I thought of her real mother lying in the morgue. Weak and defenseless, Aleisha had sent her newborn baby with Darla for safekeeping, knowing she would face Wolf's wrath when he returned. Having seen Wolf's fury, I shuddered to think how terrified she must have been. Her decision to save her child had probably gotten her killed. She would never know the simple joy of even singing to her baby. Would I have been brave enough to do what she did? Would I have to be that brave before this was over?

For two hours I played with Katie. I rocked her by the fire in the living room at the Ronald McDonald House while the two women on duty clucked over her and admired her dark curls and lovely slanted eyes. When they went back to their duties, I put her on a blanket on the floor and dangled the clown mobile over her head. She lay there with her eyes open, and she seemed to be staring at it. I grinned with satisfaction and held it up until my arm ached.

When she started sucking on her fist, I picked her up again. I was now savvy and competent. I rummaged through the diaper bag and pulled out a diaper to tuck under her chin before giving her a bottle. No way was this baby going to soak her clothes in formula a second time on my watch.

After I returned her to Loretta's house, I went to Denny's to celebrate a successful morning as a foster mother. As soon as I was seated and the waitress poured my coffee, I called Darla.

"I just spent two hours playing with Katie. She was an angel!" I said.

Darla demanded all the details about both the baby and Caroline.

I also have a new cell phone number," I told her.

"Good," she said. "And I've got my plan in place." She coughed until she was gasping for breath, but swore she was beginning to feel better. "So here's what you need to do," she concluded.

I listened, and against my better judgment, I agreed to do my part.

By three-thirty that afternoon I was at Caroline's house, sitting-cross legged on the floor of her small living room. The refugees had turned the heat up to about ninety, and a cartoon program, which none of the children was watching, was blaring on the TV. The room was littered with toys and clothing. Some sort of goat stew was simmering in the kitchen. The odor, combined with the fear that Darla's plan engendered, made me feel like retching.

Fatima, the Somali translator, was perched on the edge of Caroline's footstool. She watched anxiously as Halima, the mother of the refugee family, bound my short hair in a cloth and then pulled me to my feet so she could drape a bright, red-and-orange patterned dress over my long-sleeved t-shirt and jeans. Halima was a sturdy, wide-shouldered, large-breasted woman, and her dress hung ridiculously on my thin frame. But it hardly mattered. We weren't going for haute couture. My disguise was to be that of a refugee. Refugees wore whatever came their way.

Halima handed me a second even more colorful garment to layer over the first one. Next, she draped her yellow UN headscarf over my head and around my shoulders. The children were chattering and dancing around us, oblivious to the somber mood of the adults in the room. One of the little girls laughed and pointed at my face. Her mother's clothes could not turn a lady with a white face and green eyes into an African. Halima shook her head at her and tugged the scarf lower on my brow.

The doorbell at the side door rang, and a few minutes later Rosa stalked into the living room. Aguilar was right behind her. He was wearing jeans and sneakers, as usual, but he had replaced his leather jacket with a bright green hooded windbreaker. He stopped to distribute lollipops to each of the children. He handed me a lollipop as well. His face registered that sarcastic look which said he knew I had eaten nothing healthy all day, why start now? I gave him a sickly smile and took the candy. It was lime-flavored and it would probably turn my lips as green as my face felt.

"This is the dumbest...," he started to say, but Rosa interrupted him.

"Please, Uncle Joe, go in the kitchen with the other men. I'll handle it from here."

Aguilar rolled his eyes in disgust and left the room. I felt a smile tug at the corners of my mouth. It felt strange, as if I hadn't smiled in a decade or two.

I introduced Rosa to Fatima. Rosa strode over and shook her hand. "Thank you for being willing to help us," she said gruffly.

Fatima responded solemnly. "Caroline helps many people. Today we must help her and her daughter."

Halima was sitting on the floor, smoothing and folding her scarves. She looked up shyly and said something to Fatima.

Fatima turned to Rosa. "Halima wants to ask you how you can stop a man like Wolf from hurting Caroline's daughter tonight. He has hurt Caroline and now she is in the hospital."

Rosa, who was in her uniform, walked over to Halima and squatted in front of her. "I have a small persuader here," she said as she patted her holstered service revolver. "In America, men can't beat up women. It's against the law. And I enforce that law."

I watched Halima's eyes widen as Fatima translated. She stared at Rosa, and Rosa smiled at her and sat down in front of her. It was the first time I had ever seen Rosa smile. She, too, had seen the wonder in Halima's eyes. Maybe America really was the Promised Land.

Halima knelt and began to wrap a cloth around Rosa's long dark hair. Then she pulled bright layers of clothing over Rosa's uniform and handed her a large headscarf. Rosa put it over her bound hair. Rosa had dark eyes and an olive complexion. Once she exchanged her regulation black shoes for old sneakers, she would look quite authentic. Unless someone happened to look in her eyes and see a cop's cool assessing stare.

"Okay, Uncle Joe, if you want to be in on this, you better get in here," Rosa yelled to Aguilar. He appeared in the doorway with Mr. Mohamed. Fariq and Ahmed followed close behind them. Aguilar's dark hair, normally so carefully slicked back, was now covered with an old beige ski cap. He carried a spiral notebook, as did the other men, and a transparent plastic bag filled with a large bottle of water, paper cups, hardboiled eggs, and some oranges. He met my eyes but refrained from commentary.

What followed was a council of war. Rosa had reluctantly agreed to go along with Darla's plan, but it was clear she was running the show. She gave us our final marching orders, and Fatima translated for the Bantus.

"Remember, when we get there, we don't look around. We go straight over to the tables in the corner of the lobby where the other refugees will be gathering. We take part in the English class, we don't watch the door, and if our guy comes in, we don't give him any idea we recognize him. No one, I repeat, no one makes a move except me. Just make sure I have free access to the room. I may have to move fast. I've got my partner for backup. He'll be in street clothes sitting in an unmarked car in the parking lot. If this guy, Wolf, actually shows up, all you have to do is let me know if he's the fellow who attacked Caroline, and we'll do the rest. If he makes a move against Darla, I radio my partner and we

213

move in immediately. No one's going to get hurt. This guy's not going to do anything crazy in a room full of witnesses. But, just in case, I need you to understand no matter what happens, you all stay out of the way. So let's get moving. We want to be in place before he shows up. And...Kate? "

I jumped at the sound of my name.

"Keep that scarf around your face and your head down and your hands hidden. And keep your back to the room. I understand why you want to be there, but you don't exactly blend. The last thing we need in this charade is to spook the perp before the Mohameds can ID him."

Ahmed stayed behind at Caroline's house to watch the children. The rest of the refugees, Fatima, Rosa, Aguilar and I all piled into my SUV. I bumped up the SUV's heat to its highest setting, and we followed Rosa in her police car out into the brutally cold afternoon. I could only pray that we would all return.

Chapter Thirty-five

It was a seven-minute drive to River Park Commons, a government-subsidized housing complex adjacent to the Ford Street Bridge on Mt. Hope. The deteriorating complex consisted of two low-rise buildings flanking a thirteen-story high rise. The low-rise buildings were scheduled to be demolished in the spring to make way for new, upscale housing. For the present, the complex was home to an entrenched Bantu and Somali community who had come to America after long, hopeless years in refugee camps. For them the dismal apartments were a safe haven filled with wondrous amenities like running water and doors that locked.

I turned into the apartment parking lot, a stretch of macadam riddled with potholes and filled with salt-rusted cars long past their prime. Beyond the parking lot lay a deserted, snow-covered playground. Through the playground's chain link fence I glimpsed the Genesee River in winter spate, gunmetal gray and laced with dead branches and chunks of dirty ice. Visions of the ruined body of the young girl in the morgue flashed into my mind, and I shuddered at the memory. She had looked so much like Darla. She could so easily have been Darla.

We trudged through the parking lot under lightly falling snow. Mr. Mohamed, Aguilar, and Fariq pushed through heavy glass doors into the lobby of the high rise, and Rosa and I followed meekly behind with Fatima and Halima. The lobby was a large, overheated space with worn beige flooring and a few scraggly plants. The door to the manager's office was immediately to the left of the entrance. A large sign on the door read *Closed*. Set in the wall of the lobby opposite the door was a bank of three elevators.

As we walked in, one of the elevators opened with a groan, and a group of Africans emerged. The women wore bright, loose dresses and headscarves similar to ours. The men wore jackets and loose fitting trousers. One young woman was pushing a baby stroller with a small baby muffled in pink and blue blankets. They walked over to join other refugees who were already standing around long tables and folding chairs, chatting and laughing as they waited for the evening's ESOL class to begin. We joined the group, and the Africans from the apartment complex quickly flocked around us.

"They all have family and friends still at Kakuma," Fatima explained to Rosa and me. "The Mohameds can give them news from the camp."

A few of the women stared at Rosa and me, but when we remained silent, they ignored us and continued to press the Mohameds for news from Kenya.

Within a few minutes, the ESOL teacher arrived, an older woman with short white hair and a face ravaged by sun damage. When she smiled, the patterns of lines around her mouth and her hazel eyes indicated a smile was her usual expression. She shrugged out of her dark wool coat and pulled a pair of wire-rimmed reading glasses from her purse. That seemed to be the signal for class to begin. The refugees quickly found seats around the table and grew quiet.

I found a spot with my back to the room where I could look directly across the table at Rosa, who was perched stiffly on a folding metal chair facing the double doors leading to the parking lot. She seemed angry because she had allowed herself to be talked into Darla's crazy scheme, and she had a right to be angry. Professionally, she was taking a big risk. I was sure it was only pressure from her uncle and Caroline's plight that had impelled her to put her job on the line.

Around us, the class began their evening's struggle with English nouns and verbs, the days of the week, the seasons, and the months of the year. There was a lot of head shaking and mute gestures and embarrassed smiles, but everyone at the tables was trying. Their ticket to success in America depended on jobs, and they couldn't get jobs until they mastered this diabolical new language.

Half an hour dragged by. My stomach cramped and my hands trembled as I tried to sit quietly in my seat. Rosa shifted impatiently in hers, and Aguilar kept glaring at me as if I had the power to conjure up Darla and the man she had promised she would meet here.

The teacher had just shifted gears and was handing out bus schedules for the next part of the lesson when I felt a cold draft from the lobby doors. I furtively glanced around and saw Wolf walk in. His pale blue eyes cased the lobby, swept disdainfully over the refugees at their tables in the corner, and checked out the few other people coming and going. Seeing nothing to trigger alarm, he strode over to the elevators and leaned insolently against the wall. I shrank down in my seat and glanced across the table at the Mohameds. Their angry eyes confirmed what I already knew. This was the man who had attacked Caroline. Behind her open bus map, Rosa noted their response. She frowned a warning at me, and I ducked my head lower and stared at my bus schedule, but I was beyond concentrating on weekend arrival and departure times.

Darla pushed through the lobby doors about five minutes later, stamping her feet and shaking snow out of her hair. She glanced quickly around the room and then focused on Wolf. With a cold stare in his direction, she shrugged out of Aguilar's leather jacket and tossed it carelessly onto a folding chair by the door. I knew Aguilar had caught her cavalier treatment of his jacket because I heard the hiss of his breath. I risked a glance at Rosa. She had shifted in her chair so she had access to her radio and her gun. The Mohameds kept their eyes on the teacher, but the grim set of their faces told me they were aware of the unfolding drama. I glanced at Rosa to make sure she hadn't noticed that I'd surreptitiously shifted my chair so I could watch what was happening.

Darla coughed hoarsely as she walked across the room towards Wolf. She was wearing nothing except the thin t-shirt and the tight-fitting jeans I had peeled off her filthy body the morning I found her in the nursery. Clearly she wasn't wearing a bra, nor was she wearing my boots. Somewhere she had found a pair of fur-lined clogs. In spite of her illness, she hadn't even had the sense to acquire a pair of socks. As she walked across the room she reached up and casually pulled her long curly hair into a makeshift ponytail.

Wolf watched Darla like a predator tracking prey. His eyes held not even the slightest indication of humanity. There were those who dined and there were those who were the dinner. Darla was nothing to him but an option on his food chain. Under the overhead lights, Darla's dark skin had a sickly, grayish cast, and she continued to cough as she defiantly approached the man. Her face was set in a look of undistilled hatred.

Wolf glared back at her and pushed the elevator button. When the door creaked open, he jerked his head toward it. I held my breath, and Rosa stiffened in her seat across from me. Darla shook her head and said something that elicited a fierce scowl and an epithet. I hoped what she said was, "I'm not stupid enough to go upstairs with you."

Wolf snapped something at her and gestured angrily at the lobby. Darla shrugged and pointed toward the lobby doors. After a moment's consideration, Wolf pushed himself off the wall and followed Darla toward the heavy glass doors. As they went out into the cold, Darla wrapped her arms around her thin body. She had not even bothered to grab Aguilar's jacket before she left.

Rosa and I both jumped up the minute the lobby doors closed. Rosa tore off her scarf and yanked the two-way radio off her belt. She jammed her thumb onto one of its buttons and held the radio to her mouth. "It's him, Cisco! The Mohameds ID'd him. Darla and the suspect are coming out the door! You got 'em in sight?"

"Her partner's coded reply was instantaneous. Then he said, "What's the hell's going on? This wasn't part of the plan!"

"Tell me about it," snapped Rosa with a filthy look in my direction. She ran across the lobby, pulling Halima's dress over her head and dropping it on the floor as she pushed open the heavy doors. "What's your 10-20, Cisco?" she said into her radio.

I heard Cisco's reply because I was on Rosa's heels "I'm half way across the parking lot. Where are they headed?"

I picked up Halima's dress and rushed out the doors after Rosa. She stopped on the front steps and scanned the street. Cisco was running toward us. I looked around for Darla and Wolf. "The playground!" I pointed. "They're on the playground!"

"They probably want to negotiate out of hearing range," yelled Cisco as he ran up. "I told ya we should've made her wear a wire." Rosa's partner was a Latino, built like a cinderblock with coarse black hair gelled in a high crew cut. Rosa started to head for the playground, but Cisco grabbed her arm.

"Take it easy, Rosa. The playground's fenced all the way around. Chain link on three sides and the stone wall along the river. I checked before you got here. There's only one way out."

Dusk was falling. We stood on the steps and watched Wolf and Darla trudging across the playground in the wind. Wolf was gesturing angrily, but Darla forged ahead ignoring whatever he was saying. I assumed Darla knew we were watching, but it was obvious Wolf was not aware of our presence.

Rosa took a deep breath. "Okay. We don't need to go in unless he makes a move against her. But we've got to back off. If he sees us, he might grab her and use her as a hostage."

I turned to Rosa and clutched her arm. "How do you know he doesn't have a knife or a gun? You've got to stop him before he hurts her!"

Rosa shook off my hand in cold fury. "I told you to stay out of the way! Darla knew what she was supposed to do. We had an agreement. Remember? The Mohameds ID him and Darla walks away. We take Wolf in for questioning, and she turns herself in. She's the one who led him outside and out of range. So now we wait. We're not going in there like the Lone Ranger."

Cisco glared at me. "Did you know she was going to do this?"

"What do you mean?"

"Did you know she was going to lead him outside?"

Aguilar had followed us. He pushed his way over to Cisco and glared at him. "Back off," he said coldly. "Kate took the kid at her word just like we all did."

The wind tangled my colorful African skirts around my legs and whipped at my headscarf as we watched Darla lead Wolf to the wall along the river. Then I gasped as Darla climbed onto the stone wall and sat with her back to the river. She stared down at Wolf. I could tell from her body language she was taunting him. And it worked, because I suddenly he reached out to grab her.

Behind me I heard Aguilar curse. Cisco pushed past me, knocking me to the ground. Rosa was on his heels. I picked myself up in time to see Darla shove Wolf's hands away and laugh mockingly at him. Wolf's back was to us. He did not hear the two cops yelling into the wind to back away and freeze.

In horror I watched Wolf grab Darla's ankles and with a vicious shove, tip her off the wall backwards into the river. Then, oblivious to the approaching cops, he leaned over the railing to watch as her body hit the freezing water. "Die, you bitch!" he yelled. "And keep your eyes open when you go under. Maybe you'll see your friend, Aleisha, down there!"

I knew in an instant Darla had planned it that way. It was why she had taken off Aguilar's jacket and why she had the kind of shoes she could easily kick off. She was sick and crazy and desperate to keep Wolf away from his child. She was afraid the testimony of refugees newly arrived in America would not be sufficient to put Wolf behind bars, so she set us up as witnesses to her own murder.

Wolf whirled around when he heard Cisco run up behind him. Cisco grabbed him and threw him to the ground. I ran screaming to the wall and leaned over it. Darla was flailing against the current. I watched her go under. I tried to climb the wall and felt Aguilar grab my wrist in a bone-crushing grip. The pain barely registered through my panic.

Cisco pushed Wolf face down in the snow and jammed a knee in his back. He turned and yelled at Rosa. "Get the throw bag from the swift water rescue kit. It's in my trunk with the rest of my gear." He snapped a handcuff on one of Wolf's wrists and then dragged him to the metal fencing and handcuffed him to a post.

I struggled to get out of Aguilar's grasp. Forget rescue kits. I was going in after Darla, myself!

221

"Stay right there, Miss," Cisco hollered at me. "If one of us needs to go in, it'll be me. I'm trained for this and you aren't."

I ignored him and screamed down at Darla where the current was pinning her against the branch of a dead tree that was half-submerged near the base of the wall. "Don't let go, Darla! Don't you dare let go!" I fought Aguilar as he tried to pull me away from the wall. "She's going to die!" I screamed at him. The wind snatched the words from my mouth, and I sank down into the snow and sobbed. "She's going to die. Please, God..."

Rosa raced across the playground carrying a flotation device, a white helmet, a wet suit, and a thick yellow rope wadded in a red bag. While Cisco made repeated attempts to throw the rope to Darla, I heard Rosa radio for air rescue. Cisco was having no luck with the rope. Each time he threw it, the current dragged it out of Darla's reach. Finally he managed to snag the rope in the branch.

We all held our breath.

Darla's movements were sluggish as she tried to reach for the yellow lifeline. The freezing water had slowed her reflexes to the point of non-existence.

"She's never going to be able to hold onto it, Cisco! You're gonna have to go in," Rosa yelled as she secured the rope to the rail. "What's the ETA of the copter?" she hollered into her radio.

We all heard the response.

Five to six minutes.

Cisco swiftly stripped down and struggled into a drysuit used for cold-water diving, the flotation device, and the helmet. He climbed onto the rail and stared into the river for what seemed an interminable amount of time while he gauged his jump. Then he dropped and vanished beneath the dark, turbulent water. We all cheered madly as he surfaced.

He whipped his head around to get his bearings and then struck out for the branch where Darla was hanging limply. He used the branch to lever himself close to Darla and grabbed her with his free hand. Somehow he managed to wrap the rope around her, and then he hung on to her as the icy Genesee sluiced their bodies and did its best to suck them into the mainstream of its vicious current.

We heard the helicopter before we actually saw it in the darkening sky. It arrived, hovering overhead, its rotors whipping a frenzy of mist in the water below. A door opened, and we could see the crew moving inside. A rescue basket appeared in the doorway. The wind buffeted the basket as it was slowly lowered into the river.

A crowd had gathered at the fence. Together we held our breath and watched the chopper troll the basket in the swift current, trying to maneuver it within reaching distance of Cisco and Darla. I felt someone take my hand. I looked up and saw Halima staring at me with compassion. She knew what I was going through. She, too, had lost children to war.

It took four tries before the basket came close enough for Cisco to grab it.

Although he must have been all but paralyzed by the cold, Cisco managed to manhandle Darla into the basket. He clung to the branch, up to his armpits in water, and watched members of the crew slowly haul her up to the helicopter. Hands reached for her and pulled her inside. Then the basket, bucking and dipping in the wind, was lowered a second time.

When Cisco was finally pulled into the helicopter, the crowd cheered wildly. I looked around and saw Wolf watching the unfolding drama. He turned his head and stared at me. His face held no expression, but his pale eyes glittered with malice. I took two steps away from the crowd and vomited my bile-green lollipop into the trampled snow.

Chapter Thirty-six

The rescue helicopter airlifted Darla and Cisco to Strong Hospital at the University of Rochester Medical Center. I stayed with Darla most of the night while they set her broken arm, stitched her lacerations, and treated her for hypothermia. She was in shock, and she had pneumonia.

Rosa stopped by the hospital the next morning. I had just gotten off the phone with Caroline, and I asked Rosa if she would come to the cafeteria with me for a very early breakfast. Surprisingly, she accepted.

"I want to thank you for all you've done for my family," I told her over plates of pancakes and sausage. "Cisco, too. He risked his life to rescue Darla. I hope he gets a commendation for his bravery. He could have died jumping into that river! Have you seen him this morning? Is he okay?"

Rosa shrugged. "Yeah, he's pretty tough. It's all in a day's work." Then she added gruffly, "Darla's nuttier than a fruitcake, but she's got a lot of guts. I think they'll end up dropping all the charges against her now they've seen Wolf in action." She stirred two packets of sugar into her coffee and added, "And I guess I owe you, too."

I stared at her. "How could you possibly owe me anything? We've caused you nothing but grief."

"Yeah, but Uncle Joe finally has something to do when he's not working besides watch TV and hover over Gramps all day. It's been good for him to be involved with all of you. And the best part? He said he was going to start coming to Mass."

"You're kidding!"

A rare smile lit Rosa's face. "He said you and your family needed all the prayers you could get. Our family's been trying to get him to church for years!"

A feeling of warmth and happiness washed over me. I wasn't sure I had ever been in anyone's prayers before. Then I laughed. "I wonder if his prayers are as laced with profanity as his every day speech." Rosa laughed, too, and rolled her eyes.

That afternoon, after I had a chance to get some desperately needed sleep, Aguilar drove me back to Strong Hospital. Darla was running a high fever and her lungs were congested. She was on oxygen, IV drips, and massive doses of antibiotics. Her eyes opened when I called her name, but they appeared vacant and unseeing. Her mass of curly hair was lank against the pillow, her face a ghastly shade. Stitches ran across her cheek and up her arm where the river's swift current had raked her against branches of the dead tree that had ultimately saved her life.

I felt a wild, helpless rage as I chalked up the damage caused by one pathologically violent man. Aleisha, Katie, Caroline, and Darla. Three innocents hospitalized and one dead as a direct result of his quest for easy money. Two dead, if you counted Nomad. What made someone like that tick? What made some people like Caroline and Darla altruistic and kind and others like Wolf cruel and inhuman?

I sat slumped in a chair by Darla's bed until Aguilar stuck his head in the door.

"Someone named Rhonda Wims just called your cell phone."

I jumped up. "What did she say?"

"She said she had good news for you and to call when you had a chance."

It was good news indeed. Child Protective Services was granting me custody of Katie.

"Tonight?" I asked joyfully.

"First thing tomorrow," Rhonda Wims assured me. "How about ten o'clock?"

When Loretta Whiting handed me Katie the next morning, I was overwhelmed with emotion.

"Thank you," I breathed as I blinked back tears. "Thank you for being here for this baby and for what you do. I know it isn't easy. The world needs more people like you."

She offered me a smile and a quiet wish for good luck. Then I was out the door with Katie in my arms.

I tucked the baby into her car seat. She was restless and trying to suck on her fist through the sleeve of her blue snowsuit. "My first official decision as your new foster mother," I told her, "is to ditch that hideous snowsuit. My second official decision is to sit here in this driveway and call your grandmother. She's not really your grandmother, but don't ever tell her that!"

A nurse answered the phone by Caroline's bed, "Ms. Scholfield is tied up with the doctor at the moment. Could you call back in about fifteen minutes?"

I heard Caroline's imperious voice in the background. "Doctor Yates is an old friend. He won't mind waiting for just one minute. Please hand me that phone."

"I've got Katie!" I told her. "I'm sitting in Loretta Whiting's driveway, but I knew you would want to know that she's finally ours!"

"Bring her here!" Caroline begged. "I asked the charge nurse, and she said it would be okay."

I headed over to the hospital, but before I took Katie up to Caroline's room, I sat in the lobby on one of the couches, lifted her out of her carrier and stripped off the blue snowsuit. Then I dressed her in the pink and white outfit which I had tucked in the bottom of Aunt Myla's Portuguese purse.

I held Katie up so she could see my face. "You look beautiful in pink rabbits," I told her. "You'll knock their socks off up on West 6!"

She stared at my face and then, amazingly, she tentatively smiled. I knew I would carry that first smile with me for the rest of my life. I would also carry for the rest of my life the picture of Caroline propped up in her hospital bed holding Katie. It was the point at which the healing really began for all of us.

Nine days later, Darla was well enough to be discharged. Caroline, having been sent home two days ago, insisted on accompanying Aguilar and the baby and me for the event. It was a three-ring circus in Darla's hospital room while we waited for the doctor's last visit, prescriptions to be called in, and the final shuffling of hospital paperwork.

It was the first time Caroline had seen Darla since Darla had disappeared. Aguilar snapped pictures of their emotional reunion. Then everyone wanted to hold Katie, so we handed her around while Aguilar snapped more pictures. When word came from the nurses' station that the doctor would be delayed, Aguilar went out in the hall to find extra chairs so we could sit and talk. Darla had a lot of explaining to do, and she had promised she would wait until we were all together to tell us the story she had already given to the police.

"Honey, the first thing I want to know is where you went when you ran away with little Katie," Caroline began.

"Well, I couldn't take her to school, could I, Mom? And I couldn't take her to our house and put you in jeopardy. It was the first place Wolf would look. So I hid in the downtown library with her under my coat until the library closed for the day. Then we hung out in an all night diner about five blocks away."

"How did you think you were going to feed her?" I

227

demanded.

Darla looked at me sheepishly. "Actually? I stole formula from a convenience store. I didn't have a baby bottle, so I had to try to dribble the formula down her throat." Darla looked down at the baby sleeping in her lap. "But you couldn't swallow it, could you, sweetheart?" She hugged the baby to her. Then she glanced up at me. "I guess I'll have to go back to the store and give them some money for what I took."

"I guess you will," I said in dragon mode.

"I don't understand why you simply didn't go to the police," Caroline said.

"Because they would have handed the baby over to the welfare people, and sooner or later the welfare people give kids back to their mothers. It's what they do, Mom. I knew Aleisha would never be able to stand up to Wolf. Sooner or later she would have let him sell her baby."

"Darla," I said, my voice stern. "Just for the record, we're not dealing with the welfare people. We're dealing with Child Protective Services, and their people have been absolutely rabid about looking out for Katie's best interest."

Darla's dark eyes slitted with anger. "They're all part of the same system, Aunt Kate. And the system didn't do much for Aleisha and her brothers and sisters, did it? They always ended up back with their mother. And I can tell you it wasn't in their best interest."

"Oh, Darla," Caroline said sadly.

"Look, Mom, you rescued me from a mother who couldn't keep me. And I have always loved you so much for that. When I held Aleisha's newborn baby in my arms, it was like destiny. I had to do for Katie what you did for me."

"Your mother didn't have a psychopath on her tail," Aguilar interjected.

"No, just Immigration and the administration people

228

from Doctors Without Borders," Darla retorted.

"But when you took the baby to the hospital," Aguilar protested, "you must have known the story would come out."

"I didn't think the story would come out if they didn't have the names of her real parents. So I said she was mine. And, Aunt Kate? I named her after you because you never had a baby of your own, but you were always there for me. And ...I needed you to be there for her."

Tears welled in my eyes. "I'm doing my best. It isn't very good, but I'm trying."

Aguilar glared at me as if to stave off one of my famous crying jags. He leaned forward and said to Darla. "Where the hell did you go after you left the baby at the hospital? There were cops combing the city for you."

"I walked out to Aunt Myla's. It took me two days. I knew Aunt Myla had died." Darla squeezed Caroline's hand. "I know, Mom. I never returned your phone calls then or when Uncle Whit died, but I didn't think I could handle all your questions."

"You were just gonna live in her barn in the middle of winter?" Aguilar demanded.

Darla shook her head. "Aunt Myla never locked her doors. She didn't even know which keys matched the locks. I knew I could get in the house and find food and stay warm, but when Aunt Kate showed up, I had to hide in the barn."

"It was below freezing out there, honey!" Caroline said. She was slumped in her wheelchair. She had fought riding in it, but the tremor in her voice revealed just how weak she was.

"Yeah, it was, Mom. I've never been so cold in my life! Even Aunt Myla's raccoon coat didn't keep me warm in that barn. That's why I finally went inside the house and hid in the basement even though Aunt Kate was living there. I knew I was sick. And I had the kittens to think about."

229

"Right," said Aguilar in disgust. "Let's not forget those sorry-ass cats. Where did you pick them up?"

"Out on the road by the barn. I heard them mewing. Someone must have dumped them out of a car. There was a third kitten. It got run over or something, but the other two were okay, so I put them in the pocket of Aunt Myla's coat to keep them warm. Of course, I had nothing to feed them." Darla coughed and looked at me with that innocent expression which could wreak such havoc. "That's why I was sitting in the rocking chair in the middle of the night, Aunt Kate. I didn't mean to scare you. I was just waiting until you woke up so you could go to the store and buy some cat food for them."

Chapter Thirty-seven

After Darla was fully recovered, she returned to nursing school, but she moved out of the dorm and back home to be with her mother. I finished my class in childcare and gradually adjusted to my role as foster mother, reveling as Katie learned to laugh, began to reach for colorful toys, and struggled to sit up on her own. I held her, and fed her, and watched her brown eyes take on an unfocused stare as warm milk filled her mouth. I rocked her until she fell asleep at night and lay limp and warm in my arms. I bathed her and played with her. When she didn't sleep, I didn't sleep either. And when she cried, I stopped what I was doing to pick her up and comfort her. For six glorious months, I was her mother, and she was my child. And for Mother's Day, Darla and Caroline gave me a small gold locket with Katie's picture inside.

Wolf was in custody and was appealing his sentence for attempted murder. He had signed away his parental rights to Katie in the hope it would gain him a lighter sentence. We all hoped he would hang.

Darla had the sad task of identifying Aleisha's body. Rosa said the autopsy indicated Aleisha had been alive when she entered the water. Had she committed suicide in despair over losing her child or accidentally fallen into the river? Or had Wolf returned to the apartment to find his baby gone and, in the dark of night, thrown her in the Genesee's raging torrent as punishment? No one would ever know. Aleisha had indeed been a child lost to the system.

We arranged for Aleisha to be buried in Mount Hope

Cemetery next to Aunt Myla. "Aleisha didn't have much of a family of her own," Darla reasoned. "She and her brothers and sisters were always being split up to go in and out of foster care. Since she's Katie's real mother, I think we should treat her as part of our family."

In the spring, Katie and I visited the cemetery to put flowers on both their graves. It was just before nursing school let out for the summer. That same week, Darla called me and invited me to lunch. When Katie and I arrived at Caroline's house a little before noon, we had to park on the street. Caroline's driveway was full of cars, and people were carrying out all the household goods that had been stored in her garage.

Caroline and her new guide dog, a placid black Labrador named Percy, met us at the door.

"What's going on?" I asked as Caroline reached for Katie, then nuzzled her and whispered, "Hey Diddle, Diddle, cutie pie."

Caroline grinned at the baby in her arms and then looked up. "The Mohammeds are renting a house. Now that the two boys are working at the hospital, in the kitchen and the housekeeping departments, the family can afford to move out of their tiny apartment. And, this is the best part...Mr. Mohammed just got a part time job at the meat market owned by Joe Aguilar's brother. Pretty soon every African in the city will be shopping there for goat meat."

"That's great," I said and glanced at my watch. "But I need to get going if I'm going to pick up Darla at school and have her back for her afternoon classes." I handed Katie's diaper bag to Caroline and launched into a litany of instructions about bottles, naps, diapers, and pacifiers.

"Give me a break!" said Caroline. "You'd think I'd never taken care of a baby before. Go pick up Darla. Katie will still be alive when you get back."

Darla was waiting for me on campus just outside Miner Library. A smile lit up her lovely face when she saw my car. She was wearing what were probably size two jeans and a flowered blouse in citrus colors that enhanced her exotic features.

She tossed her computer case and a medical textbook onto the back seat and climbed into the car. "Hi, Aunt Kate. I made us a reservation at The Toad in the Hole for lunch. It's just off East Avenue. How's Katie today?"

Later it occurred to me that Darla took me to the only British pub in Rochester hoping to remind me of how much I missed London. We ordered fish and chips and iced tea with slices of lemon. I refrained from pointing out that in England no one would dream of tea with ice cubes in it. Or lemon. I smiled to myself. Motherhood was mellowing me.

I should have known that happy moments never last forever.

Darla didn't eat much. She fidgeted with her food and played with the straw in her glass of iced tea. Finally she wadded up her napkin and dropped it on her plate. "Aunt Kate," she said, "There's stuff I have to say to you."

I looked up, and when I saw her face, I laid down my fork and clenched my hands together in my lap.

Darla took a deep breath. "First of all, I hope you know how much I love you. I will never, ever be able to thank you for all you've done. But I guess you already know that. And second, I've been working really, really hard to straighten out my life. I guess you know that, too. I've been going to counseling and parenting classes, and I just finished CPR for babies. And I'm getting really good grades, so...."

"What is it, Darla?" I asked, suddenly frightened.

Darla blinked back tears. "I don't know how to say this next part, so I guess I'll just blurt it out."

I sat unmoving, dreading whatever it was she was about

to tell me.

"I want to start proceedings to adopt Katie. I love her so, so much, and I hate not being with her. I've thought of her as my baby ever since I ran out of Aleisha's apartment with her under my coat. That's why I said she was mine when I left her at the hospital. I intended to come back for her as soon as it was safe."

I opened my mouth to say something, anything, but there was nothing I could think of to say.

Darla rushed on. "I know it will be hard being in school and having a baby and no money, but I don't care. There are other girls in my class doing it, and they manage. I'll manage, too. I promise. Please, Aunt Kate. I want to adopt her more than anything in the world, but I can't do it without your blessing."

I looked down at my plate and blinked back tears of my own. Darla jumped up and ran around the table to put her arms around me. "I knew it would make you sad! I'm so sorry. You're always so tough. Please don't cry!"

I had known Darla would want to adopt Katie some day. I just never expected it would be so soon. I used my napkin to wipe my eyes. The napkin smelled of fish and balsamic vinegar and greasy fries. I tried for a smile, and once the smile was somewhat in place, I gave her my blessing.

"Darla, if it weren't for you, Katie would have...well, who knows what horrible things might have happened to her. You'll be a wonderful mother, and I just want you to know that I'll always be grateful to have...shared her with you for...for a...little while."

"It isn't over, Aunt Kate. You'll always be part of our family."

I smiled. It was a sad smile, but in her elation Darla didn't notice.

At the final adoption hearing, Rosa, members of the

church, and even Rhonda Wims of Child Protective Services spoke on Darla's behalf. The hearing went well. When the papers were finalized, I hugged and kissed Katie and handed her, dressed in a pink smocked dress to Darla, her new mother. I felt Caroline's arms wrap around me.

She knows how hard this is for me, I thought. I turned and hugged her back and tried, yet again, not to cry.

"How does it feel to be a grandma, old lady?" I whispered tremulously into her ear.

Caroline grinned. "It feels magical. But one grandchild is enough. I sure as hell couldn't live through another one."

Afterward we all went to Our Lady of Victory for a celebration in the church hall. As the party was winding down, I pulled Aguilar aside.

"What are you doing tonight?" I said to him.

"Lady, don't tell me after all this time you're asking me for a date."

"Sort of."

"Sure, doll. Where do you wanna go?"

"The airport."

"The airport? At this time of night? What kind of a date is that?"

"My flight for London leaves at nine."

At the airport Aguilar stood silently watching as I took my place in the security line. Woodenly I slipped off my shoes and placed them in a plastic bin for scanning along with my computer and my camera. I glanced back. Aguilar was still there. He looked as if he were losing his best friend. I steeled myself and blew him a mocking kiss. He shook his head in disgust and twisted his mouth into that sarcastic smile I knew so well. Resolutely, I turned away and walked through the security checkpoint back into my old world.

Why would I return to London and leave everything I loved behind? Because Darla needed the freedom to raise her child in her own way. She had earned that right. A foster mother's role is to care for a child and then give it up. It's what I signed on for. And if I had delayed my departure, I never would have had the strength to leave.

On the plane, I grabbed a blanket from an overhead bin, downed a Dramamine, and automatically checked the seat pocket in front of me for the airsickness bag. The doors of the plane closed, and the flight attendant began to review the safety features of our aircraft. Motors revved, and, as we taxied down the runway, I touched the little gold locket I was wearing.

Good-bye, Katie. You will always be the child of my heart, and I will pray for you every day for the rest of my life.

If you enjoyed **Break Point,** follow Kate Scholfield to London in the sequel.

The Smallest Things
by Amelia Grace Seiler

Sometimes...the smallest things take up the most room in your heart.
~A.A. Milne

Chapter One

Ida Lieberman froze at the sound of shattering glass. Then came even more ominous noises, the snick of a deadbolt being slipped and the grating sound of unoiled hinges as the door that led to her back garden slowly opened. The crunch of footsteps treading over broken glass confirmed what she already knew. *There was an intruder in her flat!*

Her hand trembled as she set down her teacup and eased out of her chair. She had been translating a passage from Cicero, and the book tumbled to the floor with a muffled thud. Panicked that the sound had revealed her presence, she glanced frantically around the room. The single lamp on the table by her chair cast the room in shadows, but there was no place to hide.

Fear constricted her throat as she crept on stocking feet

past the stairs into the front hall. Silently she crossed the tile floor and leaned against the front door to muffle the noise when she turned the key in the lock. She eased open the front door and felt a shock of cold air.

The hiss of winter rain sluicing off the eaves must have muffled the footsteps of the intruder because she did not hear him in the hallway behind her until he was almost upon her. Whirling around in mute terror, she found herself facing a short, heavy-set man in a black ski mask.

"You weren't supposed to be home, luv," the man said in a soft, menacing voice.

Ida turned and tried to bolt through the front door. His gloved hand clamped onto her arm and yanked her back, then slammed the door shut. She stumbled against the Victorian hall tree. Wrought iron coat hooks dug into her spine. *Did my mother and father and brother feel like this when the Gestapo came to take them away?*

"What do you want?" she whispered as a second masked man, taller and slimmer silently emerged from the kitchen.

"We want the papers your friend, Nigel, told us about."

"No!" she cried. Too late she gathered her wits and said, "What...papers?"

"Don't play stupid, old woman. We know you have them. Just hand them over, and you won't get hurt."

Unconsciously, Ida glanced towards the stairs.

The shorter man looked at his accomplice who slowly nodded and tilted his head towards the upper floor. The silent gesture made him appear even more malevolent.

The shorter fellow grabbed her arm. "They're up there, aren't they? Let's go find them. Then we can go home, and no one needs to get hurt."

In her panic, Ida could scarcely climb the stairs, but the man kept an iron grip on her elbow and forced her to keep moving. When they reached the landing, he allowed her to pause for a moment to catch her breath before he propelled her up the last five steps. At the top of the stairs he stood with her in the center of the narrow hall while his accomplice peered into the three bedrooms and her small, antiquated bath.

Still saying nothing, the accomplice shrugged again and gestured with his head in the direction of her bedroom. Ida led them woodenly through the door. She sank onto the bed and watched, helpless to prevent them from ransacking her room for the papers that were so precious to her. At one point she had to clutch the duvet to keep from crying out as gloved hands tore the cover off an old white box and dumped a child's red woolen cape onto the floor.

"Nothing," snarled the smaller of the two after long minutes of futile searching. "Keep her here. I'll go through the rest of the flat."

After his footsteps had receded down the hall, Ida reached down, picked up the red cape from the floor, and painstakingly folded it on her lap. "Please," she begged the man guarding her. "Why are you doing this?"

He shrugged and said nothing. To Ida his silence was more ominous than anything he might have said.

After what seemed a very long time, Ida heard the other man climbing the stairs. He glared at her as he entered. "Again, nothing," he said to his partner.

Ida flinched when he reached out to jerk her to her feet. He smelled of stale cigarettes and sweat.

"You gonna tell us where it is or not, luv? This is your last chance. Then we're going to get rough." He let go of her arm.

Ida backed away. "The papers...they're not here. They're in a box at a bank."

The man took a menacing step in her direction.

Ida turned and fled. Behind her she heard a curse and

heavy footsteps. At the top of the stairs she felt his hand grab for her collar. She turned to fight him off, stepped back into thin air, and fell headlong down the stairs. Through a haze of agony, she heard the two men pounding down the steps to the landing where she lay.

The man who had been silent until now said in a voice pitched high with alarm, "Oh, my God! Is she dead?"

The other squatted down and stared at Ida as her eyes flickered open. Through a blur of pain, she saw him shake his head.

"You told me she wasn't goin' to be here tonight!" the taller, thinner man said shrilly.

"She wasn't supposed to be. Do you think I'd plan a caper like this if she were going to be home? I called the British Library. They said she'd be working!"

For some inexplicable reason, as she lay there Ida felt compelled to excuse her absence at the event. "I had a...sore throat," she gasped.

The man ignored her and stood up. "We want those papers, luv," he growled. He nudged her with the toe of his boot. "You understand what I'm saying?"

Ida was in too much pain to speak further. After a moment, she simply nodded her head.

"And by the way," the man added as he and his accomplice stepped over her inert form and continued down the stairs, "One word of this to the police, and we'll break every bone in your friend Nigel's frail old body."

Chapter Two

I knew searching for a place to live in London was not for the faint of heart, but I always thought that referred to the exorbitant price of real estate. It never occurred to me that I would be risking my life for a flat in a decent part of town.

It was a dreary day in February, and rain was pattering on the glass roof of Nigel Weatherford's West London conservatory. I was sitting on a moldy wicker couch watching rainwater puddle on one of the faded cushions and then trickle onto the worn brick floor. Nigel never let small details bother him. He was dressed for the chill in rumpled slacks and the gray wool sweater which he wore during the day and his white cat, Bede, slept on at night.

"So what are we going to do about you, Kate?" Nigel said. "You can't grieve indefinitely. Where exactly have you been since you stopped by last summer?"

"Collecting material for travel articles," I told him. "Switzerland by train, sheep dog trials in Scotland, convents and monasteries as alternatives to hostels. That sort of thing. Oh, yes, and I did an article on the plight of Bali's stray dogs and cats. Then I just sat on the beach." I raked my fingers through my unruly brown hair that was fast going gray and did not elaborate on my reflections while sitting on the shore staring out at the warm, restless Indian Ocean.

"Isn't it about time you had a base here in London? Your old house is still available if you should want it."

Nigel rented flats and houses which he had inherited from his father, a perspicacious businessman who had envisioned the long-term value of London real estate. "After your husband died, his company cancelled the lease, but I've never had your things boxed up and removed. The economy, you know. Makes letting large properties all but impossible."

The wicker couch creaked as I leaned back against an array of mildewed pillows. I shook my head. "I'll just want something small now. My days as a corporate wife are over. I certainly won't miss the entertaining. And, to be honest, I'm doing my best not to miss Whit. While I was in America I learned he'd been having an affair with his secretary."

"Ah, men and their women," sighed Nigel. "It's been the same since the beginning of time, hasn't it." He sipped his drink and meditated for a while on the vagaries of infidelity or whatever men in their old age meditate on. Finally he picked up the thread of the conversation again. "So what will you do with yourself now? A novel perhaps? One of those American private-eye thrillers?"

I laughed. "Not quite. I've taken a desk job for a travel magazine so I can work from home. I'm going to adopt a baby. From India. Some orphanages there allow single, middle-aged women to adopt. The red tape has just about snaked its way through all the proper channels."

"Ah, Kate. You've missed your former foster child terribly, haven't you. But you did the right thing, allowing your niece to adopt her."

I nodded, unable to speak around the lump in my throat.

"Well," said Nigel. "A new baby deserves a toast. Sure you won't join me for one little drinkie?" Although it was only two in the afternoon, Nigel was nursing a crystal water glass of gin with a single slice of lemon.

I shook my head and managed a feeble smile as I held up my Havilland teacup. "No, thanks. I'll stick to Earl Grey." I'd downed one of Nigel's drinks before and had learned my lesson. Fourteen months ago, after two grim-faced executives from my husband's oil company had visited our London home to break the news of his death in Iraq, I stumbled down the street to Nigel's flat. Nigel wordlessly handed me a glass of gin with his signature slice of lemon. He'd added a token ice cube to the glass because I was American. I had no memory of walking home that night. Nigel had lived through the Blitz. He knew about bombs and death and grief.

Nigel ran his hand across the white bristles on his unshaven face. "So now you need a place to live." He stared out at the rain for a moment. "Ida Lieberman's flat three doors down is vacant. Perhaps it would suit you and a baby."

"Ida's gone? Where did she go?"

Ida was an elderly Jewish woman who had also survived the war. When Whit and I lived in the mansion on the corner, Ida had walked past every day on her way to Wandsworth Park. In good weather she wore a brown cardigan and sensible shoes. On inclement days she wore a yellow slicker and Wellingtons. When we first moved in, Ida often stopped to admire our front garden and to chat about flowers. Gradually she and I became casual friends and often had tea together.

"She's in a home for the elderly," Nigel said noncommittally.

"Oh, no! Is she ill?"

Nigel hesitated just a beat before he said, "She took a tumble on her stairs. She wasn't badly hurt, but as she has no living relatives, the doctors recommended she go into care."

"That's horrible. When did it happen?"

"A few weeks ago. Ida went straight from hospital to a care center in Hammersmith."

"But won't she be coming back once she's better?"

"Evidently not. All those stairs. Not safe for an elderly woman living on her own."

"How sad. If you write down her address for me, I'll

take her some flowers. She must miss her home terribly. Do you think she'd like a pot of chrysanthemums?"

Nigel was my guide to all things British. "Chrysanthemums are for funerals, my dear. I shouldn't think she's quite ready for chrysanthemums. Perhaps some grapes. Sweet and easy to eat."

While we sipped our drinks and watched the rain stream down the windows of the conservatory, I told him about my plans for the next four weeks. "I've had to sign up for a month-long, total-immersion French class in Villefranche-sur-Mer."

"Just outside of Nice. The wife and I went on holiday there. The sun was lovely. It will be a good time for a trip abroad." He gestured ruefully at the weather beyond the glass room.

I smiled. "The fellow who hired me at the travel magazine suggested it. Actually it wasn't a suggestion. It was an edict. So I'm off to France tomorrow. But I want to buy some things for the orphanage in India before I leave. If I have them sent round to you, would you keep them for me until I get back from France?"

"Certainly, Madam," said Nigel. "Whatever Madam wishes."

When I finished my tea, Nigel put his drink aside and shoved Bede off his lap. "Come on, then. I'll get the key and we can look over Ida's flat. It won't need much to set it right."

I followed him into the dim recesses of his flat. In addition to his real estate business, Nigel owned a dusty little book store in Leicester Square and frequented auctions where he often bought the contents of entire libraries. Consequently, books covered every available surface of his flat including the floor, which left only narrow paths for walking. We followed one such precarious maze into his dining room where he kept a rat's nest of tagged keys in a tarnished silver bowl.

"These are Ida's books," Nigel said with a vague gesture towards the dining room floor. "She no longer has use for them and asked if I'd sell them. Quite sad, isn't it, to give up your books. I've been meaning to sort through them."

Nigel trolled through the bowl for the key to Ida's flat. "If you decide to rent the flat, perhaps I could put Ida's books back in there for a while. There are lovely shelves in her parlor. And books give a room a warm feeling, don't you think?"

The rain had turned into a relentless downpour which sluiced off Nigel's roof and assaulted our umbrellas the minute we stepped out his front door. We hurried down the uneven sidewalk trying to avoid the deeper puddles.

Ida's flat was a typical Victorian semi-detached. In America we'd call it a duplex. Built over one hundred years ago of red brick with bay windows above and below, nothing about the building was particularly well maintained. Paint was flaking off the exterior trim, and the window sashes needed replacing, but, from what little I could see of it, the steep slate roof with its chimney pots appeared to be sound. The roof of our former house on the street had leaked like the proverbial sieve. Nigel always found workmen to sort things out, but the workmen he found tended to take their time and felt entitled to take over our kitchen on a daily basis for heated discussions of Irish politics and lengthy cups of tea.

I followed Nigel up the brick walk past Ida's bay window to the recessed front door and waited as he tried the key. The door creaked open onto a dark and narrow front hall, its black-and-white tiled floor an intricate octagonal maze. Muddy footprints could not obscure the fact that some of the tiles were cracked, and some were missing altogether.

We parked our dripping umbrellas on the Victorian hall

tree just inside the door. The hall tree held Ida's old black coat and the red felt beret she wore in winter. Did that mean she was no longer able to go walking? She'd been so lively. I could not picture her sitting all day confined to a small, stuffy room.

"The hall looks a bit worn," I commented to Nigel.

He nodded. "You'd look a bit worn, too, if you were over one hundred years old. A nice coat of paint should freshen things up."

The parlor was on the left just beyond the stairs to the upper floor. It had oak floors, high ceilings, ornate cornices begging for repair, and a small tiled fireplace which at one time had burned coal and now held an electric heater. There was a red camelback sofa facing the fireplace, a chintz-covered wingback chair in one corner near the bare shelves Nigel coveted, and a faded oriental carpet on the floor. Overhead was a crystal chandelier. It was in need of a good cleaning and some of its prisms were missing, but it lent an aged elegance to a room otherwise sparsely adorned.

"I was intending to have the furniture carted around to Lloyd's Auction House," Nigel said as we returned to the front hall. "But perhaps you'd rather it stayed. It's old, but serviceable."

I nodded. I was a nomad accustomed to living with other people's furnishings. "Right now I simply need a place that will be suitable to bring a baby. When I return from Villefranche-sur-Mer, perhaps I can invite Ida over. There must be things here she'd like to have. Has she been back since she went into the nursing home?"

"The Care Center is not a nursing home per se. She's under nursing care until she's back on her feet. Then she'll have the freedom to come and go without restriction. I've been by to see her, but she's been, well, unresponsive to any suggestions to return for her things. Perhaps you can have a go at it. When she came out of hospital, she asked me to collect a few items...." Nigel paused as if he were going to say more on the subject, but then he simply said, "Sorry, my dear, I seem to be feeling a bit tired. You wouldn't mind, would you, if I went back for a little lie down?"

"Sure, Nigel. Go ahead. I'll lock up here when I'm finished. Leave your front door open, and I'll put the key back in the bowl on your dining room table."

I heard the front door close as I continued down the tiled front hall, past a tiny powder room under the stairs, to Ida's kitchen. Kitchens, in general, held little interest for me. This one looked as if someone had been rifling through the cupboards, but it seemed to have everything one would need to cook a basic meal, including a set of white crockery with chipped blue-striped rims. For one treacherous moment, I remembered another set of blue and white dishes in a house in upstate New York, and I turned away from the kitchen and the memory. I was going forward with my life now. This was a time for anticipation, not retrospection.

A back door led to Ida's garden. The door looked as if a gust of wind had caught it and slammed it shut. Two panes were cracked and a third was broken. The muddy mat in front of the door glittered with shards of glass. I would have to tell Nigel to add it to the list of things that needed repair.

Stepping carefully over the broken glass, I peered out at withered asters and penstemons and rose bushes that had been lovingly pruned. Ida considered her flowers to be her jewels, her family, her friends. How she would miss them! Perhaps it would cheer her to know a child would soon be playing in her garden.

Humming *Hey, Diddle, Diddle, the cat and the fiddle* under my breath, I walked back down the hall, noticing again muddy tracks on the hall floor. There were muddy tracks on the stairs, too. I gave them no more thought than I had the broken pane in the back door. Nice flats in London were in high demand. Nigel had probably shown this flat several times over the past week, and he would never think to ask anyone to remove their shoes. I knew everything would be made right before I moved in.

Upstairs, the front bedroom looked as if someone had packed up Ida in undue haste. Discarded clothing was strewn across the rumpled double bed, and the bed's sheets and white feather duvet had been tossed to the floor. A dresser stood in one corner, lace runner askew and drawers half open. To resist the sudden impulse to straighten Ida's things, I pulled aside a curtain darkened by the soot of London streets and peered out the window at the familiar vista.

Across the road was an array of stately old houses. Several had been divided into flats which demanded prime rent because they overlooked the Thames, and one had been turned into an elite school for young children. It felt good to be back in London, and I thought with pleasure of crossing the Thames footbridge to the Underground station and standing on Putney Bridge to wait for buses, even in the dreary month of February.

A floorboard creaked in the hall and startled me out of my reverie. I turned from the window. "Nigel?"

Suddenly I was facing the frightening specter of a small man in a bulky jacket, gloves, and muddy leather boots. Through the balaclava he had pulled over his face, his dark brown eyes glittered with hostility. In the dim hall beyond, I caught a glimpse of a second man also wearing a ski mask over his face. I froze, too surprised to react.

The smaller of the two men attacked with astonishing speed. In a swift, vicious move, he grabbed my arm and slammed his fist into my gut. I doubled over in pain. As I sank to the floor, his boot connected with the back of my head. I must have blacked out, because when I next opened my eyes, it took me a minute to figure out why I hurt so badly and why I was so cold.

For a while I lay on the bare floor of Ida's bedroom, too frightened and in too much pain to move. My eyes roamed the room searching for something with which to defend myself. Ida's upright vacuum cleaner plugged into the wall behind the partially closed door seemed to be my only option.

I am a small woman, a pacifist by nature, untrained to muster a single martial art for my own defense. I always assumed I could use my wits for self-preservation. Now as I lay shivering on the floor, the only strategy my sorry wits could muster was to keep absolutely still and pretend I was still unconscious. The only alternative was to switch on the vacuum and Hoover the two men into submission if they returned.

After a while, hearing no sound that would indicate the intruders were still in the flat, I righted myself and limped down the stairs and out the door. I hobbled through the downpour to Nigel's flat and pushed open his front door, knowing that if Nigel offered me a glass of gin now, I would drink it.

"Nigel?" I called in a voice that reeked of self-pity.

Nigel did not answer, but Bede came running wild-eyed at the sound of my voice. He raced past me out the front door, his ears back and his white tail looking as if he had passed through a field of static electricity. I stared down in horror at the bloody paw prints left in his wake.

"Nigel!" I shrieked and stumbled through the house in search of my old friend.

I found him crumpled on the floor of the dining room, ashen and scarcely breathing. There was a horrific gash over his left ear and a bloody poker lying nearby. Ida's books were tossed like shipwrecked barges in a pool of his blood.

I knelt to feel Nigel's pulse. It was faint, but it was there. Wiping my blood-smeared fingers on my jeans, I made my way into his littered kitchen in search of the phone. The bloody soles of my shoes made squelching sounds on the linoleum.

Dialing 999 summoned help. An ambulance arrived, and medics eventually carted Nigel off, leaving a revolting puddle of gore in their wake. I rejected all suggestions to ride along to the hospital and have my ribs x-rayed. My pupils showed no sign of concussion, and as far as I knew, the only cure for battered ribs was time and suffering. Consequently, I spent the rest of the afternoon hunched over in pain in the company of two tight-lipped officers from New Scotland Yard.

I had very little information to offer other than the niggling suspicion that maybe Ida hadn't fallen down her stairs. Maybe she'd been pushed. But I'm an American, warped by a diet of crime fiction. At least that's what Nigel would say if he made it through the night.